Sinful Enemy

A Hate To Love Romance

Simply Sinful
Book 2

Vivian Wood

Author's Copyright

Chapter 1

Cate

I will never, ever understand what the big fuss is over Luca Leone.

As I sit across from him in the airport shuttle bus, rocking and swaying with the motion of all the stops and starts, I look at my best friend's older brother skeptically. I'm wedged into this three person seat, Luna Leone on one side, our other bestie from college Harper on the other. Luna leans forward, looking out the window into the still bright early evening light.

And Luca sits opposite of us with his two closest friends, the three oversized men comically jammed together on this crowded bus. One dark haired, one blond, one ginger. They are quite a matched set. I see dark-haired Luca say something to his friends and laugh, though I can't hear it. The engine is loud and the bus is packed so I can talk to Luna and Harper without being worried that Luca will overhear.

"Cate! Harper! When we get to the hotel, I call the

biggest room. It is my birthday after all." Luna grins at me and Harper, wiggling her eyebrows.

"No argument here," Harper says, muffling a yawn.

"Mm," is my only comment.

I scrunch my face up, studying Luca as he talks to Bradford and Owen. Whatever they are talking about, his expression is sly. Probably making fun of somebody, I bet.

What is Luca's *deal*?

He's tall, yeah. Probably six foot two or three, without an ounce of fat on his big frame. I've seen him with his shirt off at the pool; his six pack abs and well-muscled arms are nothing to sneeze at. He's got dark hair with just a hint of a curl. His angular cheeks have two days of dark stubble growing on them, which is kind of hot.

And then there are his eyes, a gorgeous dark brown-black wrapped in long, dark lashes. His gaze is always penetrating, making me feel like he sees right through me. Sees my darkest secrets and greatest wishes.

Swoon-worthy? Yeah, maybe. But all of that can't make up for the fact that he is a *jerk*. He's always antagonized me from the first moment that I met him when he picked up Luna and me from the mall. He pulled up in his too-expensive car, arched a brow, and uttered the words that would come to define our relationship.

"Honestly, Luna. This is who you think you should be bringing home? God, remind me to count all the silver when she leaves."

My whole body filled with shame. From that moment on, Luca was the ultra-rich older playboy and I was the girl whose family just scraped by. We were entrenched.

Ugh. His smug smile makes me feel so... so *tense.* Like I have to be vigilant at all times, to be on my guard in case... well, of *what*, I'm not sure.

I've known Luna and Luca for almost nine years, since my first day of high school. And it has *always* been like this. Luna is the adorable one, playing younger sister to Luca. Luca is the brooding, taunting one... and I'm the one that is rushing to catch up with them, desperate and flushed while trying to keep pace.

Luna elbows me. "Are you okay, Cate?"

She tucks a strand of dark hair behind one ear, looking flawless as always. She pulls off her bob and her white wrap dress so easily. I flush, looking down at my threadbare jeans. I won't make a big deal about money, though she has infinitely more of it than I do...

"Yeah, sure," I say, trying to brighten my tone. "Just worried about work. Javier wasn't thrilled when I told him I had to take this weekend off. I told him I covered my shift but he gave me this whole lecture about responsibility."

Her brows lift. "But you've never taken a sick day or requested vacation at all in the time that you've been working at the cafe! You're just one barista... what is the harm in you asking for a few days off?"

I wrinkle my nose. "I know. You would think from the amount of hassle he gave me that I'd just asked him to give me a kidney or something."

Our other best friend from college Harper leans over from Luna's other side. She's blonde and pretty, but she doesn't pull a single punch. "Your job *sucks.*"

Luna nods emphatically. "It really does. You should make Luca hire you to work at his bar. I heard one of the bartenders talking last week about how much she makes working just three days a week. Can you imagine just working the weekends and making way more than you do now?"

"My kitten Lyra would like if I just never worked again. So much more time to devote to petting her!" I joke. "Will your brother pay me just to knit and pet my cat, I wonder?"

Obviously I am just kidding; the idea of Luca being my boss makes me nothing short of queasy. I know I'm stubborn but the idea of taking anything from anyone is hard. I almost refused when Luca texted me an invite to this weekend.

An all exclusive weekend, all airfare and hotel already paid for? The idea still makes me squirm and blush. I could never afford that, not when I'm only a year out of college and making a whopping nine dollars an hour.

Well, nine dollars an hour *plus tips*. I roll my eyes to myself. Like that really matters.

Luca looks up at me. His casual smile falls just a little and he cocks an eyebrow. *What are you looking at?* he seems to say. I blush, darting my gaze away. When I glance back for a moment, he is focusing on what his friend Owen is saying.

"I can't believe we are actually in Vegas for the weekend," Luna says to me and Harper. She grins excitedly. "I might actually start my day tomorrow at the pool. Try to soak up all the sun that I don't get at home in Seattle."

"I can't believe your brother paid to fly all of us out here," Harper says. She eyes Luca, who sits between two of his best friends. She sighs wistfully. "What a birthday gift. He's paying for the flight, the hotel, and basically everything else? I am so jealous that you have Luca." Dropping her voice, she whispers the last bit. "And having your brother and his two hunky best friends to stare at doesn't hurt, either."

"Mm," I say again, giving her my most disgruntled expression. "Luca's hot, but so rude. No offense, Luna."

She shrugs. "None taken. I know my brother can be a tool."

"Well, I'm totally gonna get drunk tonight," Harper declares. "And so are you, Miss 'My Birthday Isn't Until Tomorrow' and Miss 'I'm Catholic And Perfect'."

She casts an eye over us. Luna laughs. "It will technically be my birthday at midnight... can you believe I'll be twenty-five?"

"You're so old," I tease, elbowing her in the ribs. "I won't be twenty-five until April."

"We should do something for our birthdays again this year," Harper says. "Yours is the 14th, right? Mine is April 20th." She looks thoughtful.

The shuttle lurches to a stop and Luca stands up, clearing his throat. "This is our hotel. Come on, everybody off."

The next few minutes are taken up by struggling off the shuttle bus with our bags. Our huge hotel and the

Vegas strip are a blur as we lug ourselves through the fancy marble lobby, receive our keys, and head up the elevators. To my surprise, Luca has booked two enormous suites on the same floor, one for the girls and one for the guys.

I use my keycard, stopping in my tracks with wide eyes as soon as I burst into our suite. It has an enormous window at one end, two stories high, looking down on a fancy white kitchenette and a big white living room. Everything is white and *lavish*, without a doubt.

"Come on, let us in," Harper says, gently pushing me aside with her shoulder.

"Sorry," I say, nervously moving out of the doorway. "This place must have cost Luca a small fortune to rent for the weekend. And there is one like it for the guys too?" I whistle.

Luna shrugs, looking around. "He said he got a deal. Where are the bedrooms?"

Harper is already making her way down the little hallway tucked away almost out of view. "Over here."

"Yesssss," Luna says, rolling her suitcase over. I drift behind them as they go down the hallway, opening bedroom doors. She launches herself into one of the rooms, jumping up and down on the bed. "This bed is so nice!! Oooh and look! Complimentary champagne..." She grins at me. "We are gonna be so drunk before dinner."

Smiling, I shake my head at her. Finding my identical room, I wheel my luggage in.

Harper yells from her own room. "It's time to change for pre-dinner drinks!"

"And Cate, do not come out of that room wearing jeans!" Luna calls. "I mean it! Wear something a little daring for once in your life."

No one is around to see my blush. The girls like to rib me about how I dress conservatively, about how I don't usually drink or do drugs. What can I say, I was raised to be a good, God-fearing Catholic.

Like a go to Mass on Wednesdays kind of Catholic. A visit the cemetery to talk to Mom and Dad even though it makes me super sad kind of Catholic.

So when I step out of my bedroom in a new black lace dress that barely covers my butt, Luna and Harper look at me with a fair amount of surprise. Harper pulls off a pink jumper perfectly, and Luna looks amazing in a sparkly silver dress that hugs her curves. I tug on the lace sleeves of my dress, embarrassed.

"Is it okay?" I ask.

"Oh my god!" Harper cries. "I've been trying to get you to dress like this for my whole life, I feel like."

"That dress fits you perfectly," Luna says. "It's gorgeous."

When I walk over to her, she hugs me, taking care to tuck the price tag of the dress back into the nape of my neck. I blush again; I didn't want Luna and Harper to know that I'll be returning this dress first thing on Monday morning.

"Thanks," I say, bowing my head. She hugs me for a second longer, her eyes sparkling when she pulls away. She winks at me.

Harper is already popping a bottle of champagne. It

spills over while she pours a little into each glass, delighting her. "Get your glasses!"

We rush to grab our champagne flutes from the bar, toasting.

"To Luna," I say. "May you be blessed and fruitful in the coming year."

Harper holds her glass up. "And may you get so drunk that you can't see tonight... but not spend all night puking. Happy birthday, love."

We cheers, sipping the bubbly brew. When we've downed that glass, Harper refills our flutes. "Thank God for your brother, Luna. Whatever possessed him to plan this trip, I'm so glad to be here."

Luna snorts. "I think it's more of a sign that he is over getting dumped by Madisyn than an homage to me, honestly."

That makes me sit up a little straighter. "It's been almost three months," I murmur. "It's about time he got over her. I can't believe they were almost married! She was just so... *awful*."

Harper cocks a brow. "Really? Even you didn't like her? I thought you were all, *'everyone is nice, sometimes we just can't see it'* or whatever."

An image of the gorgeous brunette with her designer clothes and sky-high heels pops into my head. Even in my mind, she has a bitchy expression. I pull a face. "She was awfully rude to me. And to Luna, even. You can say anything you want to me, but don't you dare talk bad about my friends. After that, I couldn't help but develop a distaste."

"Well, well." Harper grins. "Welcome to the dark side, Cate. It's nice here. We have the best cocktails."

Luna looks down at her cell phone screen. "Luca says that we are leaving for dinner and a show in ten minutes."

"That's enough time to put on our shoes and have a third glass of bubbles..." Harper says, her eyes sparkling mischievously.

"Wait, will one of you please do my eyeshadow?" I plead.

Luna looks between us, grinning. "I have a good feeling about tonight. We are going to have the best time, girls."

As Harper fills up my glass again, I bite my lip. Here in our hotel room, I'm fine. It's just when I get outside, when people are looking at me... that makes me anxious. No, let's be honest. The very idea of doing something stupid while Luca looks on, judging me...

That makes me *shake*.

Yeah, I'm going to have to drink a lot more to make that okay. I down my third glass in a single gulp and hurry to get my shoes from my room.

Chapter 2

Luca

"**A**re you having a good time?" I shout in Luna's ear.

She is seated beside me at the dance club, wedged into the semicircle of a booth while we watch the lights flash. We're on the second floor, a little removed from the noisy dance floor. The music is still loud as fuck, but it's muffled slightly on the second floor. Above our heads, there is a TV with a stream playing of the semi famous DJ who is spinning records on the stage below.

Luna looks up at me with a grin. "Yes. Thank you, Luca. Bringing me and my best friends to Vegas was an amazing idea."

"No problem," I call back with a shrug. "Since I own a music venue, almost everything you want to do this weekend is free for us. I scratch this club owner's back, he scratches mine. Same with the hotel; I book a few acts that the hotel manager wants to promote, he gives me a discount, etc., so forth." I flap a hand.

"Well you should get something out of it, since you work like all the time," she shouts, wrinkling her nose. "You should get way more weekends like this one."

I shrug again. "I make do."

A fast-paced song comes on and Luna squeals. "Omigod! I love this song!"

She grabs Harper's hand and drags her down to the dance floor, leaving me alone in the booth. Owen and Bradford never even made it this far, scouting people that they wanted to flirt with as soon as we got in the door of the club. I sit back with a sigh.

As much as I want to party and get drunk, a part of me is still in big brother mode. I will be vigilant no matter what, which means I'm not going to totally cut loose. Which is fine, because I'm still brooding about my failed engagement.

I try to think of what Madisyn is doing right now. Probably going out to dinner with some guy that isn't me, batting her lashes and trying to figure out his net worth. Yeah, Madisyn is kind of shallow; she is one of those girls that picks men based on good looks *and* a fat bank account... but she was *very* hot and very quantifiable.

What you see with her, you get. End of story.

I glance up from my brooding to see my little sister's friend Cate sitting down in the booth. I narrow my gaze at her; she blushes and hooks a strand of her long, wavy hair behind her ear.

Sending my gaze up and down her figure, I realize

that she's actually pretty. Pretty and extremely short. Her head probably lands a whole foot below mine.

Too bad I can't stand her. Since I've known Cate, she's been annoying and usually downright unpleasant to be around. I swear, I made one crack about her when I first met her and she's turned up her nose at me ever since.

But a vague dislike on my part was cemented into a cold, hard hate by the end of the first month that she was friends with Luna.

I'll admit that I think she's hot. I've seen her in a barely-there black bikini, her tits and ass and legs looking like a million fucking bucks.

One toss of her dark hair. One glance over her shoulder. One glimpse of those big, dark eyes set in her elfin face. And then she bent down in front of me, her eyes flirting even as she reached for the sunblock...

My brain practically melted.

Cate short circuits my thoughts by sitting on the very edge of the seat, looking extremely uncomfortable. I'm entirely sure that if Cate had her way, I wouldn't be on this trip at all.

That makes me smirk. I beckon to her with two fingers and she scoots further into the booth.

"Where's the librarian today?" I ask, accidentally getting a little too close to her ear. She reacts visibly, glancing up at me with those wide, curious eyes.

"What librarian?"

I can't help it. I rib her a little. "The librarian whose clothes you usually steal. You know, skirts below your knees, cardigans buttoned up to your neck…" I grin. "Or is it a nun who you've been defrocking?"

Her cheeks go a vivid, angry red. "I'm so sorry that I don't just strip naked and strut around trying to please you, Luca. That's not the world I inhabit. I have a purpose other than to make your jeans tight, okay?"

I roll my eyes. "Of course, Miss Feminist. But nobody said that you had to dress like a ninety-year-old lady just because you don't want to accidentally turn anybody on."

Cate gives me sour look. "That's just your opinion."

I reach for my drink, swirling the ice cubes around in their whiskey bath. "Me and the rest of the male population, you mean."

Though I'm teasing her, my eye does drop to her dress. Made of black satin, it's pretty damn short. Until now, until I actually laid eyes on her gleaming legs, I would've probably assumed that Cate didn't have legs worth noticing.

But I'm noticing them now. I'm making note of the way that dress hugs her body, the hemline barely covering the vee between her legs.

Yeah, all right. Cate is not horrible to look at. Not by a long shot, if that often-recalled memory of her is right. It's just too bad that she hides herself away most of the time.

She hasn't always been like this. Frigid and blocky. She used to merely be annoying.

"Stop staring," she mutters, blushing. She rolls her eyes a little and reaches for the bottle of champagne chilling in a bucket of ice on the table. She refills her glass, spilling a little of the bubbles. It's only then that I realize that Cate is drunk.

For some reason, that thought makes me smile. When she glances back up at me, she sees me smiling and gives me a distrustful look.

"What?" I ask, splaying my hand out. I take up plenty of space in the booth, man-spreading with a kind of glee. I know that it gets her goat, otherwise I wouldn't do it.

"You are just such a guy," she declares, looking away.

"Don't even start with that shit." I sip my whiskey for a second, eyeing her. "Is this about the Beatles again?"

Her gaze darts back to me, her eyes narrowing almost to slits. "Oh my god. You and the Beatles!! I'm a millennial, alright? I don't even know why the Beatles are a big deal. Or the Rolling Stones or like... I don't even know. U2, I guess?"

I push my glass away, disgusted. "U2 and the Beatles are not the same."

She is so *snotty*. "I'm sorry I don't like Radiohead or whoever you think is the best band ever."

I can feel my chest puff out and my brain start to overheat.

"How can you even say that? Radiohead has three of the best rock albums of all time. And one of the best electronica albums too, incidentally." I narrow my gaze. "And I'm a millennial too, you know. I'm only twenty-seven. I happen to just have good taste."

She takes another sip of champagne. "Whatever. So what? So I like the music in the top 100. Not everybody is a snob."

"People that call me a music snob have literally no perspective in music," I point out to her, grinding my teeth.

"So?" she asks with a shrug. "You're so hung up on music. I'm just not. It's like religion... I believe in Jesus, you... well, you don't. We just don't see eye to eye. We never have."

She's right. I'm definitely an atheist. "I've known you for eight years—"

"Nine," she corrects me.

That causes me to roll my eyes again. "All right, nine years. And you've been irritating every single one of them."

"Kettle, you're black." She sips her drink. It takes me a few seconds to realize she's saying the I'm the pot and I'm calling the kettle black. "Mm. This champagne is good. Did this get better somehow?"

A low chuckle escapes me. "I think you might be drunk, Little Miss Goody Two Shoes."

She looks at me with a startled expression. "Am I? I've been drunk before and I don't remember it being so..." She screws up her face. "Mmm... I feel *lovely*."

She scoots inward into the booth a little more, her face flushed. The corners of my mouth tip up. She really is pretty when she's not using her mouth as a way to destroy me.

Then she stops what she's doing and looks at me, her brows drawing down.

"Oh, I think I'm really going to regret this tomorrow. Anytime that I really enjoy myself, I pay for it later." She nods sagely, but that is a little overtaken by how drunk she appears.

I cock a brow. Is that how she sees everything in her life? Or does she just mean partying? Either way, it's kind of sad.

"You're going to have a hangover in the morning," I agree.

She looks at me, her brown eyes seeming impossibly large. "How did I end up here? I'm in Vegas. I should be partying and have a good time, not worrying about tomorrow. And definitely not telling you about it." She shakes her head. "You're the closest thing I think I've ever had to an enemy, you know that?"

Snorting, I pick up my glass of whiskey, upending the whole thing into my mouth and swallowing down. Alcohol is apparently a truth serum for Cate, which is just another thing that we don't have in common. Whiskey is my friend, even when it gives me hangovers.

When I look at her again, she is staring at her hands that she's placed on the table, spread wide.

"You are pretty annoying," I say at last.

Cate looks at me, scrunching up her nose. "You think I'm annoying? *You're* annoying. You're so bossy and domineering and... *stuff*." She hiccups.

"Well, at least that's settled." I huff a sour laugh.

"What?"

"That we are enemies. I know you're drunk but please keep up with the flow of conversation, Cate."

She glares at me. Luckily I'm saved from whatever shitty comeback she has by the arrival of the rest of our party, breathless and drunk. Owen and Bradford slide in on my left, Luna and Harper get in on Cate's right. Owen is red-faced and sweaty, but he doesn't seem as drunk as everyone else.

"Scoot over!" Luna says, bumping Cate's hip with her own. "Luca and Cate, you two can stand each other for a weekend, right?"

Cate and I move closer together, but both of us are staring daggers at Luna. Luna doesn't seem to notice. She's still glowing with post-dancing energy. Cate and I end up almost touching, with barely an inch between us. Bradford puts a stack of crinkled napkins on the table, looking proud of himself.

Owen picks one up, reading aloud from the note scrawled on it. *"You're cute af. Call me. Dan."*

Bradford grins. The second he opens his mouth, a thick Southern twang pours out. His accent always gets more pronounced when he's a little drunk. "It's not a surprise that Vegas is great for meeting hot guys. It is a surprise that I got a dozen phone numbers in the hour and half we've been here though." He pats himself on the back. "Well done, Bradford. Your hotness has been noted."

Owen nods, giving Bradford a drunken one over. "If I liked guys, I would probably want to suck your dick."

"Thanks." Bradford laughs. "We've had this conversation before." He pats Owen's arm. "I also got a girl's number. She was drunk as a skunk but very nice." He sorts through the pile of napkins. "Lisa. I couldn't even tell her that she's barking up the wrong tree."

A waitress approaches with a bottle of alcohol and a tray of shot glasses. "Hey guys! Who ordered the tequila?"

Luna shoots up her hand. "I did!!"

I give Luna a discouraging glance. "Oh, you really didn't have to do that..."

The waitress deposits the bottle and six shot glasses brimming with tequila on the table. Then she places a little plate with salt and limes on it in front of each of us. "I'll be back soon to refresh your limes, okay?"

I nod to the waitress, who gives me a meaningful wink. She hands us napkins and then walks away, short skirt swishing. I turn mine over and find her number printed neatly on it. I glance up at her, a smile on my lips.

"Hey! Pay attention!" Luna gives me a mischievous grin and picks up her shot. "It's almost midnight. That means that it's almost my birthday. Which means that if I tell you to drink, you drink!"

Then without preamble she shoots the tequila. Shaking my head a little, I shoot the tequila, eschewing the salt but biting into a lime wedge afterward. As soon as I put my glass down, Bradford is already refilling it.

"Here's to Luna's birthday," Owen says, raising his glass. He hiccups. Now I can tell that he's drunk. "And here's to not being tied to Madisyn for the rest of your life, Luca! I can't tell you how glad I am not to have to hang out with her every time I want to see you."

Just the sound of her name on my best friend's lips sends a little shiver of displeasure down my spine. Madisyn dumped me as publicly as possible, citing *irrec-*

oncilable differences. She's the last thing I want to talk about right now.

So I shoot the tequila, wincing at the afterburn. I start feeling the effects of the first shot, the heavy, numbing sensation overlaid with a thick layer of dreamy smog. I find myself chuckling though I don't know what I'm laughing at, per se.

Harper clears her throat, rising up from her seat halfway and lifting her shot glass. "We are some of the hottest people here. Honestly, the fact that—" She pauses, giggling. "The fact that none of us have never slept together is amazing."

Luna's eyes light up. "Good point. Oooh! Let's play never have I ever!"

Cate shifts in her seat, uncomfortable. "What are the rules, exactly?"

Bradford leans in towards the center of the table. "Drink if... you have ever thought about how hot someone else *in this circle* is." He eyes Owen. "I know that you have to drink, because earlier you said I was a good-looking man."

Owen grins. "Fair enough. I might have had a shit ton of whiskey first, but I meant it honestly.'

Bradford grins. "Well, I think everyone is hot."

He tips his shot glass back. Everyone else does a shot, everyone but me. Bradford slides me a look. "What are you doing?"

Rolling my eyes, I sigh. "Not taking a shot."

He pulls a face. "Seriously? Don't make me call you out."

Confused, I give him a look. "On what?"

Owen leans closer to me, his eyes sparkling. "Two years ago, we got drunk and rated the fuckability of everybody we know. You gave Cate here an eight out of ten, with the caveat that if the apocalypse happened, she would become a nine and a half."

Cate's face goes red and she looks paralyzed. I can feel my own cheeks begin to heat. I glare at Owen. "That never happened," I growl.

"Yes it did! I heard it too," Bradford interjects. Both of my friends are against me, which is unfair. I barely remember that conversation and I definitely don't remember saying that Cate was hot.

"Seriously? She's too fucking annoying to be hot! And she dresses like an old lady!" I protest.

Cate looks like she wants to slide under the table and disappear. She puts her hands in front of her face like a shield. "Please kill me."

Luna looks downright gleeful. "Drink! You know what? Both of you, drink! It's my birthday and I say so."

Begrudgingly I pick up my shot glass and toss back the tequila inside. I can feel the edges of my vision starting to go black.

The last thing I remember thinking is something Cate said.

I think I'm really going to regret this tomorrow.

Yep, she's completely right... and I definitely am.

Chapter 3

Cate

Before I even open my eyes, I'm aware of how thirsty I am. My mouth is open, my head pointed down. I'm not somewhere comfortable.

Then I shift my position with a groan, fluttering my eyelids open. It all hits me at once: the light is unbearably bright. The noise of a vacuum in the distance is so loud that I could cry. And when I shift again, I feel nauseated to my very core.

Staying still, I try to assess where exactly I am without moving. I'm on the floor, I think. There is a bed beside me on one side and the doorway to a bathroom on the other.

Vegas.

I'm in Las Vegas.

I close my eyes and breathe, every breath seeming painful and labored.

What in the hell did I drink last night?

But as soon as I wonder that, memories come flying at

me. We drank all the shots of tequila, even though it was basically the most vile substance known to man. Then we left the club and went to another bar, where... I'm not sure, but I remember drinking something that tasted like a liquid gummy bear.

Then my memory gets faulty. I only have flashes of what happened. I groan as I try to remember; even the flashes inside my head are loud, somehow.

I've got to get water. In order to do that, I'm going to have to actually get up off the floor. Breathing in and out for a second, I steady myself.

"One... two... three..." I launch myself up, staggering to my feet. Looking down at my lacy bra and panties, I frown. Where is the huge billowy nightshirt that Luna always teases me for wearing to bed?

I wasn't concerned with being comfortable last night, I guess.

It looks like I rolled off my bed and onto the floor at some point... My eyes widen and my heart stutters in my chest when I turn to face the bed.

There, spread out in all his naked glory, is a sleeping Luca. He's sleeping on his side, his rear end on display. I didn't... I wouldn't have slept with him, would I?

The fact that I'm still in my bra and panties suggests that I didn't. I glance back to Luca.

I take a nice long look, bring my lower lip. The long lean line of his back and his unclothed rear are certainly a sight worth viewing. If I was seduced last night, it would be the second time I ever...

I blush. The fact that I can't even say the word in my

head is another sign that I didn't get too handsy with Luca. At least his... *business* is covered. I wouldn't want someone staring at me when I was in that state, though.

Tiptoeing around the bed, I grab a blanket that's been tossed on the floor and cover him up with it. He stirs for a moment, his brow crinkling critically. Then he murmurs something that sounds a lot like, "thanks, sugar".

Ugh. My face wrinkles.

My head pounds, reminding me of why I got up in the first place. I feel so dehydrated at this moment that I don't know that I could even form a sentence. My tongue is too large and too dry in my mouth, and that's the first and last time I want to think that to myself, ever.

When I pad to the bathroom, I turn the tap on and stick my head under. Cool water gushes across my tongue, a relief so acute that it brings actual tears to my eyes. I stay there for a minute, gulping down water, standing on the cool tiles of the bathroom. It's dark in here at least, a nice reprieve from the bright sunlight streaming in through the giant picture window.

Finally I have my fill. Reaching up to turn off the tap, I pause.

There, on the fourth finger of my left hand, is a gigantic ring. Not an expensive one, either. It's solid light pink plastic with a sort of waffle pattern all over. I pry it off with a great deal of effort; I guess that I was less puffy when I slid it onto my finger.

"Holy fuck!"

Looking behind me, I can only guess that Luca is awake. I flush when I realize that I'm still in nothing but my bra and panties. My urge to get water into my body was overwhelming, I guess.

Sticking my head out of the bathroom, I squint into the brightness of the bedroom. Luca is sitting facing away from me, his head drooping low. I clear my throat.

"Do you think you could hand me... umm... a robe? Or a sheet?"

He turns around, a piece of paper in his hand. He glares. "*You.*"

Paling, I lick my chapped lips. I'm thirsty again. "What?"

"This was your idea, I bet," he mutters. "Fucking religious people."

My eyebrows rise. "I'm sorry?"

He shoots me the filthiest look. "You'd better be."

"No, I mean..." I shake my head. "What are you talking about?"

Luca stands up, naked as a jaybird. I raise a hand to block out his lower half from my sight, protesting. "Luca! Come on. Put on some clothes!"

He doesn't seem too worried about it because he stalks right over to me, shoving the paper under my nose. Swallowing hard, I read the title.

State of Nevada. Marriage Certificate. And below that, it clearly says Luca Leone and Catherine De Rose.

My eyes widen. My pulse speeds up. I look up to Luca, my eyes pleading.

"No." It's all I can think of to say. "I..."

He folds his arms across his chest. "Yes. According to this, we got married last night."

My eyes slip down to his... junk... which looks to be at full attention. Then my eyes bounce between his member and my semi-nude body. "We didn't... we couldn't have...?"

"Yeah, you *wish*," Luca growls. "We didn't fuck, if that's what you're asking."

He runs his hand down, cupping his erection. I rip my eyes away and put my hand in front of my face. I didn't think I could get any pinker, but I feel like my cheeks are glowing now.

"Do you mind?" I ask, exasperated. "I can't talk to you like this."

"Fine," he snaps. I hear him rustling around for half a minute, then the sound of jeans being zipped up. "You can stop hiding your face."

Even though I heard him put jeans on, I peek through my fingers. He's still shirtless, but at least I can talk to him now. He glares at me and grabs my hands. "Act like an adult for once in your life. This isn't like showing up late at your crappy little kid job, okay? This is serious."

My brow draws down. "My job isn't for little kids."

He gives me an angry look, as if he already knows everything he could possibly want to know. It makes me feel small. "Making coffee? You do the same job as when you were in college. Let's not pretend that you don't."

My mouth opens and closes a few times as I gawp up at him. "That's... that's none of your business!"

I yank my hands out of his. He lets me go, eyeing me like I'm a time bomb ready to go off at any moment. "It's is while we're married. Which is why we need to get unmarried, quick."

"Are you saying that we have to get divorced?" I go still, my heart beating loudly in my ears. "You know that Catholics don't believe in that. I... I can't get divorced."

He rolls his eyes. "I don't think that will be necessary, princess. We'll probably qualify for an annulment." Luca reaches down for a t-shirt, pulling it on over his head. "Jesus fucking Christ, I can't believe we're even in this situation."

"An annulment?" I echo. "Like it never happened?"

He looks distracted. "Cate, get dressed. I want to go see if anybody remembers where we got married. Maybe they haven't filed that paperwork yet. Since I feel like you won't do anything on your own, you had better come with me."

I scrunch my face up. "Why do I have to come with you? I want to take a shower and drink a hundred coconut waters."

Luca finds a black hoodie, pulling it on. "Because, princess. The Jagermiester shots were your idea..."

The word Jagermiester makes me suddenly nauseated. I get a flash of pouring brown liquid from a green bottle into Luca's mouth as he laughs. Something about the way the Jager shines in my flashback makes my stomach curdle.

Oh gosh.

I'm going to throw up, there is no question about it.

Two seconds later, I clap my hands over my mouth and launch myself toward the bathroom. I almost make it to the toilet but not quite, puking all over my hands. The sound of wet splattering all over the porcelain makes me heave again.

Getting to my knees, I pop the lid of toilet up and vomit for several minutes. I'm losing all the water I just drank and then some but there is no helping it.

When I finally wipe my chin and drag myself up, I turn to find Luca waiting just outside the bathroom door. I feel completely out of sorts and no small amount of self-pity. There is an impatient expression on his face.

He hands me a towel, his voice brusque. "Wash your face and brush your teeth. When you come out of the bathroom, there will be a glass of water and a couple of aspirin waiting for you. I'll be outside, trying to sort this fucking mess out."

He whirls and stalks away, letting me know that by *this fucking mess* he means me.

Great.

This is what I get for trying to let go of my strict upbringing. Go to Las Vegas one single time, come back married to a man who swears like a sailor. I pray that he's right, that whatever chapel we were at still has the paperwork.

I mean, things like this have got to happen all the time, right? People that are diametrically opposite in every way — to the point of being actual enemies — they slip up and accidentally get married every day.

...don't they?

It takes me a few minutes to brush my teeth, wash my face, get dressed in my dress from last night, and take the aspirin that Luca left out for me. I find my purse, which luckily seems to be completely intact. When I open Luca's bedroom door, I sneak out into a living room exactly like the one I saw in my own suite.

This room is at least twice as bright as the bedroom was. Shading my eyes against the invasive sun, I manage to steal out of Luca's suite unnoticed. Creeping down the hall, I realize that I don't have my keycard.

So much for being stealthy. I knock on the door, dreading talking to Luna and Harper about where I have been. The fact that I married Luna's big brother but slept on the floor of his bedroom rather than share a bed with a man... that is *so* me.

The door opens to reveal a very sleepy Luna. "Oh. It's you."

Without another word, she opens the door all the way and turns around, heading for the kitchen. I slip in, closing the door behind me. "Did I wake you?"

My head pounds. Luna is already scrounging around the kitchen. "Where is the freaking coffee?"

"Sit down," I command, although my grasp of the situation is somewhat more tenuous than my voice lets on. "I'll make the coffee, okay?"

Identifying the coffee maker and finding the filters and the grounds, I start measuring things out. Luna leans against the kitchen counter, eyeing me. "My brother has already been here."

I freeze at that, the coffee measuring scoop hovering over the filtration basket. My face grows hot. "Oh."

Luna sighs. "He looked pretty pissed. He was raving about you and how you shouldn't sign contracts when you're drunk." She winces. "I'll admit to not fully paying attention. I had the same kind of night that you guys had."

I pause, the empty coffee scoop still in my hand. "What happened, exactly?"

She sighs. "I didn't get his name, but I spent the night with this unbelievably dreamy guy. He rocked my world... and then left before I got his name." She rubs her temple, looking at me through bloodshot eyes.

"Wait, a super hot guy left before you could slip out first?" I say, trying to piece it together.

She waves an impatient hand. "Now that I'm looking at you, you're wearing the same clothes as you had on last night—"

"We got married," I blurt. Dumping the coffee into the coffee maker, I hit the button to start brewing. Then I turn to her, my cheeks pink. She is the perfect caricature of surprise right now, her eyes wide and her mouth forming an O of shock.

"You... you..." she stammers.

"Married your brother last night.' I wince at how formal that sounds. "We didn't actually like... consummate or anything—"

Luna launches herself at me, her hug taking me by surprise. "You're my sister for real now!" She tightens her embrace. "When you went through losing your family freshman year of college, I made myself a promise that I would make you part of my family." She pulls back, her eyes bright. "I never expected you to actually join my family, though!"

And that's it. The mention of my family makes me push out of her hug, turning dead eyed. "Don't talk about my family."

She bites her lip. "I know you don't like to bring them up—"

"It was a mistake!" I start walking away from the kitchen, feeling all this anger building in my chest. "Marrying your brother... it was a fluke. Your brother knows it. I know it. We'll get an annulment. End of story."

And with that, I stalk out of the living room, livid. At Luca? Certainly. And at Luna, yes.

But mostly at myself.

Chapter 4

Luca

"So basically, an annulment and a divorce are different because..."

My attorney's voice drones on through the speakerphone on my office desk. I have cobbled together a collection of awkward chairs in the dark little room, adding a desk that is buried somewhere under the avalanche of paperwork. My phone sits precariously on top.

Behind the scenes of The Attic is a mess, yeah. The office is a disaster, from the peeling black paint down to the fourth-hand furniture. It's hard to find things in the cramped area back here. And don't even get me started about the troubles of doing liquor inventory in the storage room. But just thinking about taking a day off of work to tackle all of it — and it would take a whole day at minimum, I think — the idea is just unbearable.

I lean forward in my chair, trying to pay attention to

what my lawyer says. Pinching my brow, I reach for the bottle of aspirin that I keep in my desk drawer. Somehow, I am still fucking hungover.

And still married, it seems. I tried to get the paperwork back from the chapel and the lady in the office practically laughed me out of the damn place. So here I am Monday morning, trying to make head or tails of the marriage system.

"So what do you think?" he asks.

Drinking the last of the water from a huge bottle on my desk, I sigh. I toss the water bottle in the corner, on top of the already-overflowing recycling bin. "I'll be honest with you, Dan. I have no idea what you just said. What I can tell you however is that Cate—"

"Is that the girl that you married?"

Wrinkling my brow, I frown. "Yeah. Cate is Catholic. So divorce is like... the last option. I don't want to deal with explaining to her how much easier it would be. If you had met her, you would feel the same."

On the other end, there is a moment of silence. "All right, Luca. Whatever you say. Unfortunately, annulling a marriage takes time... at the very least it will be a month from the day that we sign all the paperwork."

I rock back in my chair, forgetting that its back is broken. I'm not a small person. So when I lean back and snap the chair's back, all six foot three inches of me is thrown to the ground. Hitting the ground with a soft thump, I groan.

"Are you okay over there?" Bradford calls from the storage room. It's the next room between here and the bar

After that, the room opens up into the huge dance floor and the stage. Behind there are a few dressing rooms and a locker room for the staff.

"Yeah!" I call, dragging myself up. I refocus on the phone. "Are you still there?"

Dan clears his throat. "I am."

Perching on one corner of my desk, I stare down intently at the phone. "When can we get the paperwork we would need?"

"Let me see... just looking at my calendar here..." He clears his throat again and there is the faint sound of papers being shuffled. "I think I could messenger over two sets of paperwork by Friday at noon.'"

"Great," I say. I've said that word so much in the last twenty four hours that it has ceased to have any meaning to me. "I'll look for your packet to arrive."

"There is just one more thing."

Bradford pokes his head into the office, arching a brow. He's carrying two cases of vodka and silently asking me something, but I hold up my hand to ask for five minutes. He huffs and vanishes from the doorway.

Where Owen, the third proprietor of this business is, no one knows.

"Of course there is," I say.

Dan chuckles. "You'll just have to pick a reason for the annulment. There's a proscribed list that you have to choose from. Things like... are you related, is one of you mentally incapacitated, were you under duress... there's some wiggle room for fraud..."

My breath leaves me in a whoosh. "Jesus. It's not

fraud or bigamy, that I know of. Maybe mental incapac-itation..."

"If you can just let me know which, I can get the paperwork started."

A loud crash comes from another room. "Shit. I'll have to let you know later. I'll text you, okay?"

"All right."

I hang up, grinding my teeth. When I told my two best friends about our 'wedding' the morning after my little wedding fiasco, they laughed in my face. As a matter of fact, they are still laughing. I thought that would be the worst thing I had to face, but it looks like it's not over yet.

Heading out of the office, I pass the storage room with its shelves stacked high with boxes of liquor, cups, and napkins. The hallway into the front of the house is narrow; I pass the iPad on the wall that's supposed to stay charged so that employees can clock in. The charger lies on the floor and the iPad is dead.

Stooping to plug it back in, I sigh. My head is still fucking aching which isn't helping things at all. Among the many bad decisions I made in Las Vegas, I regret giving myself a hangover almost as much as getting married.

When I poke my head around the corner and look down the bar, I don't immediately see the cause of the crash. I see the gleaming copper-topped bar and the tall bar stools on one side. And on the other I see the bar fridges, the iPads that we use for cash registers, the towering display of liquor bottles...

And then I spot it. We usually keep our spare

stemware and glasses in racks at the far end of the bar. Apparently not only has Bradford broken a glass, he has actually managed to rip one of the racks off the wall and tumble to the ground with it.

Shit.

Jogging over to where he is just picking himself up off the floor, I survey the scene critically. "Are you okay? Watch out for all that broken glass, man."

Bradford brushes some glass out of his chin-length blond hair, pulling a face. "I'm okay. I just broke five hundred dollars of stemware though. Pulled that rack right out of the wall." He sighs. "That rack took so much work to put up in the first place. Remember?"

Looking at where he ripped it off the wall, I nod slowly. "I do. That rack was the first piece of hardware we installed when we bought the place, I think."

"Yeah. Aww, memories. We were just babies then." He purses his lips.

I chuckle. "It was only three years ago."

"Still!" he protests. He shakes his head. "Ugh. Look at this mess, would you?"

I wave him off. "Go home and change. This place needs a bar manager tonight but I'll bet that whatever you were doing can wait until tomorrow. I'll clean up this glass."

"Are you sure?" he asks, wrinkling his face up at the mess.

"Yep." I wave him off. "Go ahead. I'll see you at..." I check my watch. "Around six?"

"Okay. I love you, never change, byeeee!" He

manages to squeeze all three of his favorite phrases into a single breath as he disappears into the back hallway.

If I bring Cate on to work here, will that be a problem? I mean, it's not ideal — ever since the second time I saw her, I have carried this distaste that I just don't know how to shake.

I was driving an SUV packed to the gills with Bradford, Luna, and all the ski gear we would need for the weekend. We pulled up outside Cate's shabby little house to wait for her to come out. When she finally emerged, she was obviously still in the middle of a full blown fight with her tired-looking mother. Cate stopped and turned on her mom when she was just steps from the SUV.

I tensed. Cate raised her voice. Her mother just listened, smiled sadly, and then forced a sweater into Cate's hands. Cate shook her head but she allowed her mom to hug her. I turned away; my own parents couldn't give a rat's ass about Luna and I. They were too busy yachting in Greece to pay that kind of attention to us.

When she got in the car, Cate had the *audacity* to grumble about her mother being overbearing. God, she had no idea how precious that sort of relationship was. How when I was younger, I dreamed of having parents who cared about me even a little.

And Cate complained about her parents? No. No way.

Just like that, my brain jumped tracks. I might not have been nice before, but from then on I stopped pulling my punches. I tried to get Luna to see that she could pick a better friend than Cate, but to no avail.

So I deal. Or at least I did... until last weekend. How fucking stupid could I be?

Sighing, I go back to work.

Chapter 5

Luca

I'm sweeping up the last little bits of glass when a woman's voice interrupts me. "Did you have an accident here?"

Stiffening, I look up. There is Madisyn Montgomery herself, looking as good as ever. With skin like rich brown mahogany and a spotless white dress that hugs every curve in just the right places, she looks utterly edible. She's all smooth legs and toned arms as she takes off her sunglasses.

It's too bad that she's actually toxic.

My brows hunch. I'm a little bit at a loss for what to say to the woman. She gleefully announced our broken engagement on social media — without even bothering to inform me that we were done.

I only found out after the fact that she *invested* a good chunk of the money deposited in our joint account. And by invested, I mean she bought into a pyramid scheme.

Not only that, but she bragged to her friends about how I was her personal ATM.

My fists tighten. Since I found out that bit, I've maintained a careful wall of silence, despite the fact that my ego was pretty bruised.

I end up just saying her name. "Madisyn..." I realize that I probably sound more than a little shocked at seeing her.

Pull it together, self.

She looks around the whole bar, putting her sunglasses inside her white leather arm bag. "You've redecorated. I like the black and gold motif. It reminds me of my hometown of New Orleans." She titters, tilting her head and fake cheering. "Go Saints."

I frown at her, leaning on my broom. "What are you doing here, Madisyn?"

She gives me her most saccharine smile. "I came to invite you personally."

She's playing a game. One where she holds the answers and she expects me to puzzle them out of her. I'm definitely not in the fucking mood for this.

"You have ten seconds to tell me what you are fucking talking about, Syn." I rest the broom against the bar. "I'm still pissed at you for ending things like you did, by the way. And I would love to get the fifteen grand you owe me, by the way"

Madisyn has the decency to blush at that. "I'm sorry about that. Not the money, but the engagement ending. I'm especially sorry about announcing it on Instagram first. I just didn't want the news to get out before I told people."

I speak the language of Madisyn. What she means by that is she wanted the likes that poured in from all our friends when she declared us over. I narrow my eyes.

"Five seconds, Syn."

She rolls her eyes and shifts back and forth on her stilettos. "Okay! Okay." She fishes something out of her purse and hands it to me. I accept the plain piece of card stock from her, turning it over to read the calligraphy.

"Save The Date," I read. I glance up at her, my brow drawing down. "Mr. Reginald Jackson and Miss Madisyn Montgomery would like you to reserve March 14th for their wedding day—"

I glance up at her again, confused. She pets her long dark hair and purses her lips, the look in her eyes saying *eat your heart out.*

"Syn, what the fuck is this?" I ask.

She smiles haughtily. "Reggie asked me to marry him and I said yes. I thought that you would prefer to be told in person. Apparently you like to be told big news." She gives a pouty little shrug.

"I was under the impression that we weren't *done,*" I growl. "That's the pattern. You leave, you make a big deal about it on social media, then you sneak back in. I just deal with the blower to finances and social esteem. It's been that way for four years, Madisyn."

Syn flutters her eyelashes. "Well, this is me, telling you. It's final this time. I'm really with Reggie. Look." She flashes an enormous diamond ring at me, looking proud.

"It's two carats and princess cut, because Reggie says I'm his queen."

It takes everything in me not to ball up the save the date invitation and throw it back in her smug face. "I see," I say, jaw clenched.

I expect to feel anger. After all, anger and disappointment are the usual breakup feelings. But instead I feel a weary sort of relief.

Dating Madisyn was like going to a theme park. It was exciting for a while to ride the rollercoasters and eat the junk food, but after a couple of years, I just feel queasy and sunburned.

As she gushes about her new man, all excited to have something to rub in my face, I just sort of feel bad for whoever she fooled into proposing to her so soon.

"It's only a month and a half away, because we are just so excited to tie the knot. Don't worry, though..." she says, her expression indulgent. "I made Reggie agree that we were going to invite you. We'll even throw in a plus one... not that you'll need it, probably..."

A thought occurs to me. It's maybe not the best idea I've ever had, but standing there in a staring contest with Madisyn, it seems better than just taking whatever she hands me.

"I will need it," I say, showing her my teeth when I smile. "I'll need a seat right by my side. Where else would my wife sit?"

I swear, Syn's smugness drops away faster than an atomic bomb. "Come again?"

"My wife, Cate?" I speak slowly to antagonize Madisyn. "You do know that I got married, don't you?"

"I—" She shakes her head, looking chagrined. "No. I hadn't heard."

My smile curls into a grin. "Well, we've been playing it very low key. Anyway, I will need that plus one, okay?"

"Oh... okay..." Madisyn seems to shake off her stupor. "Well... I should probably get back to Reggie. He likes to know where I am."

"Uh huh." I'll just bet he would love to know his future wife is here, rubbing her upcoming nuptials in my face. "Sounds good. I've got this save the date so..."

She gives me the most fake smile ever and then practically bolts out of the bar. I watch her go, grinning.

That is, until I realize that Cate didn't exactly agree to me using her as a pawn in my war against my former fiancée. In fact, Cate didn't agree to my telling Madisyn that we got married.

Oops.

Maybe if I make a fuss over things, it'll take a couple of months for our annulment to go through. Or maybe I can convince Cate to help me.

It's unlikely, given that we pretty much hate each other. But it can't hurt to propose the idea to her... even if I never proposed the actual marriage.

I shake my head and go back to sweeping, puzzling over how I'm going to talk to Cate about it tomorrow.

Chapter 6

Cate

When my alarm clock goes off, I'm already awake. I reach over and silence it with a slap of my hand to the plastic case. Groaning, I sit up, disturbing no less than three cats and one very large Doberman. They all stretch, the Doberman whining when I move a cat closer to her and get out of my tiny twin bed.

"Don't start with me today," I tell her. "I can't be late to work, not even for more pets. Although if I just didn't go, my quality of life would probably be better…"

My job absolutely sucks. Not only do I sort of hate being forced to smile as I make coffee, but three people quit last week so I was forced to do the work of multiple people for the same pay. I also had to trade shifts with everyone that still works at the shop to even get the weekend off, making all kinds of deals with the devil.

"Work sucks," I say. "Then you die. Hopefully you

get to buy a house first but there are no guarantees. Right, Shaggy?"

Shaggy whines and shoves her head under my hands.

I scratch her behind an ear and then turn to the other twin bed. Carmine, my seventy seven year old Italian roommate, is already long gone. He made his bed neatly, but the two dogs and one cat sleeping on it don't care. They probably made themselves at home as soon as Carmine left.

Getting together my shower tote, a clean-ish towel, and my shower flip flops, I shuffle down the hallway toward the bathroom. My grandma is sitting outside the bathroom, waiting in her floral bathrobe.

"Ernest is taking forever!" she shouts at the closed door. She rolls her eyes and looks at me. "Hello, darling."

"Hi Grandma," I say, juggling my towel and my tote. "I'm guessing I shouldn't even ask if the shower downstairs is free?"

"Ha!" She shakes her head. "Do you think I would be up here in line for the smaller bathroom if there weren't three people in line for the downstairs one?"

I nod. "That figures."

Her face softens and she reaches over, smoothing my hair. "How was your vacation, my dearest?"

Bobbing my head, I squint at her. She's exactly the same height as me, same texture hair, same lithe frame. Looking at my mother's mother is like looking in a magical mirror that shows exactly what I'll look like some day.

"It was fine, Grandma. Although I think I do have a hangover still."

Her eyebrows lift. "Still? It's Tuesday!"

"I know. I drank half the alcohol on planet Earth, I'm pretty sure." And got married, but I don't feel the need to share that fact. Especially not since I'm pretty sure that Luca will move heaven and earth in order to not be tied to me in that way...

Grandma cocks her head. "Well, I suppose you were due for a weekend away, weren't you? You're always busy working or tutoring or volunteering... That's all quite important, but it's fun to spoil yourself for a weekend."

My face heats. "Well, consider that done."

My grandmother smiles, her lips pressed into a thin line. "Yes, well. I've tried to finish the work your parents started as best I can. They did such a good job raising you."

I press her hand. "It's okay. When they died, you took me in. Here you were, a woman who thought that she had outlived her child bearing years—"

Her lips lift. "Having you move into this commune of a house was maybe not the wisest choice for someone that recently lost their parents. But it is what I have to offer."

I smile. "Hey, if it wasn't for you, I never would've roomed with someone like Carmine. It's been interesting if nothing else."

"Unfortunately, in having you live as I do, I'm afraid I've instilled some of my tendencies in you. Your parents would probably not be terribly glad."

I don't feel like talking about my parents with anyone,

not even my grandma. When they died in an auto accident during my first semester in college, I had a choice: spend forever crying miserably, or pack up my tears and stuff my sadness deep down inside.

I chose the option that allowed me to carry on living. I stitched my heart up and guard myself at all times because...

Well, it's better to live a life without love than to lose someone I truly care for. Of that, I am certain.

Giving my grandma a stiff smile, I touch her shoulder softly. "You did great. I'm going to be late for work if I don't hurry. I guess I'll skip the shower this morning."

"Whatever you think, my dear." She returns my smile and then picks up a section of the paper, putting it close to her face in order to make out that small print.

Wandering back down the hall to my bedroom, I lock the door and start changing clothes. A blue skirt, yellow knee socks, a matching yellow shirt, and a darker blue cardigan. For a second, I am reminded of the black dress I wore in Las Vegas. After wearing that for a night, it feels like all my other clothes are dull and ordinary.

After another second, I switch the yellow socks and shirt for a light pink camisole. I know it's not a big deal for some people, but for me I've made a huge change to my wardrobe.

My orange tabby Lyra appears from beneath my bed, chirping for attention. Scratching her under her chin, I check my phone. I have a text from Luna waiting.

Feb 2ⁿᵈ, The Seattle Stadium, Billie Eilish. Should I snag us tix?

Rather than replying right away, I put my phone down. I can't afford to see Billie Eilish, but I also don't want Luna to just buy me a ticket. Luna's family are so wealthy that they have a Swiss ski chalet and houses sprinkled across the States. Even back when my family was alive, I usually watched her family go on their yachting trips and getting a new Mercedes when they had a birthday. I've never had that kind of wealth, nor wanted it.

And after my parents died, I was left with my grandma and precious little else. So I have to really put my foot down with Luna, because of the house.

I go over to my bedside table, lifting the lid on my mahogany jewelry box. I pull out two pieces of paper: one a worn photograph and the other a full sized sheet of paper that has been unfolded and refolded so many times that it's falling apart.

In the photo, my parents hug me, an unremarkable little one story house in the background. I unfold the sheet of paper, which is from the realtor. There lies an updated version of the house, quaint ivy overgrowing the tan brick façade. It had to be sold when my parents died...

But one day, I'll get it back. I smooth the little bend lines at the corner of the photograph, briefly running my fingers over my family. I already have eighteen thousand dollars saved up toward the down payment.

So while seeing Billie Eilish sounds great, owning my family home sounds even better than that. And I know that Luna would buy the tickets without even thinking twice because she's gracious like that, but I don't want her to.

Heading over to the door, I unlock it again. Carmine is really only particular about one thing, and that's having access to his space. Which is fair, everything considered.

I pick up my phone, unsure what I'm going to say to Luna. Can I just be frank and honest with her? That shouldn't hurt her feelings, right?

As I am wondering just what to write, my phone rings. It's my manager from work Javier, and he's video calling me. That's very weird. Javier pretty flatly dislikes me. Why would he call me? Is it a pocket dial?

Taking a huge breath, I answer the phone. "Hello?"

Javier's scowling face appears on the screen. "Cate. You are *late*. Again."

I screw up my face. "I switched with Dawn. Remember, you signed off on it?"

"Dawn got fired yesterday," he says, a satisfied look on his face. "So any deals you might have made with her are null and void."

Shaking my head, I am at a loss. "I'm sorry, but no one told me."

"It's your responsibility to reach out to her. And now it's a bit of a moot point anyway, because this was the last straw." His lips curve up into a smile. "You're fired, Cate De Rose."

I don't believe it. "But... but I've never even had a negative review! On the customer comment cards, they all love me! And the other managers love working with me..."

Javier shrugs. "Too bad. There a million eager young baristas waiting to fill your shoes." He clears his throat. "I'll need you to return your work shirt and keys before I can release your last paycheck."

I scowl, still a little taken aback. "For the record, you are the worst manager I've ever had. Like *ever*. And before this I worked at McDonald's."

He rolls his eyes. "Yeah, all the employees I've fired say that. Listen, I'm gonna need your shirt and keys this week—"

I press the end button and his face vanishes. What a jerk! I mean, who fires someone over the phone in the first place? My eyes well up, although I know that Javier really did me a favor. It's just hard to look at it any way but as a personal slight at the moment.

I take a few deep breaths, trying to remind myself that I kind of hated the job anyway. I just relied on it for a steady income, but other jobs can offer that.

Grinding my teeth and wiping my eyes, I toss my phone at my bed. A second later, Carmine pops his head in the room, looking like nothing so much as a grape that has withered with age. When he speaks, his voice is hoarser than it usually is. It sounds like someone grating a particularly hard cheese.

"Eh, Cate. You got a friend looking for you downstairs." His accent is Italian, so thick you could spread it on toast.

My eyebrows fly up. "Yeah?"

"Eh." Carmine turns and hobbles back down the hallway, his cane clicking faintly on the hardwood floors.

I take a deep breath, willing myself to calm down. It's probably Luna, all excited about the Billie Eilish show. One part of my mind is whirling, trying to think of all I have to do: update my resume, compile a list of coffee shops, and start plastering every single place on that list with a picture of me attached to my resume.

I head downstairs in the meantime. It's still early in the day. Plenty of time to head to the library and use their computer and printer.

Gosh, it really grinds my gears that Javier was so rude. I trudge down the stairs, angry at the whole world just now.

Chapter 7

Cate

Clenching my jaw, I hit the bottom floor and round the corner, expecting to see Luna waiting there.

I pull up short, startled. Luca is there, looking every bit the part of the bad boy in his dark jeans and leather motorcycle jacket. He glances up, catching my eye. His gaze automatically narrows, but his expression is blank.

"Hey, Cate," he says. For just a second, the throatiness of his voice makes my heart speed up. His expression turns hesitant, which I don't think I have ever witnessed before.

"Hi?" I ask, folding my arms across my chest. "I didn't even know you knew where I lived." My brows draw down. "Did you bring a form for me to sign or something?"

Luca glances behind me, pulling a face at the sound of the vacuum firing up in the next room. "Want to take a walk?"

Now I'm growing suspicious. "Uhhhh...." I glance behind me, biting my lip. Grandma's friend Cynthia pokes her head in, looking gently surprised. I turn back to Luca with a shrug. "Sure, okay."

Slipping on a pair of Grandma's clogs and one of her heavy woolen coats, I follow him out of the house. It's *cold* out here, Seattle in the winter cold. So I can see my breath and there is a thin layer of snow on the ground.

It's definitely no Las Vegas, that's for sure.

I can feel Luca's gaze on me, judgmental as ever. In the cold light of midmorning, he seems cool and impenetrable, as if nothing in the world bothers him. I take in his oversized features and his dark, brooding look. The thought of being on the wrong end of one of his glares sits heavy in the pit of my stomach.

Shivering, I shake my head at myself. So he's handsome. So he's moody. So he's attractive. That's no reason to get bent out of shape, is it?

I wrinkle my nose. "So?"

He glances away for a moment, seeming to steel himself. "I need a favor," he admits.

Tilting my head to the side, I frown. "From me?"

"Yes." He folds his arms across his chest. "It's to do with the annulment."

Shoving my hands deep into the pockets of my coat, I try to imagine just what he's getting at. Another chill slides down my spine. "Well, anytime you want to get around to naming it, that would be great."

He shoots me an annoyed glance. "Alright. I need

you to agree not to annul for a little while. I need a month before we can start the paperwork."

I pull a face. "Okay… that's not really a *favor*, though. That's just being patient."

He closes his eyes briefly. "Well… that's not all. I also need you to attend a wedding with me." He clears his throat, his dark eyes flashing with intensity. "My ex's wedding."

Now I am officially surprised. "The one who dumped you recently?"

His cheeks color but he just grows more gruff. "Yeah. Madisyn. She's getting married in a month and a half and I…" He pauses. His throat works as he swallows. "I told her that I was married. Which is true…"

That gives me pause. On one hand, my heart immediately goes out to Luca. He's admitting to being upset by Madisyn's treatment of him, which I think was poor. But on the other hand, he's proposing lying to her.

To what end exactly, I can't say.

"I mean… *technically* we are married," I say, looking at him skeptically. "I'm guessing you didn't fill her in on the fact that you got drunk and wed someone you don't even like, huh?"

Luca looks at me as if I was actually torturing him. "No, I didn't. But you have to know that I wouldn't ask you if there was any other way." He hesitates. "I could make it worth your while, though. I could give you a job at my bar. And… I don't know… a cash bonus when you finally sign the annulment paperwork, maybe?"

My eyebrows go up. "A bonus?"

He rolls his eyes at my response. "Yeah. If that's what needs to happen, sure."

I bite my lower lip, thinking for a second. "Let me just be sure that I've got this right. You're offering me a job and a cash bonus for just... not pursuing the annulment for a month?"

His head bobs. "You would probably be legally bound up for two months total. But yeah, that's about the breadth of it. I'd be willing to pay you five thousand dollars."

Puffing out my cheeks, I exhale slowly. That's a lot of money to me. And I can't think of any downsides offhand, honestly. I've already made the mistake of marrying Luca. I might as well get something out of it in the meantime.

"Two months. Five grand. Sounds like a good deal." Thrusting out my hand, I give him an uncertain look.

His lips curl up at the corners as he takes my hand. He steps closer, his expression intense, making me feel small next to him. His palm feels warm and a little rough where it presses against mine. "All right. We're agreed, then."

He grips my hand for a second too long, looking down into my eyes. And me being me, I blush. Then he releases my hand, turning and pacing away from me. I stand still, unsure how to proceed.

Luca is on the ball, though. "Do you need to make arrangements with your current job?"

My cheeks turn pink and I look down. "Nope."

A hint of a smirk appears on his face. "Right. Well... can you come into the bar tomorrow, then?"

I nod, drowning in my embarrassment. "Yep."

"Great." He looks like he means the opposite. "See you then, Cate."

He turns and heads to a sleek black motorcycle parked in front of the next yard. I roll my eyes; of course that would be his bike. The fact that Luca drives a two-wheeled death trap should surprise exactly no one.

As I watch, he mounts it, puts on his helmet, and revs the engine. I'll admit it to myself: right this second he is tall, dark, and oh so very handsome. Enough to make some girls swoon, I should think.

Then he pulls off, quickly disappearing. I stare after him for half a minute, then shake my head.

Staying married to Luca won't be that bad.

It will only be two months at the most.

And at the end, I'll get a little more cash to bundle into my nest egg. I'll be that much closer to buying my house.

I would consider that a win-win.

Shivering against the cold, I turn and head back inside.

Chapter 8

Luca

At one forty five the next day, I glance at my watch. For some reason I've been keyed up all morning. Drumming my fingers, tapping my foot, staring at the front door of The Attic.

I guess I'm searching for a sign of whether hiring Cate was a terrible idea or not.

Will she flout the rules? Will she drop every bottle of liquor handed to her?

Will her big brown eyes and elfin features distract me from my work?

More importantly, will she even show up in the first place?

"Hey!" Bradford says, snapping his fingers. "Earth to Luca. We're having an ownership meeting here, buddy."

"Sorry," I mumble. "I'm just distracted,"

I look at Bradford and Owen, both of them sitting with their papers spread out on the little table before us.

Owen looks up from his calendar notebook, his brow creasing.

"I was asking whether the twelfth of February will be too early for a staff appreciation party," he sighs. "I want to close the whole place down and have the bar open late the next day."

"Uhhh..." I look down at my calendar, which is basically covered with post its and scrawled notes. Checking beneath several piles of post its, I shrug. "I don't think I have anything booked for that day..."

Bradford narrows his eyes and looks down his nose at me. "I don't trust you, Luca. Your management style as a whole is wonderful, but you are absolutely the worst when it comes to keeping a calendar."

Owen nods in agreement. "He's right. I don't want to announce a staff appreciation day and then cancel it at the last minute because you realize that you've double booked us. *Again*."

Rolling my eyes, I stretch. "That was one time, guys."

Bradford is ready. "No, it was two times. I think you secretly have it in for the staff."

He crosses his arms and gives me a dirty look. I wave him off. "Send me the date in an email. I'll block the day off, okay?"

"And the next day," Owen reminds me.

"Yes, mother." I glance around, my gaze ending up on the empty doorway once more. I grind my teeth; I have a dozen things to worry about that are more important than when precisely Cate walks through that door. "Are we by any chance done here?"

Owen rolls his eyes, closing his notebook. Bradford just frowns. "Yeah, all right."

"Hello?" I turn around to find Cate waiting at the bar, biting her lip. She spots the three of us and looks a little relieved. "Oh, there you are."

"Where did you come from?" I ask, irritated with her already. Cate comes around the bar, dressed in an ankle-length gray skirt and a long sleeve gray cotton top. "Jesus, what did you do, rob a nunnery?"

She immediately turns bright red, tucking her wavy dark hair behind her ear. "You didn't specify that I needed to dress any particular way. And I came from the employees' entrance out back."

I stand up, shaking my head. This was a bad idea, I can already tell. Cate nods to Owen and Bradford. "Hey guys."

"Hey, honey..." Bradford says to her, arching a brow at me.

Oh. Yeah, it would probably have been a good idea to tell my business partners that I brought someone new onto our staff. By the angry look I'm receiving from Owen, I can see that I should've brought Cate up before right now.

"Cate's going to be working here," I say, pretending that her hiring is totally normal.

Yeah, it's absolutely the norm to hire someone I got drunk with and married to the weekend before. No, I'm not going to regret this at *all*.

There is a look shared between Owen, Bradford, and I that says we will definitely get into this later. For her part, Cate looks like she's drowning over by the bar. I sigh.

"Come on," I say to her, stalking back behind the bar. "Let's get you in the computer system, I guess."

Heading back to my mess of an office, I try to figure out where the fuck I'm going to stash Cate. Casting an eye over her choice of wardrobe, I shake my head a little bit. She can't dress like that, first of all. I should've thought of her clothes yesterday, but I was too busy plotting against Madisyn.

So for today, I can't have her waiting tables or anything. Which kind of sucks, because I was just going to dump the responsibility for training her in Bradford's lap. He likes new people. At least he would get along with her, probably.

"Sit down," I rumble, pointing to a chair that is almost entirely covered with a big pile of white buffet bunting from something we did at Easter this year. "Just move that to the ground."

Cate eyes the pile with some suspicion, but eventually moves it to the ground by tilting the chair. The bunting slides off into a graceless pile. She gives me a cool smile as she sits down.

Rooting around in one of my desk drawers, I produce a new employee packet. Flinging it across my desk, I favor her with a dry smile. "Bring this back tomorrow filled out. And make sure you bring your identification, too."

She leafs though it with a frown. I unearth an iPad from under some stacks of paper on my desk and start keying her basics in to the system.

"What am I going to be doing here, exactly?"

Looking at her frankly, I shrug. "I don't know. We don't exactly have any positions for baristas. I figure that we'll find you something that fits for the next few months. The absolute worst case is that I pay you for nothing and you just stay at home. You would have to be pretty bad at everything for that to happen, though."

She shoots me a glare. "I plan on pulling my own weight thank you very much. I don't want your charity."

That earns a raised eyebrow from me. "I thought you only agreed to do this for the money."

The apples of her cheeks flush. "I want to be useful."

She ducks her head. I stare at her for half a minute. "Is this a Christian thing or something?"

Cate gives me a dirty look. "No."

I shift in my chair. "Because this is a bar, princess. We are not interested in judging our patrons. Or musical acts. We book whoever we want, whenever we want. And we don't dress..." I wave my hand over her. "...like *this* when we do it, either."

Her look shifts to a glare. "I said it wasn't a Catholic thing, okay? Everyone likes to be useful and productive."

I raise my brows. "I think you're giving people way more credit than they are due for."

She just rolls her eyes. Shaking my head, I finish plugging her into the computer system. Then when I'm done, I frog march her out to the bar. "Come on. Let's see if you are a decent bar back."

"Bradford!" I call out. He turns around, his pen poised over his inventory list.

"What?" he asks, eyeing both of us skeptically.

"Try Cate out as a bar back tonight. She can prep fruit, stack beer cans, wash glasses, clean the bar..." I stop, giving him a desperate look. "Please take her."

Bradford gives me a look, holding his arm out to Cate. "Come on, darling. Let's get you set up juicing oranges and lemons. Citrus fruit is the best way to start any shift."

Cate looks at me, her brown eyes wide. She goes along with Bradford, who keeps making stern eye contact with me until I turn and leave.

Heading back into my office, I start sifting through a whole pile of artist-venue contracts. I put the ones that need contacting to the side and then start to plug all the finished ones into a spreadsheet on the iPad. It's boring as fuck, but it'll make Owen happy. As the money manager of our threesome, he is always moaning that none of us put anything in Excel.

And if I'm not paying enough attention, I know it's something I can't screw up too badly. I keep my eye on the door at first, relaxing after a few minutes. Still, I feel like I've barely started when Bradford and Cate are in my office again.

Cate is nursing her right hand and looking paler than usual. Bradford looks like he wants to sigh about people testing his patience but thankfully doesn't.

"We just got Miss Cate here all bandaged up, didn't we? You're gonna need to find somewhere else to work today, hon," he says, pursing his lips. "Cate just gored her own hand when I was trying to teach her how to zest a lime."

"I'm sorry," Cate tells Bradford. "I know I already said it, but I'm so sorry bled on your pants."

"It's okay, honey." Bradford pats her on the back. "I'll tell people I was tussling with a wild bear. No one will know the difference."

"Fuck. Are you okay?" I ask.

"Yes," Cate mumbles. "Just clumsy, I guess."

"Hm." I scrub my hand through my short hair.

Bradford shoots me a questioning look as he leaves. I'm going to have so many questions to answer when Cate isn't around. Pushing myself to my feet, I consider what to do with her next.

"Ummm... I need the stock room organized... or I guess there is the filing room..."

She perks up a little. "Filing? I can file in my sleep."

Blowing out a breath, I shrug. "Yeah, all right. Come on. Just... prepare yourself. It's a little bit of a zoo."

I walk right next door, opening the door and flipping on the light. The filing room, more of a closet really, is an absolute disaster. So is the stock room. So is my office.

But just thinking about the time it would take to reorganize everything brings on a splitting headache. So... I just deal with it.

"It's not great," I say with a shrug. "It drives Owen crazy and Bradford won't even look in here."

I turn, expecting to see some sort of horror written on Cate's face. But instead, I see a light turn on behind her eyes. She looks at me, animated. "Oh, I'm gonna conquer this mess."

She pushes up the sleeves of her cardigan and pushes past me, picking up one of the files closest to her.

"Do you need—" I start.

She cuts me off by raising a hand. Without taking her eyes off the file, she starts to close the door. "I'm fine. Go work. I'll come see you if I have questions."

Hesitating, I watch Cate for a second until the door closes on her. What could she really screw up? Nothing that's not fixable, I guess...

Slinking back to my office, I return to my seat and try my best to focus on the contracts and the spreadsheet. At one point, I field a phone call from an irate manager. He's mad because he doesn't have finalized details for a set booked in late January. It takes me a while to uncover the band's file and by the time we are done haggling, it's early evening.

Cate has been going at the organization of the file closet for almost two and a half hours. Frowning, I decide I should check on her. Before I can though, Owen pops his head into my office.

"Have you seen your wife's organizational skills?" he asks, widening his eyes. "I think you should think twice about divorcing her, Luca."

"We're getting an annulment," I say with a sigh. "And no, I haven't seen her work. What is she screwing up now?"

Owen waves me over, so I get up out of my chair. When I round the corner, Owen pushes the door of the file closet open a little more. Cate's ass is the first thing I see, poking up as she reaches for a file at the very bottom of a filing cabinet.

All around her, folders are neatly sorted into stacks. It's really not bad for a couple of hours of work. She senses us behind her and freezes, then shoots to her knees. When she turns to face us, her cheeks are stained pink.

"Hi," she says, patting at her hair. She has a streak of dust across her right cheek. Reaching for her cell phone, she says, "What time is it? There are no windows in here."

Owen glances at his watch. "Just past six."

"Ah. I have a tendency to get caught up in projects that involve organizing." She turns around, dusting herself off. "Is there something I should be doing instead?"

"Oh, look at this!" Bradford says, crowding into the doorway. "Girl! This closet has been a wreck for years. It's time that somebody did something with it, honestly. Good job!"

Cate blushes. "Well, it's hardly done. I have a few types of files..."

Owen looks down at his phone. "I gotta take this call guys. Excuse me."

Cate adjusts the waist of her long skirt, seeming not to realize the fact that her nipples are poking through her camisole. There is something so innocent about that, so lacking in pretense.

What would it be like if I laid her down right here and took her, hard and quick and dirty?

"Well..." she says, frowning. "What now?"

Bradford is already headed into the storage room. That leaves me, staring down at Cate. She meets my gaze, licking her lips. "Luca, any direction you would like to give me?"

Yes, is my first instinct. There is something about her being on her knees and asking that question that makes me think dirty thoughts.

God, am I really lusting after my little sister's best friend? Ugh, I really need to get laid.

Clearing my throat, I shake my head. "No. It seems like you have things well in hand here."

Her eyes narrow on my face. "You don't have to make fun of me, Luca."

"I'm not," I shoot back, defensive.

Cate rolls her eyes and begins to shut the door. "Come get me when it's time for me to leave."

Before I can say anything else, the door closes with a click. My phone rings on my desk next door, so I just sigh heavily and head to answer it.

But in the back of my mind, I'm still wondering if the idea to have Cate work here was terrible or not.

Chapter 9

Cate

"**O**h no. No way am I wearing *that*." I'm in the employee dressing room, and I'm mad. Well, less *mad* and more *wildly uncomfortable*. "I've worked here for a week and nobody other than Luca has had anything to say about my wardrobe..."

Standing at a rolling rack full of clothes that Luna has picked out, I'm staring at a bright pink tube dress on a hanger.

It turns out that Luca said something to her about how I don't dress to match the *bar vibe*, whatever that means. So today when I showed up for work, Luna was already here. And she came prepared with all kinds of clothes.

She's a clothes horse for sure; most of this rack just came from the back of one of her closets.

Luna rolls her eyes, but she's still beaming at me. She's actually been beaming nonstop since Vegas. I don't want to crush her dreams, so I just stay silent about the fact that I'm still getting an annulment from her jerk of a brother.

"We're gonna take this in baby steps, okay? No glittery pink tube dresses but maybe..." She brushes my shoulder as she flips through the garment rack. "How about this?"

She pulls out a bright red one-piece pantsuit, her eyes sparkling. It has a very low front and back and appears to be made of parachute material. "This is conservative, sort of. Well, less *conservative* conservative, but it's got pants!"

"Luna, that thing has a plunging neckline instead of a collar. It would show off all kinds of boob. It's not happening." I pause, my head tilting. "What kind of bra do you even wear with that?"

Luna sighs, putting the jumpsuit back. "You don't. And you're right, it's probably too advanced for you."

She pushes a few hangers aside one by one, looking thoughtful. I clear my throat. "Maybe something with a skirt, at least? I've worn a skirt for my whole life and I don't see any reason to stop now." I pause. "And for the love of god, no more plunging necklines."

"Ooooh," she says, pulling out a black cocktail dress. "Simple. Basic. No crazy neckline. It even has sleeves... and it's made of cotton."

I wrinkle my nose. "It's so short."

"No more protesting! Just think of it as your work wardrobe. Now go change into this," Luna commands. "And I think I have some black high heels in my car that are your size."

"Thanks," I say, although I don't really mean it. Luna flashes me a big grin and hurries out of the room. I hurry through changing, thanking the Lord that I decided to wear my good bra and panties today.

Turning to look at myself in the full length mirror, I frown. This dress falls to mid-thigh and shows off an eye-catching amount of cleavage. Is this really my uniform for working at this bar?

Luna bursts back in the room, unworried about my privacy. "So I think if you like that dress—" She stops short, the black heels hanging from one hand. "Daaaamn. That dress looks dope on you! That's it, I'm ordering five more in different colors."

"Luna," I warn. "I only agreed to this because you promised me it wouldn't cost anything."

"Pssh," she says, beaming. "They're only like $120 each. That's a total bargain!"

Flushing, I grab her hand when she pulls out her phone. "That's six hundred dollars, Luna. That's a ton of money to most people. Please don't spend that kind of money. I will feel obligated to pay you back and I really can't afford it."

Her brow furrows and she sighs. "Alright, fine. But you are totally taking that dress. I thought it looked good on me, but seeing it on you, I'm like... *damn.*" She hands me the shoes she's carrying. "Here, put these on. And I'm going to put some mascara and lipstick on you. Not a single word, okay?"

I curl my lip but step into the heels anyway. They're uncomfortable but I can walk in them. After I begrudgingly allow Luna to do my makeup, she beckons me to the mirror.

"Ready to see?"

I take a moment to thank her. "I just want you to know that I'm grateful for this, Luna. Even though I hate subscribing to other people's beauty standards, I'm glad that I have you to dress me up. Thank you."

"Are you kidding? I've wanted to do this forever. Besides, you make a great doll." She fluffs my hair. "Now look."

Glancing in the mirror, I'm a little surprised. The girl that stares back at me is an absolute knockout, no doubt about it. But she also looks a little... dull. Like someone drained all the personality right out of her and replaced it with hotness.

I pull a face. "I need something—"

"Got it," Luna cuts in. She offers me a sparkly pink and blue stegosaurus made out of sequins . It's about the size of my hand and it has a handy pin on the backside.

I look at her, my lips curling. "How did you know?"

She shrugs. "You always did like to be individualistic. This definitely says something more than just the black dress."

I take a second to hug her and then affix the pin to the right side of my chest, just above my breast. Looking at it makes me laugh, which is good. I was almost sweating bullets without it.

The door bursts open, revealing an all-black wearing Luca. "Cate!"

He stops in his tracks when he sees us, his eyes widening. His eyes go right to my cleavage. "Jesus."

I feel completely naked under his gaze, and not in a good way. My hands tug down the hem of my dress.

"The nuns can finally dress in their own clothes, huh?" he says. "It's really nice of you to dress your age and leave the long skirts to them."

I shoot Luca a glare but don't have a good comeback.

Luna leans close to me, stage whispering. "That's the initial reaction you want everyone to have, in case you were wondering. You're a fox."

He glares at his sister. "Very funny. We are short a server tonight, so Cate, that's where we'll put you in. Come on, Bradford has to run through things with you."

Nodding, I start following him. I turn to Luna as I go. "Text me later?"

"Of course," she says, smiling at me again.

As I hurry to follow Luca, I can't help but notice the fact that there is a hole in his jeans. On the inside of his leg, only a few inches down from his crotch. Is that fashion? Is it just laziness?

Whatever reason that hole exists, it is making me stare at Luca's ass for a prolonged period... so I guess there is that. Yanking my gaze away, I throw myself into the training Bradford is about to give me.

Twenty minutes later, I'm trying to remember it all. "Go to a table." I take a deep breath. "Write down the table number. Carry the order back to one of the iPads. Order the drinks. Pick up said drinks from the bar. Take them to the customers."

Bradford leans against the bar, looking pleased. "Rinse. Repeat. Multiply by a few hundred. You'll do fine. If not, it doesn't matter. It's a Wednesday so it'll be slow. Besides, Bonnie will be back tomorrow to take her usual shift."

Luca stalks out of the back, looking even more annoyed than usual. "Hey. Miss Not-A-Nun—"

I flush. "Better a nun than a slut. If there are only two ways a man can look at a woman, I'll take the more innocent one, every single time."

"God, she's so right," Bradford sighs. He gives me a high five.

Luca rolls his eyes. "Christ. I have a private party of fifteen coming in tonight. Usually I would ask Bradford to take them, but he's also training a new bartender."

"Lucky me," Bradford mutters. His sarcasm is missed by no one.

"Come with me. I'll help you set up their table." He starts off, leaving me to trail in his wake.

In the back of my mind, I'm still a little off-kilter over the fact that Luca demeaned my dress again in public. Worse than that actually... because I have to work with these people.

When he reaches a table, I catch his elbow. He gives me the same look that a king would give a dirty peasant, but I don't care. I'm *pissed*.

"Hey. Do you want to lay off a little?" I ask, whispering angrily.

One of his brows rises. "Excuse me?"

I lean closer to his smug face, pointing a finger at him.

"You just can't help yourself. I'm dressing how you want me to, okay? Isn't that enough? Do you really have to keeping bullying me about every little thing?"

He glares, moving closer so that he's right in my face. He reaches out and lifts up my pin. "I didn't realize that sparkly dinosaurs counted as what I wanted. This thing is ugly as sin."

I yank my body back. "Don't touch me."

He actually laughs in my face. "You are such a nun! Admit it!"

"I am not!" I can feel my face turning red. "It's not prudish to tell a man to keep his hands to himself."

Luca's dark eyes gleam. "But what about your husband?"

Fuming, I smack him on the arm. "I swear, this whole *please stay married to me* thing is just... stupid!"

He glares at me, opening his mouth. Luckily at that moment Bradford calls out from across the bar. "Save it for the bedroom, guys! We open the front door in less than five minutes!"

Luca narrows his eyes at Bradford, but he does shift his stance to grab another table and pull it close. "We're not finished here, princess."

"Whatever. You should just be glad that I'm going to be busy all night." As soon as the words leave my mouth, I'm scrambling to clarify. "Because otherwise I would... you know... beat you at sparring. Err... verbally..."

Luca grins. "You know what? Maybe princess is the wrong nickname for you. Maybe it should be Old Lady."

"That's not fair!" I protest.

"Cate!" Bradford calls. "Come get an order pad, please!"

Giving Luca a foul look, I head across the venue and take one of the paper pads that Bradford holds out to me. He gives me a look, head to toe.

"Honey, I know that you're all giddy because the boss man is totally in love with you. Seriously, it's amazing. Any other time I would thank you. But right now, I need you to get your game face on. I'm about to unlock those doors and I need you to pretend that you have the minutest smidge of experience, okay?"

"Oh, that's not... we're not..." I laugh. "I mean, we are getting an annulment," I finish lamely.

"How nice for you. My point is, put all your personal stuff aside for the next five hours. Look, Levi is unbolting the door... And there is the first guest..." He shoos me away from the bar, turning away to stack copper mugs.

I have to straighten my dress, walk a little taller in my borrowed heels, and go greet the first customers of the night. After that, the night speeds up, going into warp drive around ten. By then I'm waiting on the entire room by myself and I'm way too far in the weeds to so much as think about Luca.

I do catch a glimpse of him, bussing a table here and bringing someone water there. And I have to wonder...

What did Bradford mean when he said that Luca was in love with me? Obviously if he'd been listening, he would know that not a single sweet word crossed Luca's lips.

Is he just crazy?

By the end of the night, Luca is long gone, leaving me and Bradford to clean up. We do twenty minutes of light cleaning, during which I'm too tired to even process that I had a question for Bradford.

I head home, so tired that I'm about to drop. Only when my head is on my pillow, my eyes closed, does Bradford's statement float back up to the top of my mind.

The boss man is totally in love with you, he said.

Yeah right. I fall asleep with a smile curving my lips, thinking about what Luca would act like if we didn't absolutely hate each other.

Chapter 10

Luca

"**Y**ou push the cart like a bitch."

I eye Owen, grunting. "These carts are tiny. If you don't like how I do it, you push the cart."

I let the cart go, forcing Owen to grab it before it runs into a huge display of apples. "I hate going to the grocery store. Can't we just make a list and send one of the employees to do our errands?"

"No," I say, stopping at the citrus display. I pick up a lime, squeezing it. "We are going into the spring season, which means we need to change our bar menu. This is how I get inspired, man."

Owen crosses his arms and grumbles. "I don't know why you had to pick right now to go grocery shopping."

"You want to watch the Seahawks game on the big screen? This is the price you pay." I sweep a bag of lemons and a bag of limes into the tiny cart, then throw a couple of grapefruits in for good measure. "Besides, this

75

store is in such a weird part of town. I never drive by this place, I only come here on purpose."

"It's expensive as fuck." He looks unimpressed. Then his head turns and his brows lift. "Is that Madisyn?"

My heart seizes up. I look over and there she is, at the other end of the produce area. She tosses her long hair, looking displeased, and points at her cart. She's not alone, of course. No, Madisyn is with a big, ripped dude that's wearing a Seahawks jersey.

"Fuck," I say.

As if she feeds off of my unhappiness, Madisyn turns away. Our gazes clash. And the biggest smile overtakes Madisyn's whole face.

"Ah, shit. She's coming over here," Owen complains, shoulders sagging. "Like I need to be dressed down right now. I had a long day."

"Hello boys," Madisyn chirps, striding up to us. "I'm not sure you've met Reginald, my fiancé?"

She motions to the guy ten paces behind her, who is having a hard time controlling his cart.

"Hey," I say.

Owen stays quiet, watching Madisyn through slitted eyes. They never got along very well. I can't say that Owen was sad in the least when Syn dumped me. He crosses his arms reflexively, tugging on his dark blue hoodie.

"I see you're shopping..." Madisyn looks around. "I don't see your wife, though. Where is she?" She pulls a sad face. "She isn't fake, is she?"

Owen snorts. "Cate is realer than your fake ass handbag."

She shoots him a glare, adjusting the big purse on her elbow. "This is a Birkin, you cretin."

He leans forward but I silence him with a hand gesture. "We're shopping for the bar. Trying out a few new recipes."

"And she's... what, at home?"

I shrug. "I don't know. I don't keep tabs on her. We're in a healthy relationship that relies on both us wanting to come back to the other every day."

Owen coughs and I eye him. Yeah, I know it was a lie. So what?

Madisyn gives me a bored look. "I want to meet her. See what my life would have been like if I hadn't... you know..." She makes a face. "Broken your heart."

"Okay," Owen says, rolling his eyes. "I think I should go look at something... somewhere else. I'll be in the next aisle, man."

"Mm," I answer, narrowing my gaze on Madisyn. "You'll have to catch her some other time."

She makes a sad face again. "That's too bad. I really want to meet her before my wedding. Make sure she's not a psycho before I let her into a ballroom full of my loved ones." She pauses, thinking. "Maybe I'll try to catch her at your house!"

That catches me by surprise, as I'm sure it was intended to. "My house?" I echo, my face showing a little of the horror I feel. I can just imagine Madisyn coming by the house to meet Cate and concluding that she isn't real.

"Yes, silly." She rolls her eyes.

"Well... you can... but Cate is in the middle of moving in still. Boxes everywhere, that whole thing. I don't think she would take kindly to a visit. I feel like she would think that you're being an intrusive busybody."

I just let that lie, putting my insult onto Cate. Madisyn glares at me. "I think that's an excuse. Either she is real and you live together or she isn't and you don't. Which is it?"

"The first," I say. My gaze slides around the store. I can feel Madisyn wearing down my edges. She already knows that listening to her talk about any topic for more than three minutes will bore me to death.

"Well then," she says brightly. "I'll just feel free to pop by and try to meet her sometime soon."

"Well, you should call first. I mean, you have to realize what you might be interrupting. Cate is so fucking hot and it hard for us to keep our hands off each other."

There, that one was only a partial lie. Cate is hot. It's only the touching each other part that is completely untrue.

She rolls her eyes. "I'm willing to risk it."

Eyeing a very bored-looking Reggie, I shrug. "Doesn't your man Reggie have any concerns about you coming to my house? After all, you did practically live with me for a year..."

She looks completely smug. "Nope. Reginald knows where his bread is buttered, okay?"

She giggles, glancing at Reggie. Reggie shrugs and nods, which is apparently enough to satisfy Madisyn.

"See?" she says. Her phone chirps and she peers inside her giant purse, looking for it. "Anyway, I've really got to get moving... so much to do for the wedding, so little time. Right Reggie?"

"Yup," he rumbles.

"I'll be seeing you soon though, don't worry." Madisyn gives me a cheesy smile. "Bye bye, Luca."

With that, she starts walking toward the front of the store. Reggie dutifully wheels the cart in her wake, utterly unbothered by anything at all. I stare after him for a second, shaking my head.

Maybe Madisyn would never have dumped me if I just went along with every stupid thing she said. If that's what she was looking for in a mate, I'm very glad that we broke up when we did.

Very, very, *very* glad.

I hurry to find Owen, my mind spinning. Do I just hope that the wedding hoax works cut and Madisyn never finds out? Or do I escalate things by asking Cate to move in with me for the duration?

I mean, it really wouldn't be a big deal to have her move in. My place is huge. We could practically live together and never see each other. And Cate's home life is... well, from what little I know of her situation, it seems like it's chaotic at best.

Really, I would be doing Cate a favor. At least, that's what I tell myself when I decide to ask her to move in.

Once I drop Owen back off at the bar and unload the groceries, I head to Cate's place again. It's a drive, way on the very outskirts of Seattle, in a big old house next to a set of railroad tracks. I pull up out front and walk around the vegetable garden growing in her front lawn.

A very old black lab watches me skeptically from a dog bed on the front porch when I pound on Cate's front door. After a few seconds, I'm about to knock again.

The door is yanked open by Cate, wearing a bathrobe, a towel in her hair, and a face mask. "Yeah, yeah," she starts. Then she sees me and stops. "What... what are you doing here, Luca?"

She pulls the edges of her robe closer together, as if I care about that. I clear my throat.

"Move in with me."

The surprise on her face is clear. "What? Why?"

I shrug. "Because. You're my wife for the next seven weeks. We should present a united front." I look behind her, where three dogs are fighting over a rope toy. "Plus it would be your own space for a while. I doubt that this place can boast that."

She sucks her lower lip into her mouth. "I don't know, Luca. Won't we be tripping over each other just the same at your house? At least here, I know I'm not... you know, *unwelcome*."

Rolling my eyes, I challenge her. "I have a ton of space. And you'd be doing me a favor."

Arching a brow, she crosses her arms. Her little pink bathrobe hitches up on one side, showing me more of her hip than she probably wants me to see. But I can be gentleman, and to prove it I keep my eyes raised.

"How much of a favor?" she demands to know. "Are

we talking an extra bonus? Because I'm pretty comfortable here already."

My nose wrinkles. "All right. Let's say... eight thousand dollars, as opposed to five. At the end of the whole thing, for your signature on the annulment papers."

"Ten," she fires back. "And I get to bring my cat."

Grinding my teeth, I pause for a second. The cat is no thing, but... is Madisyn not being able to find out that we're not married *really* worth an extra five grand? Well, not married in the long term, anyway.

Blowing out a breath, I concede. "Fine. But you have to start moving in immediately."

Cate narrows her gaze on my face, as if she knows that I'm up to something but can't quite figure it out. She sticks her hand out, and I shake it briefly. Her hand is warm and soft in mine. When I lean closer, I get just a whiff of vanilla scent.

Mmmm, I think. It's automatic, just enjoying the clean smell of a freshly showered Cate.

"I work tonight. You know what the boss can be like." She smiles, pursing her lips. "Tomorrow I can move my stuff in, though. There isn't much."

"All right." I glance at my watch. "I have to stop by my house and then go to work... I guess just call me when you're ready to move tomorrow."

"Okay." She closes the door without ceremony.

I can't be too worried about that, because I'm officially running out of time. Work is in less than two hours and I have to squeeze a shower in before then. After driving back to my side of town, I pull the car in the driveway of my three story white colonial and sprint up to the house.

I stop briefly to check the mail and then flip through it as I let myself into the house. It's mainly junk, but there is a large padded envelope from someplace called Chapel of The Bells. I recognize that name; I tried to go there the morning after I woke up next to Cate, wretchedly hungover.

Setting the rest of the mail aside, I tear open the envelope. Inside are a thumb drive and several sheets of photos. I brace myself for the photos: surely we're good and toasted by this point in the evening. Who knows what we've had to drink, how we got to the chapel, or what we are even wearing.

I'm expecting… I don't know, one of us to be wearing a foam finger and the other to be dressed as an alien, or something. Red faced, sweaty, looking like we are about to puke. Maybe even mostly passed out.

But when I look at the photos, I'm surprised for a different reason.

In every single photo, I'm staring at Cate like she is the only woman I've ever loved. Like she's the reason for my existence, something I've never felt for anyone. And her eyes are glued on me as she beams. In the photos, she's wearing a round pink piece of plastic on her fourth finger and looking blissed the fuck out.

Sure, we're a little intoxicated. But we are both bright eyed and bushy tailed, so to speak. There is absolutely no reason that anyone wouldn't marry us, especially a Las Vegas chapel.

Wow. When have I ever been that happy before? I guess never, which is why I had to be extremely drunk for those pictures to be taken. Still, it's better if no one else sees the photos. Especially not the judge that we are about to plead incapacitation to, hopefully.

Shoving the pictures back in the envelope, I drop the entire envelope into the fruit bowl in my kitchen. That's as good a spot as any while I decide what to do with the photos.

The expression on my face in the pictures keeps coming back to me as I shower, though.

What did she do that made me so happy? And vice versa, how did that happen exactly?

As the shower washes away my shampoo, I know I can't do anything to make myself remember, but I would really like to know.

Chapter 11

Cate

I haul a box of my things through the front door of Luca's house, ignoring the little voice inside my head. The one that screams as I walk into Luca's foyer. The one who whispers nasty things to me as Luca shows me around.

"This is the living room," he says. "There's a more formal parlor around the corner, but I never use it."

And the little voice, the one that sounds just like my cranky grandpa before he passed… it whispers, *don't even think about getting comfortable here. You know that someone as rich as Luca has a dozen girls lined up, ready to take your place the second you falter.*

I take a deep breath, carrying the box through the open concept living room and up the stairs to the right. The floors are covered with pristine white carpet, the walls are very muted jewel tones. Even back before my parents died in a car accident, we never had the kind of money that this house suggests.

I can just imagine my mother's face as she looked around this place. *So light! So airy! I bet it gets good sun.*

My mouth twists. My mom was fairly obsessed with the amount of light a room affords her plants.

I really, really miss her a lot right now.

Turning a corner, I nudge my bedroom door open and drop the box of stuff on the bed. Luca is right on my heels, dumping a fourth box on the bed. He frowns at the boxes.

"Is this really all you have?"

My cheeks flush. I don't mean to, but I automatically go on the defensive. "Some of us weren't born with a lot of money, okay?"

Luca flinches just a hair. "I didn't mean that. I just mean, did we leave something behind? It seems like you should have way more stuff."

Cheeks burning, I shake my head. "This is it. Everything I need for the next seven weeks, anyway."

Okay, it's everything I have period, but he doesn't need to know that.

The voice in my head snickers. *You're just lucky you happened to get drunk and marry him. Look at how wealthy he is! Don't expect it to last.*

I clench my teeth. Luca shrugs. "Okay. Just checking." He glances at his phone. "Shit, this is the manager for the Tells. I've got to answer this."

"Go," I wave him off.

He gives me an odd look as he heads out of the room, answering the phone. "Hey, Jared? Yeah, man. Yeah, I was just hoping..."

The sound of his voice fades away. I turn back to my boxes, exhaling. It shouldn't take me very long to get them squared away. Not long at all. I stare at them for a second longer, my face glum.

I reach into one of my boxes, pulling out a little wooden crucifix. That goes on to the bedside table, along with a stack of books. The Amazing Adventures of Kavalier and Clay, partially read. A copy of Sherman Alexie's autobiography. Both copies were checked out of the library just a couple of days ago.

To that list, I add my well-thumbed bible. My dad always said that he could sleep anywhere his bible was unpacked; I guess I feel that way too today.

The little voice in the back of my head laughs. I ignore it.

After unpacking the rest of my stuff and putting the flattened boxes in the closet for later use, I glance at my cell phone. Just enough time for a quick shower in my new bathroom before I have to run to catch the bus.

Every other Tuesday I give my evening to the women's shelter. I volunteer wherever they can use me, usually leading a prayer group at the end. The bus going to that part of downtown only runs once an hour, so I will have to be economical with my time.

I sprint through showering and change into my regular old clothes. I like the fabric of my new work dress, but going downtown on the bus... it's just better if I don't attract any attention.

Wearing a long gray skirt and a buttoned up black cardigan achieves exactly that. I make sure to grab my coat as it promises to drop below freezing tonight. Snagging my shoulder bag, I hunt around inside it for my necklace. My head is down as I reach the living room, frowning. Then I find what I was looking for.

A skinny silver chain with a little silver cross, given to me on my confirmation day by my parents. Of course I immediately drop it on the floor right in front of Luca, who gives me another odd look. He bends down to pick it up, eyeing my outfit as he rises again.

"Where are you going dressed like that?" he asks. "I thought we had moved beyond the librarian's garb, princess."

I give him my best glare. "I have to catch the bus. I'm going to be late."

He dangles my necklace within my reach. He's so much taller than I am that it's a little ridiculous, him standing there holding it over my head. I reach out to grab it, but he has other ideas. "Uh uh uh. You didn't answer my question."

Gritting my teeth, I give him an answer. "I'm going to First Hill."

He pauses, cocking his head. "You're going to that part of town right now? It's a little late, don't you think?"

"Give me my necklace," I snap. "Or you can find someone else to play house with. I swear to the Lord, I will walk away from this marriage."

Luca's brows rise, but his hand does drop. "Touchy, touchy."

I grab the necklace from him. "My parents gave me this necklace, you complete jerk."

"Oh." His smile falls away. "I'm sorry. I didn't realize."

Stamping my foot, I glance at my phone. Then I roll my eyes. "Oh *crud*. I just missed the bus. That's just... do you even *know* how much more an Uber will cost?"

I make an infuriated sound and then manage to drop my necklace again.

Luca is too fast for me, picking the necklace up again. "I'm sorry, Cate. Here, turn around. I'll put your necklace on for you."

Eyeing him angrily, I heft my coat and my shoulder bag. "No."

"Please?" he asks. No smirk this time, no humor at all.

I still. That may be the first time I've heard that word ever leave his lips. Huffing a sigh, I pull a face. "Fine. But hurry."

I turn around, shifting things in order to lift my long hair away from my neck. But Luca is no slouch; he helps me bundle my hair up and then smoothly brings the necklace around my neck, clasping it fast. He smooths it down onto my neck with his calloused fingers. The heat they leave, lingering on my nape just for a second, causes me to shiver.

He pauses for just a second, his fingers staying there. I wonder what sort of illicit thoughts he's having as we stand there, frozen in place.

It's the first time that I've actually thought that he actually finds me attractive. Not just hot, whatever that means, but attractive enough to fantasize about. If only for a moment.

I feel my cheeks begin to heat. Then before I can protest he withdraws.

"Alright," he says, moving away. "Now get in my car. I'll drive you to First Hill."

Shaking my head, I move toward the front door. "I'll just take an Uber—"

"Will you stop being such a pain?" He heads toward the kitchen. "I said I'm driving you. Just let me grab my keys and coat."

I stick out my tongue at him and he rolls his eyes at me. He's as good as his word though, ushering me outside into his Porsche Cayenne. I climb in the passenger seat of the luxurious vehicle, a little intimidated.

The seat warmers start heating up the second he starts the car. He presses a few buttons on his lit up center console, then looks at me. "Buckle up."

I slide the seatbelt across my body, already giving myself a pep talk. It's just a car. It may be fancy, but I shouldn't be worried. In any event, I only have to be inside for twenty minutes, tops.

Luca pulls out of the driveway. "Where are we going exactly? Do you have an address?"

Squinting, I try to remember what the intersection is. "Columbia and 9th, I think?"

He punches it into the car's navigation system. "All right. You don't seem entirely sure."

Raising one shoulder, I shrug. "I know the place by sight. I've been going there for almost two years now."

He gives me an annoyed look. "Are you going to tell me what this place is?"

Looking away out my window, I sigh. "It's a women's shelter, all right?"

Silence reigns in the car. I glance back to him. His brows are pulled down, his expression intense.

"What?" I ask.

He shrugs. "I guess I just didn't see you as a volunteer. That's like... really..." He searches for a word. "Compassionate, I guess."

"That's me," I say, pulling a face. "I'm known for being exceptionally compassionate."

Luca glances over at me. "I'm starting to think..." He scrunches up one side of his face. "I've known you for eight years, but I didn't actually know shit about you."

That earns a half-smile from me. "I know. What have I been telling you this entire time?"

He smiles, looking straight ahead at the road. "You know I don't listen that well."

I roll my eyes, but I'm still smiling. "Whatever. Just remember, in seven weeks we go back to being enemies. So just keep that in mind."

His low chuckle gives me a funny feeling in the pit of my stomach. I sit back, enjoying the heated seats. Luca turns on the radio. I stare out the window as buildings pass by, blobs of color.

If this is a draw, both sides having exhausted themselves, I'm content enough with it for right now.

Chapter 12

Luca

"If you'll turn to page five of the contract you provided me with, I can go down the list of clauses that the band will have a problem with."

God help me. In fact, God help us all if this deal doesn't go through. I'm in my office standing near my desk. My phone is on speaker, the voice of manager for The New Deals echoing against the walls. He's about a million years old and exceedingly cranky.

Marvin clears his throat loudly. "Now, the first clause, the definition of performer— that will obviously have to go..."

I am literally about to punch something. This is the third time that I've been on the phone with him in the last ten days. Every day is more irritating than the last. How do The New Deals get anything done?

Their manager is over here, telling me that the most basic language in my boilerplate contract won't work.

Who has time for this fucking bullshit? If I didn't want the band so badly, I would just hang up right now.

Marvin drones on. "The thing about defining who the performer is... it's bull. And let me tell you why..."

"Marvin," I interrupt him. "Is there any way at all that I can get you to just send me a marked up draft of the contract?"

He sighs. "No. I hope you are making notes, because I only want to go through this once. I feel like you are young enough to learn something from it."

I couldn't roll my eyes any harder. Could he be any more condescending? "Yeah, listen. I'm going to have to call you back, Marvin. I don't have anything to write on here."

That's distinctly a lie. I cast an eye over my notepad, open to a blank page, ready for my notes. I'm just not interested in having some old geezer lecture me about anything at this point.

Marvin clears his throat again. "Should we set an appointment for you to call me back?"

"Look for an email from me," I say. Then I disconnect the line.

Rolling my shoulders, I walk to the office door. Across the hall, Owen's light is on.

"Are you busy?" I call out.

There are several seconds of silence, then he yells back. "Come in, Luca."

Striding across the hall and pushing his door open, I see Owen at his desk. His computer screen is open to a spreadsheet and there is a tired look on his face. He puts his hands behind his head and pushes back in his seat.

"What's up, man?"

Shaking my head, I sigh. "You know that band, The New Deals?"

He squints. "Yeah, I think so. They're new, right? Out of Houston, really grunge-y sound?"

"Yeah. I like to think they are a mix between the -era Stones and a heavier Nirvana."

He nods. "Yeah, okay. I trust your judgment on that. What's up with them?"

I lean against the metal doorframe. "Their manager is not from this era. Or the last, even. And he expects me to sit in my office and take notes on all the things in the contract that he takes exception to... and he's so fucking condescending too."

I make a strangled noise.

Owen's eyes tighten. "That sounds like a drag."

"Yeah. It really is. I really want the band to play here but I also like... I don't let people talk to me any kind of way. He approaches me like I'm a kid or something. I'm a whole-ass adult that owns The Attic." I make a face. "Marvin should be glad that I want to have his band come play a show."

"Well, you own *part* of The Attic. Bradford and I own shares too." Owen's mouth curls up.

Rolling my eyes, I sigh. "You are ever the money guy, Owen. I just meant to say I'm not unsuccessful."

He sits upright, arching a brow. "Do you want to have

a drink? It's only early afternoon but I'm about to go cross eyed if I look at another list of numbers."

"God yes. Come on, we can grab a drink and pretend that our offices don't exist together." I turn around and head down the hall toward the front of the house. When I get out to the bar area, I stop for a second.

Down at the other end of the bar Cate stands with a guy wearing a shirt with the logo of our liquor delivery company. Cate is already full dressed for work, in her short dark dress and tall high heels. When I see Cate grin at something he says, hooking a strand of her hair behind her ear, my gut reaction is straight up jealousy.

I never felt that way before Madisyn dumped me. It just didn't occur to me to care. Why would anybody I dated have any complaints? As far as I know, I'm basically perfect boyfriend material.

But now I'm broken. Seeing Cate talking to another guy, knowing that she doesn't really belong to me... something inside of me twinges and curdles. Owen claps me on the shoulder, looking at me as if I've grown three heads.

"You'll have to keep moving if you want to get to the whiskey."

Shooting one final glare down to Cate and the delivery guy, I swipe a bottle of Four Roses and two glasses from off the bar. "I'm going, I'm going."

I turn and head to a table two dozen feet away, setting the whiskey and the glasses down. When Owen gives me a questioning look, I shrug. "Privacy."

We both sit down at the high top table. Owen glances

at Cate and the delivery guy, pursing his lips. I pour out two fingers of amber liquid into each glass. Then I slide one to him with a frown.

He raises his glass, waiting for me to do the same. I clink my glass against his, shooting Cate another dirty look before I turn the glass bottom up, drinking the whole shot in one gulp.

Owen frowns. "If it's bothering you so much, go say something."

Narrowing my gaze at him slightly, I shake my head. "Not until he leaves. I'm sure our liquor distributor would be interested to find out that their driver has so much time, though."

He shrugs. "She is your wife, man. At least technically. Isn't that the deal you guys have worked out?"

Pursing my lips, I pour myself another shot. "We don't have any rules about flirting with other people."

He sighs exasperatedly. "Obviously you should, though. Look at you. You're so tense. I would laugh at you if I didn't think you would punch me in the face."

I slide my gaze to Cate again. "I should set a boundary. Just until the marriage is dissolved, I mean. No flirting with other people. It looks bad."

Owen sips his whiskey, shaking his head. "Like that's the only reason."

I snort. "What, are you calling me stupid? Look, I know that I am a control freak—"

"You like Cate." He grins and finishes his glass.

My expression goes dark. "I do not."

He seems unworried. "You do so. You can admit it. She is your wife, you know."

"We're getting a fucking annulment, for fuck's sake!" I snap.

He nods to Cate. As I look over, the delivery guy leaves. She smiles to herself a little bit.

"Look, now's your chance. At least set some basic rules, dude. You have bigger things to worry about than who Cate is giving her number to. Like, for instance, The New Deals. And a million other things, probably."

I shoot him the dirtiest look. "Fuck off."

Pressing himself up, he picks up his glass. "I think I hear the spreadsheets calling out my name."

Waving him away, I finish my second shot and follow him to the bar. When Owen sets his glass on the bar and heads into the back, I scoop his glass up. Putting the Four Roses away, I take the dirty glasses down to where Cate stands, unloading one of the dishwashers. As she unpacks each glass, she gives it a wipe down, making sure it's dry.

Only then does she put it back behind the bar. She eyes me curiously.

"What's up?"

I set the glasses down, trying for a neutral tone. "I saw you talking to that guy."

For a second, her brow furrows. Then she puts the pieces together. "Oh, you mean Justin?"

Folding my arms across my chest, I sigh. "Yup."

Cate shakes her head a little bit. "He introduced himself. It turns out that we went to neighboring high schools. We know a lot of the same people."

"I don't care," I say. "What I do care about is not looking like a fool."

She stops wiping one of the glasses and cocks her head. "Okay?"

"I don't pay you to flirt with every guy that comes in here. Especially not delivery guys." I frown.

She throws her towel down and faces off against me. "I didn't flirt with him. I was just nice. There is a difference."

I take a step closer. "Not to Justin. And you can just bet that he goes back to the liquor distributor and tells the guys there that the owner of The Attic has a new wife who seems easy."

"Ahh!" she makes an angry sound. "That is unfair. If he were to tell the guys that, it would be making a big leap of logic. Just because I was nice doesn't mean I want anything more to do with him."

As if to punctuate her point, she crosses her arms. I shake my head, laughing a little.

"Cate, you don't get how guys work. You're nice to a guy? Well, in his mind, you just gave him permission to hit on you. You encouraged it."

She rolls her eyes. "So his imagination runs away with him. So what? That has nothing to do with me. Maybe he does think that but the second he starts acting like some kind of pick up artist, I'll set him straight."

I scowl. "You're not listening. I'm talking about me and my reputation here."

Cate steps forward, jabbing me in the chest with her index finger. "No, you're the one not listening! This isn't about you at all. It's about how I interact with other people. Who do you think you are, anyway?"

Reflexively I grab her hand and back her against the bar. My breathing is a little faster than usual, my pulse racing. She just knows how to make me so *mad*. I lean over her, relishing the way her head drops back and her eyes widen. She's sexy like this, shaking her head defiantly.

I press my hips against hers lightly, glaring down at her. "I'm Luca Leone," I growl. "And for the next six weeks, I'm your husband."

Her eyes glitter. "So?"

She's taunting me. Daring me. She thinks that I won't do anything?

Oh, she's wrong. So damned wrong.

I press my lips against hers, just to show her that I can. She tastes sweet, like she's just been eating berries. I press further, bending her back a little. Cate struggles, slapping me in the face, but for some reason that just makes me want to kiss her harder. So I breathe in deeply and sink my hand into her hair, pulling her against me as hard as I can.

I kiss her again, my lips working against hers. She's not exactly made of stone either; I feel her lifting up on her tiptoes, her mouth moving in time with my lips and tongue. I hear her panted breath. The blush on her cheeks. I feel her small body pressing against mine.

Fuck. She tastes good.

Not only that, but she feels good in my arms.

Who would've guessed?

At that moment, Bradford walks in. "Hey Luca, do you have..." He stops and stares. "Oh, I didn't mean to intrude—"

Like a flash, Cate worms out of my grasp. "Let go, Luca."

And I do. I step back, watching her flee toward the locker room. She doesn't look back, but I can still feel her heat on my lips. Her delicate rose scent is still in my nose.

"Like I said, I didn't mean to interrupt anything," Bradford says. He's smirking at me.

I feel my face begin to heat. "Shut up."

Bradford makes a face and then huffs off to the back. I'm left to stare after Cate, my body tense and my brain full of confusion.

Chapter 13

Cate

Long black skirt, grey knee socks, a gray blouse. The standard wardrobe of a very boring person. So Luna and Luca say, anyway.

I'm dressed for mass, although it's not the fancy Sunday one. It's late Wednesday afternoon; the sun is just beginning to set, the cool Seattle shadows growing longer and longer. I pick up my shoulder bag, heading down the stairs toward the front door. It's funny how I have only been here in Luca's for a few days but already I have a routine.

Get up early, find something to do outside the house. Come back when I'm already tired. No time to spend lazing around the house or looking as if I'm inviting Luca's company. Actually, it isn't that different from my grandmother's house, come to think of it.

What can I say, I do love a schedule. It's human instinct I guess. Plus, it limits the amount of time I spend thinking about Luca... and that kiss.

Oh, that kiss. The one that curled my toes and sent heat shooting through my veins. The one that got my blood pumping, especially when he ground his lower hips against mine.

I've said it before and I'll say it again: Luca is sexy. He's just also a total jerk.

I catch myself remembering what it felt like when he caged me against the bar and kissed the daylights out of me. I mean, I think about it every few minutes on average. Every single time that I do, I sternly remind myself.

It's never been a problem with the way Luca looks. The problem is with his personality, which totally sucks. Estimating the number of times he's been mean to me would be impossible. There is a very good reason we're enemies. I just have to remember that.

Thundering down the stairs, I make it all the way outside before almost running into the man I've been trying so hard to avoid. I can tell from the way his motorcycle is parked just behind him, his hair messy from the helmet, that he just climbed off the bike. He stands at the bottom of the stairs, arms folded, surveying me boldly.

How he makes me blush while I wear my most conservative outfit, I don't know. A little smile plays upon his lips as he considers me.

"Where are you going, princess?" He folds his thick arms across his broad chest.

I swallow. "Out."

He glares at me. I can feel my cheeks begin to heat. "Out isn't really an answer."

Rolling my eyes, I hitch my shoulder bag on my shoulder. "I'm going to mass."

There is a note of surprise in his voice. "Isn't that on Sundays?"

I shake my head, tucking a piece of hair back behind my ear. "I don't go on Sundays. It's too crowded. I prefer the Wednesday services."

"You actually go every week?" He looks fairly impressed. That makes me scowl.

"Yes," I say, pushing past his big body. "Twice, sometimes. Confession is good for the soul." I cast a glance at his motorcycle. "Are you still riding that thing?"

Luca chuckles. "Yes. I'm all alone for a while when I ride. It gives me time to think."

Turning to walk away, I sigh. "You could say the same for going to mass. It's quiet. It gives me time to work out problems, in between singing prayers. Now if you don't mind..."

I start heading for the bus. Luca is quiet for a second, then he calls out to me. "Hey. I'll go to mass."

What the what? I turn, making a face. "I'm sorry?"

"I said I'll go. I've never been. I can't really shit talk the Catholic faith without any firsthand experience." He narrows his eyes. "But you have to do something for me in exchange."

I shake my head. "Why would you think I care about whether or not you go to mass?"

Rolling his eyes, he gestures. "Come on. Ask what I want in exchange."

Exhaling a long stream of air, I open my arms. "Okay, I give. What do you want in exchange, Luca?"

He smiles, turning to indicate his motorcycle. "I want equal consideration. You say that you like church because it's calm and meditative. That's why I like my bike. So tit for tat." He pauses, his smile turning rueful. "It's that or a Radiohead concert, okay?"

Crossing my arms, I narrow my gaze on his bike. "That's it? You just get to take me around the block?"

"No." He shrugs. "I'll drive you somewhere special sometime."

I check the time on my phone. "Will you let me get to mass now if I agree to let you take me on a ride?"

Luca sighs. "Yes. Actually, I will drive you there. In the Porsche, that is."

I arch a brow. "Fine. But you're going to need a suit jacket."

He smirks. "I keep an extra in my car. I'm not a farmer, Cate."

"Fine." I press my lips together.

He gestures to the car, digging for his keys in his pocket. I head over there and he opens the passenger side door solicitously.

"Thanks," I say automatically. I glare at him, wondering what he wants.

His smile gives nothing away. "See how we can get along when we want to?"

"Oh, good lord in heaven." I make the sign of the cross as he closes the door and jumps in the driver's side.

The whole ride there I stare out the window, trying

to puzzle out why Luca even cares about what I think. I quickly become aware that this car smells like him, the light scent of musk and cinnamon combined with lemons.

My thoughts inevitably end up being tugged back to that kiss. That heart-racing, breathtaking kiss, bodies pressed together type of kiss. The type of kiss that makes me wonder about what Luca's body is like underneath his leather jacket and dark jeans. Then I mentally scold myself for my brain's perversity.

Really, though. I won't let my mind remain forever in the gutter. Even though my brain keeps returning to dirty thoughts obsessively.

Before I know it, we are pulling up around the back of the huge gothic cathedral that I named when Luca asked me where to go. As I climb out of the Porsche, I see a homeless guy on the corner that is absolutely glaring at me.

My face flushes. This is maybe the first time in my life where I've been embarrassed for appearing *rich*. Of course, I'm not rich. Not at all.

But I can't exactly explain that to the homeless man that is giving me the evil eye, can I? Nor can I do anything about the five or six homeless people we will undoubtedly encounter on our way into the church. We're in the poorest part downtown, near where Luca dropped me off the other day.

This block is especially popular with that population because the church serves hot meals three times a week. Homelessness is just a fact of life in this part of town, though it makes my heart ache each time I encounter it.

As we head down the sidewalk, I lock at Luca. He's not concerned one bit with the homeless people we pass. Instead, he looks up at the cathedral's spires.

"Pretty," he muses.

I follow him around the front of the building. "If you like that, wait until you see the stained glass. Each window is breathtaking."

Luca reaches the bottom of the church steps, waiting just a second for me to go ahead. "After you."

As I head up the stairs, I'm conscious of his presence right behind me. I clear my throat, pointing to the first window made of stained glass. "Look. That one is Joan of Arc, receiving the word of God before she rides into battle. See, she's kneeling there. While outside her tent is the waiting army, ready to be led to victory."

Luca looks impressed. "You're right, it is beautiful."

"And old." I smile at him, pausing for a second at the big oak doorway of the cathedral. "Ready?"

He just nods. I turn and go inside, hanging my coat up by all the others. Already from here I can hear the organ playing. The air smells like incense, probably leftover from a noon mass. Luca follows me when I head through the double doors into the nave, looking around.

To the left and right there are twenty long oak pews, shining dully in the dying light from the windows. Up ahead is the chancel and the sanctuary, with the organ and player to the right. This service is sparsely attended with only a few people sprinkled throughout the pews.

I sit in the same spot as normal, sliding into a seat in the third row. Luca is right beside me, a little frown on his face. If he is dissatisfied though, he doesn't voice his concerns.

I thank God for that.

The organ music swells as I make myself comfortable in the hard wooden pew. I grab a hymnal from the back of the pew before me and point to another. Leaning over to Luca, I whisper. "You'll need one of those, I expect."

His lips curl upward an inch. "I'll just look over yours."

I almost roll my eyes, but I stop myself in time. The Lord doesn't appreciate that kind of sarcastic expression in his church, I expect. "Fine."

There is a change in the music, making me automatically sit more upright. Father Duncan sails down the aisle toward the altar, followed closely by his altar servers.

Once he ascends the short steps to the dais before us, he turns around and begins the service by crossing himself and greeting us. I've been watching Father Duncan perform masses for five years now; he wastes no time in changing the topic from the glory of God to asking us to bow our heads in prayer. He doesn't rush exactly, but neither does he spend an extra second on anything he doesn't have to. I've gotten used to that by now.

I notice that Luca isn't bowing his head, so I elbow him in the ribs pretty hard. He glances at me and shakes his head, but he does lower his eyes. I'll take what I can get, I guess.

The rest of the mass trips along at a fair clip. Father Duncan reads the first two pieces of Scripture, one each from the Old and New Testaments. Already out of the corner of my eye I can see Luca getting fidgety; one time in particular he shakes his knee so hard that it causes several people to look back to see what the racket is.

I stop his shaking with a hand on his knee, then blush and yank my hand away. When I look at Luca again, he grins at my hasty reaction.

Eventually we reach the homily, or the part where the priest talks a bit more casually. Father Duncan clears his throat.

"Today, I want to talk about forgiveness. To forgive is divine. Have you heard that phrase? I want to tell you a story that starts off poorly. It begins with a young girl whose entire family had been killed in a car crash."

I tense up. I know Father Duncan can't be telling my story. I know that.

Even so, I clench my fists in my skirt. The priest just continues on with his story.

"The family was driving home one night when they were killed by a distracted driver. There was no alcohol at play, nor malice. It's like that sometimes. In this case, it was a text message. The driver looked down at her phone for a spilt second, and BAM! A violent collision. The driver who had been distracted walked away with bruises. The family, mother and father and little brother, all died instantly."

My mom and dad's faces are in my mind, pushing at my thoughts. That feeling of great grief still pushes at me, a sharp reminder of why I don't let anyone get too close.

Their passing was so painful for me. I won't be that vulnerable ever again.

"The young woman had a choice to make—" Father Duncan cries. "To forgive the driver — or to hold her hatred tight like a fist."

Oh God, please forgive me. I can't listen to the priest any more. I can't forgive the driver of the car that killed my parents, even though he wasn't drunk. Even though he died from his injuries, I still live with hate and anger.

Tears are in my eyes. I can't breathe. I shoot to my feet.

I have to get out of here *now*.

Luca looks at me, his brows descending. "What do you need?"

I shake my head, the tears blurring my vision, and start to push past him.

"You may think that the young girl could not forgive the driver who had killed her family—" Father Duncan pauses, probably noting my tearful departure. He clears his throat and continues. "After all, the young girl was orphaned by someone looking at a text message. How does anyone begin to forgive that?"

Launching myself out of my pew like a shot, I barrel down the aisle, heading for the back of the cathedral. I'm still clinging to my hymnal as I run through the wide double doors, looking for somewhere private.

I turn right, stumbling into a coat closet. My heart squeezes painfully. My grief is still very much at the forefront of my mind. It's messy and raw and not for public consumption.

Luca is right behind me as I push back into the coats, sobbing. "Cate..."

He sounds like he doesn't quite know what to do with me. I push my face into my hands, blocking his face out from my view.

"Can you please leave?" I ask, strangled. God, let him just go, not witness my total loss of control. I squeeze my eyes shut.

There is a second of hesitation. Then he just says, "No. I can't."

I feel his big hand on my back, rubbing gently in circles. I struggle to control my tears, but the more I struggle, the more forcefully they come. I feel naked right now, crying while I'm pressed among the coats, unable to help myself.

Luca is the last person that I want to see me like this, so weak and unprotected. Without my armor up, I don't even know how I'm supposed to exist.

"It's okay," I hear him murmur. His hand keeps rubbing my back reassuringly. "It'll be okay."

Eventually my bawling quiets to a sniffle. I am able to pull myself upright, wiping at my eyes. Turning to face Luca seems dreadful.

Is he going to laugh at me? I swear, if he so much as smirks in my direction, I'm going to lose it.

But when I wipe my face and move away from the coats, Luca surprises me. He looks at me, entirely somber, and clears his throat.

"I'm sorry." He lifts a shoulder.

My brows rise. "For what? You didn't do anything."

His mouth pulls down. "I'm just sorry." He hesitates, then shrugs again. "I wish I could've made you feel better, that's all I mean."

I look up at him, my heart starting to pound. He stands there, brooding and dark, thinking thoughts of me that are nicer than I could have imagined.

For some reason, my only response is to hug him. I burrow my face against his warm chest for just a moment, catching a whiff of his scent again. But then I pull away, my cheeks already beginning to heat. From the look on his face, we are both embarrassed by a moment I could only describe as very *human*.

"We should go," I say, straightening my skirt.

"Yup." His answer is quick and precise.

"Lead the way." As I watch him turn and push out of the coat closet though, I start to wonder.

How many more human moments could Luca possibly have in him?

And what if it is far more than I thought?

Chapter 14

Luca

I've figured out that Cate has a certain system for avoiding spending time at my house. Maybe it was learned at her grandmother's, I don't know. But it generally involves dashing out of the house as soon as she wakes up and returning when she's ready to go to sleep.

Time to shake her up a little. After she broke down crying at the cathedral, she's sort of avoided me except for at work. She even snapped at me a couple of times when she was waitressing.

All of which made me curious about seeing her somewhere new, someplace that I'm the only person she knows.

Will that make her less prickly?

I hear her footsteps now. Before Cate even gets downstairs, I'm waiting for her at the bottom of the staircase, a motorcycle helmet behind my back. To my surprise, she's not wearing her nun outfit. Instead she's wearing her black work dress with a pair of pink leggings.

"Where are you going?" I ask.

She brushes her dark hair out of her face, looking at me suspiciously. "To the grocery store. I'm hungry. Why?"

I show her the helmet. "If you can wait a few minutes, I think I can take you somewhere to eat that you'll like."

Cate's eyes narrow. "Oh, Luca. I don't know…"

"Hey, I went to mass. Fair is fair." Holding the helmet out to her, I smirk. "Come on. I can almost guarantee that you won't hate it."

She rolls her eyes. "That's not much of a guarantee."

She does take the helmet from me though, adjusting her shoulder bag. I wink at her, which makes her cheeks flush.

"Right this way, princess."

I stride toward the front door. She follows me, grumbling about her nickname. I open the front door and then usher her down the stairs to my bike. In a flash, I am climbing on it, patting the seat behind me.

As I pull on my helmet, she clambers onto the seat behind me. She gives me almost half a foot of clearance, sitting on the very back of my bike. I can't speak, so I just yank her forward, until she's snug against my back.

I can feel her tension as I start the motorcycle. She's mad that I picked an activity that not only seems dangerous to her, but means that she has to have physical contact with me the whole time.

Yup. She's just going to have to figure out how to deal with it. Smiling just a bit, I gun the engine. Then I reach behind me and pull both of her hands to my waist. She's probably muttering a lot more now.

I take off, in no hurry as I test her reserve on the side streets. At first her posture is stiff against me as we get on the interstate and cruise by a lot of slow-moving cars.

But then, bit by bit, I can feel her begin to soften against me. Not relax, exactly. Just quit being so resistant to me and the G-forces pressing against us both.

It's a pretty drive out to the little place that I want to eat. We get off the interstate for a little two-lane highway, driving out along the northernmost coast, running into the Pacific Ocean.

Out here, it looks a little marshy, alternating with beachy areas. It's a little cold as we motor along the coast; I didn't think of bringing anything heavier than my leather jacket, but I'm pretty sure that Cate starts trembling against me pretty quickly. It is winter, after all.

Damn, I should have brought extra layers to keep her warm.

Luckily we only have a few more minutes to go before I pull off the highway, slowing as I maneuver the bike down a little commercial strip. The ocean is to our right, the view somewhat blocked by a few two story buildings. To our left are a row of two and three story buildings, most looking a little worse for the wear.

When I pull the motorcycle into a spot at the last building on the right, Cate jumps off the bike before I've even turned the engine off. Pulling her helmet off, she immediately complains.

"It is so cold!" she declares as I pull my helmet off.

She hugs herself, shivering. She frowns at me. "You should've warned me that it would be freezing!"

I roll my eyes a little bit. "Sorry. Come on." I nod to the restaurant we parked next to. "Let's go warm up. I think the restaurant has a fireplace."

Cate needs to hear no more. She's off like a bullet, heading for the front door of the restaurant. I have to pick up the pace or be left behind.

Making it to the doorway several seconds after Cate, I follow her inside. She looks around with wide eyes. It looks like a cabin, but it has one giant plate glass window facing the water. There is in fact a fire crackling on our left, leaving the rest of the restaurant space for little red and white checkered cloth tables. It's not really prime eating time, so there is only one table occupied at the moment.

"Whoa. It's huge," Cate says. "Oh, look at the view!"

She shivers. A blonde woman approaches us with a smile. "Welcome to Antonio's. Two?"

"Please." I give the waitress a smile. Watching Cate shiver, I nod at a table near the fireplace. "Do you mind if we sit there?"

The waitress gestures and Cate looks at me gratefully. We are seated, the waitress dropping two menus and disappearing to get water. The chairs we're put in are uncomfortable for someone as big as I am, but I don't complain.

After all, I chose this place. And Cate agreed to come...

"Do you eat anchovies?" I ask as Cate opens her menu.

She eyes me over the top. "Yes... I mean, there is almost nothing that I won't eat."

"How about prosciutto?"

She closes her menu. "Yep."

"You should let me order." I wiggle my eyebrows. "You'll have to trust me on that one, though."

I watch her study me for several long moments before she finally shrugs. "All right."

It's hard not to tease her. "Are you sure?"

She pulls a face. "No, not remotely."

I laugh. "All we can do is see how it turns out, I guess."

The waitress comes back with a couple glasses of water. "Do you know what you would like?"

"Yeah. A big Caesar salad and a large pizza with prosciutto, funghi, and ricotta." I look at Cate, then smile. "And a glass of your house red for my friend here. She needs to relax."

Cate shoots me a look but she doesn't argue. She just thanks the waitress and hands over her menu. When the wine is put in front of her, she takes a sip. She's still shaking a little as she puts the glass back down.

"Are you really still cold?" I ask.

"You are a jerk, you know that?" Cate glares at me. "And yes, I'm still cold."

I unzip my jacket, shrugging out of it. "Here. And you should move your chair closer to this side. The fire is so warm I'm about to start sweating."

She looks a little offended. "No."

"Take the jacket," I say sternly. "And move. Don't be stupid."

"No," she says, pouting.

I start to stand up, which makes her jump a little. "Take it."

"Fine!" she whispers, giving me her best death glare. She's still shivering, which reinforces to me that I am right.

Retaking my seat, I watch her put on my jacket. There is something primal in that, watching her wearing something that is mine. I smirk. "Now move. Don't make me get up again."

"You are so bossy!" Cate complains. She does move her chair around our little table though. When she sits back down, she purses her lips. "Where do you get that from?"

My grin fades. "I don't know," I lie. But Cate seems to see through that.

"You forget, I'm best friends with your sister." Her lips lift at the corners. "And from her description, your dad is pretty domineering as well."

I roll my eyes. "Yeah, well. He and I are nothing alike, okay?"

"Touchy, touchy." She seems pleased to have found something that bothers me. After the waitress drops the Caesar salad and two side plates, she digs in. "Just because I'm starving and ready to eat does not mean the subject of your father has been forgotten."

Scowling at her, I help myself to a little salad. She

makes a sound as she takes the first bite. She looks up at me, her eyes wide as she chews and swallows. I nibble on a piece of romaine, savoring the umami bomb that goes off in my mouth. Anchovy, egg, and cream, cut with a heavy dose of lemon.

It's so good that it makes my mouth water.

"Oh my gosh," she says. "This dressing is just amazing." She takes another forkful, *mmm*ing at the flavor.

"Just wait till you try the pizza," I advise. "This place does very few things, but it does them perfectly."

As if summoned, our pizza shows up seconds later, carried by the waitress. She sets it down and I dish a slice up for Cate before digging in to my own piece. The crust is thin, stretched out to hold the ingredients. Eyeing my slice, I take a bite.

I taste the earthy sweetness of the mushrooms, the salty fat from the prosciutto, the sweet creaminess of the ricotta, and the tang of perfectly balanced tomato sauce. On that first taste, I nod, bouncing my head up and down like an idiot.

Cate tries her pizza with the same results. "Oh *man*! What is this made of? It tastes way better than any pizza I've ever tried before..."

I take another bite, then have a bit more salad. "My grandfather used to bring us here sometimes. Just me and Luna, that is."

She chews, looking thoughtful. "Was your grandfather a bully like your dad?"

A bully.

Cate doesn't know it, but she's just nailed exactly what my father is. I shake my head.

"Nah. Grandad was a busy guy — he owned most of the shipping companies here in the pacific northwest. But he wasn't a bully. Not to us, anyway. He was just..." I picture my grandfather's face, his mouth downturned, the little frown he perpetually wore. "Serious, I guess. Serious, but generous. When my parents decided to take what would turn into their endless European vacation, Grandad took Luna and I in without a fuss."

Her lips curve upward. "That sounds like me with my grandmother. Obviously the circumstances were a bit different, but my grandma is a stand up lady."

"Well, at least now we have something in common," I joke.

She rolls her eyes but laughs as she bites into her pizza again. The conversation goes on, stretching comfortably between us while we finish lunch. On the whole, I have what I would call a pleasant lunch.

After a cup of coffee to wash it all down, we head outside. "Hey, I think that there is a place across the street that sells leather goods. Maybe we can get you a coat and some gloves."

Cate smirks at me, nodding her head to the rocky beach behind her. "In a minute. We came all this way. Might as well enjoy looking at the water while we're here."

She starts walking down to the shore beside the restaurant. And I follow, faintly amused at how she just does what she wants and expects me to fall in step.

She stops a few feet from the water, poised on a rocky outcrop. Looking out over the Pacific Ocean, she covers her eyes against the glare from the late afternoon sun. A gentle breeze stirs her hair and the cold brings up the color in her cheeks. She looks small and fragile just now; my fingers itch to touch her.

She turns and pins me with her gaze. "It feels like we have some things to hash out."

That gives me pause. "Oh yeah?"

She looks out to the ocean again, her expression unreadable. "I know that things between us are changing. But how did they get so bad in the first place?"

My brows rise. "You're asking me?"

A tiny wrinkle forms just above her eyes. "Yes. You were always so... well... you were just a jerk the very first time I met you! I never understood that."

I move closer, my mouth turning down. The ocean lulls me, lapping and receding in a rhythmic pattern nearby. I take a deep breath.

"I was a jerk," I admit. "I was like that to a lot of people. Anybody new, anybody different. And you were both. If it helps at all, I thought I was looking out for Luna's best interests."

She pulls a face. "By making fun of me for dressing like I didn't come from money? You were so vicious! And you only got meaner the longer I knew you, it felt like."

I blow out a breath, looking at the horizon. My heart beats a little faster. "Well... you had something that Luna and I didn't have, and I did not want Luna to spend a lot of time obsessing over it."

Her eyebrows lift. "What would that be?"

My cheeks color. "Your family, Cate. The first time I saw your mom, it was because she followed you out of your house. And you were pissed off at her. I could tell from your body language. You just... you had someone who cared enough about you to chase you outside, and yet... you just ignored her and got in the car with us."

Cate's eyes widen. "That was it? That's why you were so mean to me for so long?"

Shrugging, I shake my head. "That's what I consider to be the root of our issues, yeah. You have to understand, at the beginning I was just trying to protect Luna. And then it just... it became a comfortable habit."

She's quiet for several beats, long enough to draw my gaze back to her face. "I remember that argument." Her lips lift at the corners. "Luna invited me to go skiing. My mom didn't want me to go because there wasn't a chaperone and there were going to be boys on the trip. My dad said that I was old enough to decide right from wrong. So I went."

"When you got in the car with us, you complained about your mom for half the ride. And when I looked at Luna, she looked sad." I look down at the ground, nudging a rock with my boot. "I'm supposed to protect her."

She exhales. "Well, if by protecting Luna you mean being a terrible bully, then you got something right."

Squinting, I glance back at the building. "I'm sorry. I really am."

Her lips quirk. "I can forgive that, Luca. The past is the past."

A few beats slip past us. Acting on pure instinct, I reach out and grab her waist, drawing her close. I bend down, bringing my mouth close to hers, letting her close the gap. Her eyes meet mine, pausing for a second before she pushes up onto her tiptoes.

Her lips brush mine, timid. Sweet and warm. I cup the back of her head, relishing the softness of her hair, and press my lips to hers.

She sighs ever so softly as I kiss her. That emboldens me to pull her flush against my body and explore her mouth, tasting her sweetness and stroking her tongue with my own.

Only now do I realize how badly I've wanted this exact thing to happen. I'm flooded with images of what could come next: stripping her down, tasting her everywhere, being inside her as she clutches my shoulders and calls out my name.

My fingers tighten in her hair and at her waist. Cate is my wife, after all; even she can't have any objections to me while she carries my name.

But too soon, she pulls back, her breathing grown a bit wild. "Luca..."

I ignore her, kissing my way down her jawline to her neck. I suck at the sweet spot there, making her breathing stop altogether for a moment.

But only for a moment. When I move my mouth further, she shoves me away with both hands. "Luca, stop!"

I growl. "Don't make me stop, Cate."

"You don't really want this," she says, slipping out of my arms. "You're just having fun, Luca. And let me tell you, I'm not interested in games. Have your fun somewhere else."

"Oh, come on," I say, aggrieved. "You want me right now. Admit it."

She flushes a darker shade of red. "I won't. And if you know what's good for you, you'll drop it." Turning around, she starts up the slope to the road.

"Cate..." I call after her. I can still feel the warmth of her body against mine.

But she's determined, shaking her head and picking up her pace. "Come on, you owe me a leather jacket before we ride back."

Sighing, I reluctantly follow her back to the road.

Chapter 15

Cate

Why do people even do this? Surely nothing is worth feeling like such a failure...

Luna and I are laying on mats in the middle of twenty other sweaty bodies, our feet raised the barest inch off the ground. My jaw is clenched, every muscle in my body is straining.

Luna of course looks perfect, winking at my when she catches my eye.

This was a bad idea. Why did I even let Luna talk me into taking this class?

I ask myself that for maybe the tenth time as the Pilates instructor clears his throat. He paces between the rows of miserable women, trying their hardest not to let their feet touch the floor. "Come on, ladies. Let's see some hustle here in the last minute... Do ten more seconds than you think you can..."

An alarm goes off. At the same time, everybody lets

their feet drop to the floor, collectively sighing with exhaustion.

"My abs are going to *hurt* later," I complain, turning onto my side and circling into a ball.

Luna pops up, grabbing her mat with a grin. "Maybe. But you're going to look so good, you won't care."

I scowl up at her. "The likelihood of that happening is very, very slim."

I push myself up, grabbing my mat and rolling it up. Luna is high on endorphins and she does a little dance as she rolls up her mat. "I'll take those chances!"

I roll my eyes. "Come on. There is a fancy coffee shop next door and you're buying."

Luna pokes me in the back with the end of her mat, giggling. "Sold."

We grab our coats and slip our shoes back on, then file out the door into the cold air outside. Luckily I'm so hot from exercising that I don't even flinch at the weather outside. I point out Heart coffee and Luna skips ahead gleefully.

Over our well-earned lattes, Luna looks at me curiously. "So how is it living with Luca so far?"

I can feel my face heat. Sipping my latte, I shake my head. "I can't wait until it's over."

She puts her cup down, her mouth turning down at the corners. "You really hate it?"

I look at Luna, a perfect blonde with innocent green eyes, and I shake my head. I don't want to offend or hurt her, so I'll have to tread lightly on this topic. "Not hate. That's too strong of a word. I'm just tired of being Mrs.

Luca Leone." I scowl. "Plus your brother keeps pushing my buttons. I know I'm anti-violence, but I'm about to sock him right in the mouth if he doesn't quit it."

"Stop what? Pushing your buttons?"

I nod. "Yeah."

"In what way?" She cocks her head, sipping her coffee again.

I blow out a breath. "In the way that I might technically be married to him, but we all know it's not permanent. It was a mistake to get married, just like it would be a mistake to..." I stop, trying to decide how to phrase what he seems to want.

"Omigod," Luna says, her eyes glowing with excitement. "Did you guys bang?"

I make a disgruntled face. "We definitely did not bang. Get your mind out of the gutter."

She purses her lips. "You thought about banging him, though. Right? I'm assuming that means you guys sucked face."

"Luna!" I protest. "Sucked face? And bang? Where are you getting this lingo?"

She giggles. "I've been watching a lot of Bravo lately. Reality television is full of colorful phrases like that."

"I would be extremely grateful if you never said sucked face to me again." My lips turn up at the corners. "And maybe lay off the reality TV for a while, okay?"

She gives me a dissatisfied look. "No. And don't change the subject! We were talking about how you had imagined doing it with my brother. Gross, but there it is."

"I didn't say that I had thought about that," I hedge.

Luna lays her hands flat on the table, staring me down. "Cate, look at me." I meet her eyes, guiltily glancing away. "You and I have been friends for nine years. I knew the third time we hung out that we were going to be besties. So when you look me in the eye, I know whether you are being truthful or not."

She's staring at me with such intensity that I wish I could writhe and escape her gaze. My cheeks flood with color.

"Look at me," she demands. "Tell me the truth."

"Fine!" I confess, throwing my hands up in the air. "You want the truth? I think Luca is ridiculously good looking, okay? He's painfully handsome. But I still think he's a complete jerk..."

"Aha!" she says, looking smug. "I knew it. You have a secret crush on the man you 'accidentally' married."

She does air quotes when she says it, which makes me roll my eyes.

"Shut up." I cross my arms. "I know that might be unChristian to say, but just be quiet about. that."

Luna grins. "I won't tell Luca that you totally want to bang him, if you're worried about that."

"I wasn't saying—"

She cuts me off. "I won't tell him that you want to kiss him and bang him and have all of his weird babies."

I cover my face with my hands. "This? This is why I never tell you anything."

She laughs, taking the final sip of her latte. "Worth it." She wiggles her eyebrows. "You should go for it. If you can't even screw the man you are accidentally married to, who can you screw?"

I roll my eyes. "Yeah right. That would be... I mean, it would complicate everything, even more than it already is."

"How do you make 'oops, we got married in Vegas' more complicated?"

I pause, thinking. "I'm not sure, but I know that sex only complicates things."

A wrinkle appears between Luna's brows. "You know what I think?"

I sigh, pushing my latte mug away. "No, what do you think, Luna?"

She shifts in her seat, waving her hands a little. "It sounds like you are too scared to find out what liking a guy is like. Not just liking, but having a physical relationship with him."

I wave my hand. "No, that's not it."

"Yes it is. When we were in high school, you were boy crazy. You always had a boyfriend, even though you were Catholic and they're pretty disapproving as a whole."

I shrug. "So? Maybe I got more religious."

"No, what you got is scared. You lost your parents over winter break. By the spring semester, you had sworn off guys. But it's not because you suddenly became a more strident Catholic."

"Oh no?" I wrinkle my nose. "By all means, keep telling me about myself."

"I'm serious, Cate. I've actually put a fair amount of thought into this. You were so hurt by losing your parents that you decided, consciously or not, to exclude any people from your life that you don't already know. Which leaves you with basically me and Harper and your grandmother."

"Oh, I don't know—" I huff.

Luna grabs my hand, leaning across the table. "But you didn't plan for Luca, did you? He was already there, you just didn't pay attention to him. And then one night Luca turned his head and saw you — I mean, really saw you. And you weren't ready for it at all."

She sits back, looking pleased. "Thus, getting drunk and getting hitched in Vegas. I'll hold now for applause..."

I stare at Luna, a little taken aback. Is any part of what she just said to me true? If so, am I willing to admit that out loud?

"I don't know what to think," I answer honestly. "Really, I don't."

"That's not an answer," Luna says, rolling her eyes.

"That's because I'm just speechless." I bat my eyes, taking a sip of my coffee.

"Think about it. You can thank me later for having such amazing insights into your personality." She grins and poses cheerily.

"Yeah, well. I will literally do anything you want if it means we can change the conversation. Literally anything!!"

Luna sighs. "Well, if you don't want to talk about how

hot my brother is, how about his friends? Bradford is gorgeous, as always. Unfortunately he's gay as fork." Her eyes twinkle. "But how about Owen?"

"Owen?" I echo. "Boring, works across the hall from Luca, doesn't drink before seven p.m. Owen?"

"The one and only." She slides me a sly grin. "I think he's hot, in an insufferable old man sort of way."

Luna's admission makes me cackle. "What?" I say, laughing. "You can't be serious!"

"Dead serious." She beams at me. "I have spent no less than two weeks trying to figure out why I think so, because he's pretty grumpy. Even to me, and I'm the nicest person any of you know."

I push away the remainder of my latte, checking the time on my phone. "Speaking of work... if I don't get going, your brother will kill me for being late."

"You should totally cite your reasons for tardiness as wifely business." She giggles.

"If only that could resuscitate my lifeless corpse," I joke. I push myself up from the table. "I do have to go, though."

"Okay. Think about what I said, though. Don't let yourself be too scared to experience something new. Especially love."

She stands, hugging me.

"I'll think about what you said," I sigh. "Not saying you're right though."

As I turn and head out of the shop, Luna calls out to me. "I'm totally right! You'll see!"

I grab my coat, forcing the sleeves onto my arms, and

try to clear my head. All the while though, I am wondering.

Could Luna be right?

And if so, what do I do about it?

Chapter 16

Luca

I'm at work when Cate arrives. Part of me didn't actually think that she would show; I guess there is some little part of me that is waiting for her to let me down.

When she shows up I'm filling in for Bradford behind the bar, prepping everything I will need for my shift. I see her come in, her eyes scanning the bar critically.

"Where's Bradford?" she asks, her arms full of her coat and purse.

I exhale loudly, not sure what footing I'm on with Cate at the moment. "He wasn't feeling well. I'm filling in at the last minute."

"Oh." Her brows pull down but she doesn't exactly make a fuss. "All right. I'm going to go put my stuff down and clock in. Then I'll be ready for whatever you want me to do."

I cock an eyebrow at her phrasing. She gives me a

long look, then shakes her head and disappears into the locker room.

Well, at least she isn't pissed at me for the other day. If Madisyn had been in her position, I would've been groveling in apology before we could even speak again. I guess it's an important thing to remember, the fact that Cate and Madisyn are worlds apart in temperament.

Cate comes back into the bar area, tying one of the stiff black leather aprons that I keep for staff around her waist. She puts her hair into a messy ponytail, which looks very punk rock to me.

She looks up from her grooming to see me grinning at her and narrows her eyes. "What?"

"Nothing. I've just never seen you wear your hair up before." I shrug, amused. "It looks nice like that."

She blushes, seeming not to know how she's supposed to respond to that. "Uh... thanks?"

I lift a crate of citrus fruit onto the bar, eyeing her. "How would you like to try bar backing a little tonight?"

She comes a little closer, pushing onto her tiptoes to peer inside the crate. "What does that mean?"

"Bar backing? It's the step between waitressing, which you're already doing, and bartending. I know that when it gets busy we'll need you and April to wait on tables. But before and after the rush, I could start teaching you the trade." I screw up my face. "Plus I have to do a mountain of prep work today anyway, to get us ready for the weekend. But when you master this, you are ready to move on to bartending..." I wave my hands over the oranges, my tone turning silly. "You too could be the master of this citrus crate."

She rolls her eyes but she smiles too. "Sure. Yeah, I would actually love that."

I grin at that. "We'll see how you feel after your first shift."

She shakes her head, smirking. "Put me to work, Mister Boss. I'm ready."

I nod to the crate of oranges, lemons, limes, and grapefruit. "Let's start here. We need five quarts each of lemon and lime juice. And one each of orange and grapefruit."

Cate scrunches up her face. "I'm guessing that you have some way to extract the juice?"

I jerk my thumb behind me, to the juicer in the corner. "Right there. You start by cutting a bunch of lemons in half. Then you put them in the press and push down the top." I smirk. "I hope you brought all your upper body muscles, because this is a really physical part of bartending."

She lifts her eyebrows. "Show me how you do it. I'll just copy whatever you do."

I pull out two cutting boards and grab two kitchen knives. Then we set to work, cutting up citrus and juicing it into empty quart containers.

Then we make a lot of lemon and lime slices for garnishes, stocking the three wells of the bar with them. I add fresh thyme and whole oranges to the wells, then show Cate how to fill everything with ice from the back.

"That's pretty much it," I say, grabbing a stack of

cocktail napkins. "Bradford probably has a more thorough routine but that's the gist. Now, as a bar back, you'll want to make sure that my ice wells are full all night. Clean and polish glasses anytime you have a free second. And maybe ask me whether there is anything we need from the storage room a couple of times."

"Juice the citrus," she recounts. "Do garnishes. Make sure there are ice and glasses behind the bar. I think I can handle that."

I lean against the bar, grabbing a polishing rag for glasses. "Now just add a thousand customers into the mix and you've got yourself a proper shift."

She purses her lips and narrows her eyes, but I can see the humor that she's trying to hide. "I guess so."

Customers start coming in after that, packing the bar and the tables. I put my head down and work, running the service well and attending to customers at the bar. A lo-fi garage rock band starts playing at some point, only increasing the noise level and the number of patrons waiting for drinks.

I lose myself in the work, pouring and mixing and shaking drinks. Cate checks in with me a couple of times and keeps pulling clean glasses out of the dishwasher. I run out of ice once but even as I am gritting my teeth, she comes in with a full ice bucket.

Alice shows up to wait tables for a few hours; she's experienced and can almost run this whole bar by herself. She even jumps back behind the bar and makes drinks a few times. Once she's here, I feel a little less pressured.

Owen pops his head out of the back during the rush. "You need help?"

"Can you just pour wine and open beers?" I ask, using the peeler and an orange to pull a long rind for an old-fashioned.

"Sure thing." He eases behind me, heading to the other end of the bar. "I know it's a Thursday, but it's pretty slammed in here."

I shake a gin martini, nodding. "Yeah. Luckily I have Alice and Cate." I purse my lips. "And now you. Together we can do it."

Owen raises his voice to be heard over the band. "We should have scheduled you a bar back!"

Not three seconds later, Cate comes in with a fresh bucket of ice. "Hey Owen." Her head bobs. "Do you guys need anything?"

"Just to take these drinks out to table twenty," I say, nodding as I pour the gin martini into a glass. "Wait..." I pull a little sliver of lemon peel, twisting it up and dropping it in. "There you go."

Cate doesn't even blink. "Thanks." She picks up the tray and starts carrying it off.

I look at Owen, who is considering me with an indulgent smile. "What?"

He smirks. "You like her."

I clear my throat, giving my head a little shake. "No. I mean, I don't hate her, but I don't..." I stop. "You know what, man? Just shut up."

Owen grins but doesn't say anything else. He stays

just until the rush ends, right as the band is done playing. After that everything wraps itself up pretty quickly.

Owen vanishes, Alice leaves, and I can finally fucking breathe a sigh of relief. The whole venue empties out pretty fast, leaving just a few people to finish up their drinks.

I look at the time. It's already midnight somehow. I forgot how much faster life moves when it's insanely busy.

"So…" Cate says, setting down a tray on the bar and stretching. "That was bananas."

"Yeah, it was. You were a big help though." I hesitate, trying to figure out where I am going with this. Am I just complimenting her now? "Er, you know. The whole staff helped. It was… good."

Cate peers at me like I've grown a second head. "Okay… Well, what now? I would guess that we have to like… sweep and restock the fridges and stuff."

"You got it. I'll restock if you sweep. And keep an eye out for any customers that need to close out."

"Got it," she says, moving to find a broom in the back hallway.

Twenty minutes later, the bar is restocked, clean, and most importantly, empty.

"Finally!" Cate says, pulling her apron over her head. She finds a seat at the bar, kicking her shoes off. "My feet are killing me."

I glance up at her, counting the last till. "We made a lot of money, though." I finish sorting the tip money, then pull out two glasses. I pour two fingers of whiskey in each. "Here. Shift drink."

Cate shrugs and takes the tumbler. As I come around the bar to sit beside her, she glances at me. "You're awfully cool and collected after all of that."

I smile, raising my glass. She clinks hers against mine and I take a sip, the amber liquid burns exactly the way it should on its way down. I make a satisfied sound, smacking my lips.

"Mmm. Tonight was busy, yes. But this is far from my first insane night at work. Besides..." I turn, pulling a little pile of money across the bar and pushing it over to her. "I did already say that we killed it, right?"

Cate's eyes go wide. "This is mine?"

"Every cent." I take another sip of whiskey. "The bartenders usually tip out the bar backs, in addition to whatever they make hourly. And in this case, whatever you made in tips as a waitress."

"Whoa." Cate puts the cash away in her order pad, then takes a big gulp of whiskey. "Thanks for taking a chance on me."

My eyes sparkle a little. "Well, you are my wife. I guess if I'm going to roll the dice with anyone—"

Cate leans forward, stopping me by putting a hand on my chest and pressing her mouth to mine. I'm a little surprised at first. But she tastes sweet and spicy, the whiskey on her lips like warmed honey.

I ease forward, sliding my arm around her waist. She opens her mouth under my explorations, her free hand coming up to bury itself in my hair.

God, how does she taste so damn good? How does her tongue against mine feel so fucking erotic?

Growling a little bit, needing more from her, I pull her closer. And she seems more than ready to give in to my demands, her breath hitching when I cup her tits through the thin dress she's wearing. She blows out the breath she is holding in a low moan, letting me know that I have her full attention.

Well, that and the fact that I can feel her nipples harden under my fingers. My whole body tightens, my cock hardening.

I'm going to fuck Cate, right here at the bar. That knowledge slides through me, a hot knife twisting in my gut.

I pull away, just to suggest we move to a more private place. My office, right the fuck in the middle of my desk, for instance.

Then I hear the creak of the front door.

"Hello?"

I freeze. "Chloe?"

Chloe peeks her little blonde pixie head out of the back. She's as gorgeous as she ever was and she's beaming at the sight of me. "Hey! I was hoping you would be here!"

I feel Cate withdraw a little, clearing her throat and patting her hair. She's still breathless; hell, I am too.

But then Chloe runs over to hug me, wearing a ridiculous combination of a sparkly barely-there skirt and an oversized gray sweater. "Hey! How are things?"

She hugs me for a second too long, then turns to

Cate. "I'm sorry, I'm Chloe. I worked here for the first two years it was open."

Cate clears her throat again. "Hey. I'm Cate."

No explanation. No territorial behavior. If Madisyn were in her shoes, she would've oozed all over me physically and made a big deal out of the fact that we were married.

Technically married, but married nonetheless.

And Madisyn would also somehow know that Chloe and I were almost an item... that is, until she got a great job offer in Portland.

Chloe grins at both of us. "Amazing. Well, I'm in town for the next few days and I just wanted to stop by—"

"Chloe!" Owen barks, appearing from the back.

Her eyes light up. "Owen! Ah!"

She runs over and hugs him. Something sour stirs in my belly, though I'm careful to smother it.

"It's so great to see you!" Owen says. "I want to hear about the new bar you opened up down in Stumptown."

I look at my watch. It's after one. "Hey, why don't we take this somewhere else? The cleaning crew should be here any minute..."

"How about your place?" Owen says. "It's the closest place that doesn't have a last call."

I see Cate make a face, but I shrug. "Okay, sure. If Chloe will come, that is..."

"I'd follow you two anywhere," Chloe says with a wink.

And just like that, Chloe, Owen, Cate and I are headed to my house.

Chapter 17

Cate

We get to Luca's house a few minutes ahead of Owen and the bubbly, beautiful Chloe. The ride home has been mostly a silent one, with Luca glancing at me every few minutes and then sighing.

My stomach twists every single time he does. I saw the way that Luca and Chloe looked at each other. If by some miracle they never slept together, I wouldn't bet on things staying that way.

And yeah, maybe Chloe also made eyes at Owen... but my guts aren't tied up in knots over how she acted. I'm only worried about him.

See? This is why I've been alone since my parents died. I just don't have the sheer amount of time that feeling angsty takes up in my life.

As we get out of his Porsche, he tries to explain.

"You know, Chloe is just a friend." He pulls out his keys and unlocks the front door.

I shake my head. "Okay."

"Really, Cate. There was a time where maybe she could have been more... but she moved away. Madisyn came after her."

"Okay." I bite off the word, sighing. "I think I'm just going to go to bed."

"Oh, come on. Don't be a party foul. Stay downstairs. Have a drink with us." He throws his coat down onto the back of a couch.

I cross my arms, feeling like a little girl. "Have you thought about how you are going to explain my presence to her?"

His surprised expression tells me that he hasn't. "Uh... no. I wasn't planning on explaining anything to her unless she asks, I guess."

I run my tongue over my teeth. "Owen is in the car with her right now, alone. Who knows what little facts she'll be filled in on by the time they get here."

Luca shrugs. "So what?" He pats the sofa. "Come here. Take off your coat. Sit down. I'll make us a round of drinks."

Wrinkling my nose, I soften to his suggestion. If he'd been weird about Chloe finding out that I'm his wife, I probably would have stormed off. But he was totally chill, so I feel stupid not accepting his offer.

"Okay," I say at last. "But can you please make me something fruity? Enough straight whiskey. That stuff is so harsh."

Luca grins, already heading for the kitchen. "Your wish is my command, princess. I'll be right back."

That word, princess... it raises the fine hairs on the back of my neck. Luca is gone too fast to say anything back, but I can see him still through a large cutout in the kitchen wall.

He bounces around, in a good mood despite having worked for a solid eight hours, on his feet the entire time no less. I scowl.

What does he have to be in a good mood about?

The front door opens behind me. I turn to see Chloe and Owen letting themselves in.

"Hiiii," Chloe says. She holds up a bottle of amber liquid. "Look what we brought..."

They come into where I am in the living room, shedding their coats. Chloe sits opposite me in a chair, winking at me.

"Let's make the men get us drinks," she stage whispers, giggling.

"I just need some glasses," Owen says, plucking the bottle from Chloe's grasp. "Where's Luca?"

I incline my head toward the kitchen. "Getting drinks."

Owen frowns. "I should help him."

He heads to the kitchen, leaving me and Chloe alone. She smiles at me, clearing her throat. "So... you and Luca, huh?"

I turn redder than a beet. "Oh no. Luca and I... that is, we aren't like... romantic or anything..."

Chloe's perfect brows rise. "Is that right?"

Scrubbing my suddenly damp palms across the

bottom of my dress, I nod. "Yup. We are like... totally, completely just friends."

She makes a face. "That's not what Owen says."

"Well, Owen is wrong," I declare. Meanwhile, I wish that I could crawl under this couch and die. Then I decide to finish with, "Luca's a total jerk! Ew, who would want to kiss him?"

As soon as I say it, I become aware that Luca is approaching with a tray of drinks. I catch his eye and he scowls but he doesn't say anything.

"Here, the first round is something fruity," he says, handing me a glass. "Cate requested it."

Chloe accepts her glass, looking at me oddly. "Well, if Cate requested it..."

My cheeks burn. I sip my drink, which is pink and frothy and honestly tastes exactly like a pink starburst.

"Mmm," I say, almost involuntarily.

Owen takes a big gulp, then winces. "Oh man, this is so sweet. I'm definitely going to regret drinking this tomorrow."

He sinks onto the couch beside me, forcing Luca to choose a chair at the end of the couch.

"Well, I like it," Chloe says diplomatically. "It reminds me of summer in a glass."

Luca pulls his chair closer before he sits down. "Thanks. It's an older Trader Vic's recipe so you know it's actually really fucking strong."

Owen nods, taking another gulp. "I'll definitely keep that in mind."

"So..." Chloe sits forward in her seat. "God, tell me everything that I've missed in the last... what, almost three years? I can't actually believe any time has passed at all."

I sip my drink, watching a tense look between Luca and Owen.

"I got my pilot's license," Owen says.

"Yeah. And I was engaged and then dumped pretty spectacularly."

Chloe hesitates, looking puzzled. "Owen said you and Cate are married, Luca."

I flush again. For several seconds, I'm waiting for Luca to try to worm out of our arrangement. But he surprises me.

"Owen is totally right," he nods, setting his drink on the floor. "You know what this party needs? Some music."

Owen rolls his eyes and looks at me. "That's his nervous tic."

"I heard that!" Luca declares, walking over to a long mahogany sideboard. He opens it, revealing a very nice record player. He just starts the record that is already on the table, dropping the needle.

Rock music starts playing. Luca turns, looking pleased. "That's better," he says.

Chloe looks at me, biting her lower lip. "Cate, tell me about yourself."

My cheeks color and I sip my drink. I'm starting to feel the effects now, a warm pleasant buzz. "What is there to tell?" I shrug. "I was raised here. I went to college with Luna at Marymount University…"

"Ah! So you know Luna, then?"

"Yep. We've been friends for years. Like since middle school."

Chloe looks between me and Luca, pursing her lips. "And how did you two end up getting hitched, exactly?"

"Booze," Luca says.

I shoot him a look, smoothing my skirt out. "We were drunk. I actually don't remember anything from the night that it happened."

Luca tips his glass all the way back, finishing his drink. "Yeah, all we have are the photos."

I look at him, canting my head to the side. "What photos?"

"Our wedding photos. Apparently I thought it was a good idea to have them sent here."

Owen and Chloe stare at him. I frown. "Do you want to share with the rest of the class, Luca?"

He rolls his eyes. "Yeah, sure. They're in the kitchen." He looks at his empty glass. "Does anybody else want another glass of anything?"

"Go get the pictures!" Chloe says, growing aggravated. "And bring back whiskey."

Luca heads to the kitchen with a sigh. I'm still trying. to wrap my head around the fact that there are pictures of an event that I thought was lost forever in the recesses of my drunken mind.

When Luca comes back, he's juggling a large white envelope with four glasses of whiskey, the bottle tucked under his arm. I jump up and grab the photos from him, my brow hunching as I slide out a thick sheaf of glossy sheets of paper.

Chloe and Owen get up, crowding in as I page through the pictures. There is one of Luca and I making out. In the next one, we gaze into each other's eyes, our faces flushed with alcohol and excitement. Then there are a dozen more of Luca and I posing together, most of them taken when we were kissing each other.

A vague memory surfaces of having fun and kissing someone... but that's it. I definitely don't remember staring deep into Luca's eyes and saying I do.

Luca speaks up. "I don't remember ever being that happy." He has set the glasses of whiskey down on the floor.

"Me neither," I agree, looking up from the pictures.

"You two are like... super cute in these photos," Chloe says, taking them from my hands.

"Yeah, I don't think I've seen you look that way at anyone, ever," Owen says.

I roll my eyes. "We were drunk. So drunk that we don't remember any of it. I probably would have gazed at a freaking can of soup like that, given the chance."

"Mmm," Luca says, sipping his whiskey. "I am tired of this topic. Let's talk about something different that won't lull me to sleep."

Chloe looks at me. "You should frame this photo. You guys both look amazing in it."

She pulls out the photo of Luca and I kissing and looking happy, wriggling her brows. I can't help but smile as I take it from her. It's hard not to like her a little bit, especially because she seems to have backed off of Luca entirely despite my protests.

"Thanks." I bite my lip. "Maybe I will."

Luca sighs, aggrieved.

"Chloe, tell us about the bar you opened," he says, his voice loud. "We all want to hear about it."

Chloe rolls her eyes and hands me the rest of the pictures, then flops on the couch. "Okay, Luca. So when I moved to Portland—"

I sit back on the couch, rifling through the photos once more while Chloe tells her story. I'm not really listening, I'll admit.

I am more interested in the photos. Proof that Luca and I got married intentionally for some reason.

Looking up at Luca as he talks to Chloe and Owen, finishing the rest of my drink, I have to wonder...

Did I really just agree to marry him based on his looks? Because yes, he is very very attractive. Plainly, obviously so.

Something inside me says that I wouldn't have done that. Then again, who knows?

Maybe he kissed me. That could be it, honestly.

I mean, he is a really good kisser. Earlier, when he pulled me closer and growled, I honestly thought I was done for. I was convinced that we were going to have sex, right there in the bar.

Luca looks up, catching me appraising him. His lips lift in a smirk. He adjusts in his chair, staring at me directly, his gaze burning right through me. It's like he's suggesting something indecent, but he hasn't said a word.

His gaze drops to my lips, then lower to my breasts. I can almost feel the scorching path of his touch on the column of my neck, on my collarbone, on my suddenly-sensitive breasts. He bites his lower lip, meeting my eyes again.

I swear, my nipples pebble with excitement. How does he do that?

Owen stands up, stretching. "I think we should go, Chloe." He pauses. "Actually, I think we should get an Uber. I've had too much to drive safely."

Chloe rises, eyeing me with a secretive smile. "Yeah, I agree. We should leave these two to... you know."

I blush and bite my lip. "Are you guys sure? I mean, we have a ton of rooms here..."

Luca stands up. "I'll get your Uber, guys."

If Owen and Chloe leave, that will just leave me and Luca to... do *whatever*. That is such a bad idea. Frowning at Luca, I try again. "Seriously, these beds are here. And they're awesome..."

"Get out," Luca says, talking over me. "Have a good night. Your Uber will be here in less than a minute."

Chloe grins. "It was nice to meet you, Cate. I'm sure I'll see you again soon—"

Owen starts pushing her toward the front door. "Goodnight, guys."

My heart beats faster. I call out to them. "Goodnight!"

Then they're out the door. I bite my lip, looking at

Luca a little helplessly. He prowls over to me, bending down to whisper in my ear.

"There is only one way to settle this tension building between us." He nips at my earlobe, biting it hard for the barest second. "Come to my bedroom."

I swallow and shiver, the sensation sliding down to my breasts and the vee between my legs. "What for?"

Luca rolls his eyes. "Don't act like you don't want me to fuck you. You do."

His lips are by my ear. I can't decide whether I want to turn my head and kiss his lips or slap his mouth for the way he's talking to me. He kisses my neck ever so slowly, turning my knees to jelly.

He moves around to my front, scooping me up without another word. I make a soft sound of protest, but he just heads upstairs to his bedroom. I won't lie, the feel of his hot mouth on my neck and my collarbone makes me want more.

More kisses, yes. But also more of him.

I want to see what he looks like naked.

I want to explore his body and let him touch mine.

That's what I'm thinking while he carries me to his bedroom. Once he gets there, he tosses me on the bed.

"Get fucking naked," he growls. "Now."

Shaking, I start to lift my dress over my head. I'm nervous, goosebumps breaking out over my whole body. My breathing is already too fast, my heart beating in my throat.

Luca strips his shirt off over his head, not breaking eye contact with me the entire time. I swallow. As I slip off my bra and panties, my eyes widen when Luca shoves his jeans down his hips and kicks them aside.

My mouth goes dry as I take him in, fully nude, his cock jutting out proudly.

I know what's going to come next. I've been waiting for this moment for too long.

Now it's finally time.

Chapter 18

Cate

My pulse races.

My body hardens under Luca's touch.

My pulse races when he knots his hand in my hair and pulls me closer. I look up at him, tall and dark and broad, his eyes full of desire.

He delivers a kiss to my lips, if you can even call it that. His touch is devastating and rough.

This is it. This is what I have been wanting ever since I got drunk in Vegas. Luca and me, nothing separating us anymore. Skin touching nothing but bare skin.

I close my eyes, preparing myself. He's just going to force my legs open and have his way with me. I know it. I figure that even Luca won't know what I like this first time we have sex, and I'm okay with it.

He surprises me though, pulling back slightly. He brushes his nose against mine.

Then his fingers graze across my cheek. The gentleness of his touch is surprising.

Luca is not gentle. Or at least, I didn't think he was.

When his thumb slides across my lips, a shiver goes down my spine. His lips graze my neck and I let out a soft gasp, my eyes opening and fluttering closed.

He chuckles softly, his voice husky. He doesn't stop touching me.

I feel his lips graze the side of my neck, and his fingers stroke up the center of my body. His hand stops just short of the place where I want him to touch the most. "Want you to enjoy this," he murmurs against my skin.

I shiver, goosebumps racing along my arms.

He moves back slightly, looking down at me. Then he leans forward, his lips crashing down on mine. I let out a whimper, and he pulls me closer, deepening the kiss.

This time, he is gentler. He moves slowly, savoring each and every touch. I'm breathless, unable to do anything but react.

His fingers graze the soft flesh between my thighs, and he groans, the sound rumbling through me.

I'm aching, so very ready for him. He strokes me with his finger, finding the small pearl that heats me up from the inside out. He touches it lightly, making me shiver.

His eyes flash with need, his body tense with anticipation.

"Luca," I breathe out.

He moves forward, his lips meeting mine in another bruising kiss. I feel his cock press against my thigh, and I gasp, arching against him.

He growls, his teeth grazing my bottom lip. "Can't fucking wait to taste you."

He trails kisses along my jaw, down the side of my neck, and to the valley between my breasts.

His tongue swirls around my nipple, his teeth gently grazing it. His hands caress me, teasing me until I'm panting, desperate for more.

I can't stop moving, squirming beneath him, my hips rocking in need. He chuckles, and the vibrations send a shudder through me.

His mouth closes over my nipple, his tongue flicking and swirling, and I let out a cry of pleasure.

He continues his exploration, kissing and licking and nibbling his way down my stomach. I'm shaking, the sensations overwhelming me.

When he reaches the top of my mound, he pauses, looking up at me. "You smell so fucking good," he says.

His voice is rough and deep, and it sends a jolt through me. I moan, unable to form words.

His lips graze the sensitive skin just above my pussy, and his tongue darts out, licking me. He lets out a growl, his fingers digging into my thighs.

The sound, the pressure, his mouth on my most sensitive parts...

It's all too much.

"Oh my God, Luca," I gasp, doing my best to hold back the orgasm that I can already feel building inside me. "It feels... feels so good."

The sexy grin he flashes me is pure sin. He continues

his assault on my senses, his tongue moving lower, circling around my clit.

I can't stop myself from writhing and moaning, my fingers digging into his hair. I'm on the verge of exploding, and I know I won't be able to hold out much longer.

He slips a finger inside me, curling it up and hitting the perfect spot. His mouth moves up, capturing my clit between his teeth.

And then, as if sensing exactly how close I am, he pulls back.

"Not yet, sweetheart," he whispers.

I cry out, the denial nearly driving me crazy.

But then he lowers his head again, his mouth returning to my pussy. His tongue teases me, his fingers thrusting in and out of me, bringing me back to the brink.

"You're close," he says. It isn't a question. We both know it's true.

"Let me suck you," I whimper, reaching for him, desperate for more—anything, as long as I can keep riding this wave of pleasure.

He groans, the sound vibrating through me. He moves up, letting me grab his hips and pull him close.

I wrap my hand around his length, and he hisses, his eyes rolling back.

I can feel his cock throbbing in my palm.

I lick him slowly, tasting the saltiness of his precum. His hands tangle in my hair, guiding me, controlling the movement. I'm completely at his mercy, and it's thrilling.

"So good," he murmurs, his eyes hooded with pleasure.

My own eyes flutter closed, and I give myself over to the sensations, letting them carry me away.

I suck and lick and swirl my tongue around him, feeling him grow harder and thicker in my mouth.

He's close, and so am I.

"Cate," he groans. "Fuck, baby. That feels so good."

His hips thrust forward, and his cock hits the back of my throat.

I choke and gag, the sound bringing a deep, rumbling growl from his chest.

"You like that?" he asks, his voice strained.

I moan around his length, and he starts fucking my mouth, the rhythm steady and relentless. I move faster, my hand working his shaft in time with my mouth.

"Yes," he hisses, still guiding me up and down, up and down. "That's it, baby. Don't stop."

I'm not sure I could even if I wanted to. I'm lost in a sea of ecstasy, waves of pleasure crashing over me.

He tightens his grip on my hair, his movements becoming more erratic. I know he's close.

"That's it," he groans, his voice a ragged whisper. "So fucking close."

He's barely hanging on, his control slipping. I want him to lose control, to give in to the pleasure. But just when I think he's about to take us both over the edge, he pulls back.

I whimper, the sudden loss of his cock in my mouth making me feel strangely empty.

"Not yet," he says, his voice husky and raw.

He moves down, pressing his body against mine, his

hard length pushing against me. He captures my mouth with his, his kiss deep and passionate.

I'm trembling, and I know he can feel it.

He pulls away, and his eyes lock on mine.

"On your hands and knees," he commands, his voice leaving no room for argument.

I comply, the thrill of anticipation making me shiver. He moves behind me, his hand cupping my ass.

"God, you're so fucking beautiful," he says, his fingers tracing the curve of my spine. "I can't wait to bury myself in your tight little pussy."

His words send a rush of heat through me, and I press back against him, eager for more.

"Please," I beg, my voice coming out as a breathless whisper.

He groans, the sound low and feral. His cock presses against my entrance, and he pushes inside, the feeling of fullness overwhelming.

"Oh God," I gasp, my hands gripping the sheets.

He moves slowly, his pace agonizingly torturous. I push back, desperate for more, but he holds me steady, his hands firm on my hips.

"You feel so fucking good," he says, his voice a low rumble. "I want to make this last forever."

He keeps moving, his cock hitting the perfect spot with every thrust. I'm on the edge, and it takes everything I have not to give in to the pleasure.

"Luca," I pant, his name a plea.

"Just a little longer," he murmurs, his fingers digging into my hips.

He picks up the pace, his cock filling me over and over, the friction sending me higher and higher. It feels like he really might be able to hold out forever, and I just hope I can keep up. I'm way past the point of stimulation overload, but in the best possible way.

My entire body is buzzing with electricity, and the pleasure is so intense it's almost painful.

"I can't," I moan, my body trembling. "I can't... Oh God... Luca, please!"

I'm begging, pleading, and I don't even care.

"Almost there, princess. Be good for me." He slams in deep, and I let out a cry, the sensation ripping through me.

Again, deeper and harder, making my head fall forward and my vision blur. I open my mouth but my breath catches in my throat as he slams into me one more time.

"Are you ready, beautiful?" he asks, leaning in and pressing his body against mine so he can nip at the back of my neck. "Ready to come for me?"

I nod frantically, my eyes squeezed shut.

He reaches down, his fingers stroking my clit as his cock fills me, the combination pushing me over the edge. I scream, the orgasm tearing through me like a tidal wave.

Luca growls, the sound primal and possessive, and he thrusts into me, his rhythm becoming erratic. "That's it, baby," he grunts. "So perfect. So fucking good."

I can't even speak, my body quaking as the waves of pleasure wash over me. Luca is relentless, his cock slamming into me over and over, drawing out my orgasm.

"I can't..." I trail off, unable to finish the thought.

"Yes, you can, sweetheart," Luca growls, his voice husky. "You can come for me again. One more time. I know you can do it."

I'm so overwhelmed, my body shaking, my mind reeling, and yet I know he's right. I'm already climbing higher and higher, his words sending me to the stars.

"Luca," I moan, his name like a prayer. "Please. Please, yes. I'm so close. Please, please."

"Come for me, princess," he commands, his voice deep and gravelly. "One more time. Come with me. Now."

And just like that, I shatter, my entire world exploding in a shower of light and color.

Luca grunts, his cock throbbing as he fills me. We're both lost, drowning in pleasure, and I never want it to end.

It seems to last forever, our bodies connected, the waves of pleasure crashing over us again and again.

I collapse on the bed and he settles beside me, his breathing ragged. He stretches out and puts his hands behind his head. I turn onto my side, cooling down. My heartbeat still races as I eye Luca's naked body.

Damp from perspiration and flushed from exertion, his body is something to behold. His arms are heavy ropes of muscle. His chest and abs are smoothly defined, pointing down to a perfectly chiseled vee at his hips. His long legs are toned...

And then there is his cock. Even now, still glistening

from being inside me, it's impressive; long and thick and perfectly pink.

"That was long overdue," he rumbles. I look up at his face, perfectly sculpted cheekbones with a couple of days' worth of stubble, that expressive mouth of his that causes no end of trouble. And his dark eyes, long lashes growing over them...

It was his eyes that really got all of this started.

"Hmm?" I ask absently.

He smirks at my distraction. "I mean, if we had just fucked when we first met, we wouldn't have spent so many years hating each other."

I shoot him a look, then sit up. "That's debatable."

When I start to move off the bed, he pulls me back with a growl. "Where are you going?"

I raise my brows. "To shower. And then probably to bed."

He narrows his eyes. "What if I'm not done with you?"

I swallow and lick my lips. "This was nice, but—"

He makes a face. "It was a fucking lot more than nice and you know it."

I roll my eyes. "Alright, it was really great. And yes, it was overdue. But now that we... let off tension, or whatever... it can't happen again."

Now it's his turn to look surprised. "Is that right?"

He reaches out, skimming his hand down my naked hip. If I were being completely honest, the caress feels good. His hand is warm against my cooling skin. And it's hard not to lean into that touch.

To be known by him. To be cherished, even if it's only temporary.

But that's what it is. My mouth twists and I pull away.

I know that there are other women he's still enthralled with. I know that he married me by mistake and now he's just going along with it because it's easier. I know that this meant nothing to him. So it should mean nothing to me... right?

"I agreed to pretend to be your wife," I say, standing up. "But I never agreed to be your... your temporary distraction."

He looks confused. "What?"

"This?" I point between us. "That's what this is. You're still hung up on Madisyn, or Chloe, or whoever else. And I'm not interested in changing who I am to slip into the place that she left empty."

He scowls. "It has nothing to do with anyone else. We just fucked because we needed to."

I shake my head. "You are delusional if you think that this wasn't a mistake. A one-time only slip up." I find my dress, pulling it down over my head. "Not to be repeated."

"You know, you are fucking hot," he spits out. "It's too bad you always open your mouth and ruin it with words."

I laugh a little, rooting around on the floor for my panties. "Yeah, that's not helping. That just reminds me of how much of a jerk you can be."

"Go, then!" he hisses. "Go lie in your bed, alone. And when you're horny, you can fucking masturbate about the time you were with me." He looks furious. "That's the only action you'll get from me from now on."

Giving up searching for my panties, I huff. "Fine!"

"Fine!" he says.

I storm out of his bedroom angrily, wishing that we had never laid eyes on each other all those years ago.

Chapter 19

Luca

The next week of work is a nightmare. Missing liquor shipments, employees calling out sick at the last possible moment, artist's managers being hard to touch base with.

But by far the worst thing is having to watch Cate running around my bar, showing absolutely zero signs of regret for what she said in my bedroom. It kills me to be this fucking stressed out and know that when I go home, she'll still be there. And she'll be fine.

Smiling at everyone else but me. Chatting with them, getting really comfortable in her new job as a bar back slash waitress.

It pisses me off to no end.

Even now, as I finish prepping some extra lemon and lime juice for Bradford at the end of a rush, I spend the entire time glaring at Cate.

I mean, who does she think she is? With her easy smile and her quick service, she's becoming one of Bradford's favorites. But she essentially ignores me and avoids me, which really fucking irritates me.

I'm the one paying her. She's living in *my* house. It's only a few weeks until Madisyn's wedding but I'm seriously considering just giving Cate her money and having my lawyer file for the annulment sooner than planned.

"Hey!" Bradford says, snapping his fingers. "You are bruising all the oranges!"

I look down at the crate of citrus I'm holding and realize that he's right. I've been pressing the lid down on the crate and staring off into space for a few minutes.

"Sorry," I say with a shrug. "It's been one of those weeks."

Bradford frowns and takes the crate out of my hands. "You don't have to take it out on the innocent citrus fruit. They didn't put your panties in a twist."

I roll my eyes. "Is there anything else you need me to do?"

He purses his lips, giving me a once over. "We're almost out of chai-infused shrub... Honey... maybe you should just go home. We're at the end of the rush anyway."

I glare at him. "You're telling me to go home now?"

He crosses his arms, looking at the crowd skeptically. "I have no idea what exactly has crawled up your ass. I can only assume it has something to do with your wife. But honestly, I'd rather deal with being in the weeds alone than put up with your huffing and moping for another second."

That sets me back for a second. Bradford is usually so

cheerful. He is the last person on the staff to hassle anyone unless he thinks they're intentionally being lazy or unhelpful.

Before I can formulate exactly what I'm going to say, the front door of the Attic opens. I turn, expecting it to be more bar flies.

But I freeze when I see my mother and father breeze through the door. They are dressed eccentrically, like a wealthy and dapper couple straight out of the 1950s. My mom is in a dark grey coat with a pink dress peeping out of the bottom. My father takes off his hat, his dark suit and dark overcoat making him look like Cary Grant.

"Shit," I mutter. "This is not what I need right now."

My father looks around with a scowl while my mother just looks confused; my mother has had so much Botox in the last few years that she can't frown anymore.

The sourness in the pit of my stomach turns to acid.

Bradford straightens when he sees my parents. "Hey, isn't that your mom and dad?"

My father spots me, making me clear my throat nervously. I nod.

"Yeah." I look at Bradford. "I didn't expect them, and yet... here they are. In my bar, which they hate."

As my parents approach me, I hurry out to catch them before they hit the bar. "Mom!" I say, bending to kiss her on the cheek. She accepts my kiss, patting my arm.

"Hello, Luca dear. I see you've still got this old place." She turns her nose up at the patrons milling around her, smiling vaguely. "Would you be a darling and get me a gin martini? The ride here was dreadful and now I find myself a bit parched."

I force a smile. My mother is rarely without a drink. It's always been that way. "Of course."

My father extends his hand. "Son."

I take his hand, shaking it firmly. As usual, he turns it into a show of strength, squeezing my hand so hard that my fingers turn white. It's important that I don't react, though. I learned that very early on.

"Dad," I greet him simply.

He looks around at the now-empty stage and the slowly dispersing crowd. "It's too bad about this place. Really solid idea, I suppose. But maybe your next venture will pan out."

His analysis sets my teeth on edge. "We're doing just fine here, Dad."

He looks at me, an air of puzzlement surrounding him. "Oh? Well you wouldn't know it. Maybe we are just used to something different. You know, we've been on the Continent for so long now, spending our days at sea and our nights in establishments that are more..." He sniffs, casting a glance at the crowd. "Elegant."

The way he says the last part gives me rage. But I do what I always do and stuff it down. I only see my parents every couple of years; there is no reason that the couple of days they'll stay should be unpleasant.

I cross my arms and say nothing.

"Do you mind getting me that drink, dear?" my mom chimes in. "Or should I perhaps try that little place down the street? It looked like an adorable sort of wine shop—"

"Your mother needs to sit down," my father says, looking around with a frown. "Preferably somewhere that's not in a dusty old attic."

My jaw clenches. I shoot a look at Bradford, then raise my arms toward the doors. "Yeah, that wine bar is fine. Let's go there."

My mother is already heading for the exit before I finish the sentence. I roll my eyes, wishing like hell that Luna was here. She is the golden child and usually helps to bail me out of this kind of situation.

I almost make it out the door before I hear Cate behind me, calling my name. "Wait, Luca! If you're going home, I need a ride there—"

I cringe and then turn toward her. "Not now, Cate."

My father doesn't miss a single trick. "Who is this, Luca?" He casts an eye up and down her body. "Some kind of angel that you know?"

I'm surprised by that. I hadn't thought to introduce Cate to my parents. Honestly part of me fears whatever kind of judgment my parents will pass on her. They have always hated anyone I chose to introduce them to as my girlfriend.

Especially Madisyn.

But my mother comes tottering back inside the front door to see what's holding us up and now she and my father are looking at me expectantly.

I clear my throat. "Mom, Dad, this is Cate. She's... uh... living with me."

Cate flushes, extending her hand to my mom. "It's

temporary! Just while I figure out... you know, what needs figuring out."

"Nice to meet you," my father booms. "You've got a nice handshake there, sweetheart."

My eyebrows rise. Sweetheart? And since when does Cate have such a magical handshake?

"So nice to meet you guys," Cate says. "I was just trying to catch Luca—"

My father barks at her. "Nonsense! You must be close with Luca here if you're staying at his house. Come have a drink with us."

"Oh yes!" my mom says, lighting up. She grabs Cate's elbow and starts steering her out the door.

"Oh no," Cate tries to protest. "I am still working—"

My father claps me on the back so hard that it stings. "Luca will forgive you for cutting out early. Isn't that right, son?"

He doesn't wait around for me to agree though. He pushes through the heavy door, rushing to catch up with my mom and Cate.

I trail after them, watching anxiously as my mom leads the way into the dimly lit wine bar. The place is pretty romantic and intimate, with lots of little black leather booths and a few tables peppered here and there. Behind that is a wall of wine bottles, organized by wine varietal and region.

Without waiting to be seated, my parents pick a booth, my dad squeezing in with my mom on one side. I sit beside Cate across from them, a sigh on my lips.

"Is there even service here at all?" Mom asks, peeling

her coat off. "I swear, Luca, once you've been in the Greek Isles for a while, you get used to their style. They like fast service, bam bam bam."

She squints around. A waiter comes up as she is saying it, smiling pleasantly.

"Good evening," he begins.

"Yeah, look. We need a bottle of your finest beaujolais, stat," my dad interrupts. "And some kind of bread."

The waiter looks unruffled. "Very good, sir. Four glasses for the table?"

"Yes!" my mother says. "Now go, go go."

She shoos him away. "I'll tell you, I wish we were back home. They know our order without asking us. When we get into any restaurant, they have someone opening our bottle before we even sit down."

She waves her hand. I glance at Cate, who looks like she thinks that if she's quiet enough, she will legitimately disappear.

Under the table, I put a reassuring hand on her knee. She blushes but when she looks at me, she seems grateful.

I repress a sigh. "That's nice, Mom. Speaking of that, why are you two in town? And with no notice on my part..."

The waiter comes back, pouring the bottle of wine into four glasses and setting down a basket of breadsticks. My mom immediately gulps her wine, so my father steps up to answer.

"We have to spend at least three days here to maintain our residency. Don't worry, we'll be on a plane tomorrow to Hawaii."

My mom smiles. "We haven't been there for almost eight years! Aloha."

"Wait, I thought you had to be here for three days?"

"Well, we have been. We've just been busy." My father sips his wine, staring at his glass. "I'm not sure that this is what I asked for."

So they were in the state of Washington, they just couldn't be bothered to tell either of their children? I would be shocked, but honestly that's pretty typical for my parents.

"Cate, dearest, tell us all about you," my mom says. "Where did you grow up?"

Cate goes red, pushing her dark hair out of her face. "Here in Seattle."

"Oh really?" My mom takes a sip of her wine. "Where did you go to high school?"

"Gatewood High." She blushes again. "I have been friends with your daughter for eight years, ma'am."

"Luna?" my dad says. "You have good taste in friends, then."

Cate ducks her head. "Yes sir."

He laughs. "And polite? I'll wager this is the best girl-friend you've even introduced us to, son."

"I'm not—"

"She's not my—"

We start protesting at once, but my parents don't listen. Truth be told, they aren't even paying attention. My mom drains her wine glass.

"Be a darling and flag that waiter down, will you?" she asks my father.

I glare at them, unsure how to even respond. Then I feel Cate put her hand on my knee.

I glance at her. She gives me a sympathetic look, squeezing my hand.

Then she puts her hand back on my knee and sits up straight. "You know, Luna and I went to college together too."

My father and mother both look at her.

"Oh yes?" my mother asks, beaming. "Luna is so smart, isn't she? Going for her medical school degree is tough stuff."

Cate smiles. "Totally. I'm always in awe of that. When we were in college, I had one semester of biology before I cried uncle."

"She gets that from me," my father brags. "I could've gone to med school if I wanted."

"Definitely," Cate says, nodding. "Luna is really smart. She's going to make a great doctor. And she's also very pretty..."

My mom reaches across the table and grabs Cate's hand. "She is so pretty! And I am so glad to meet you!" She shakes a finger at me. "You hold onto this one, Luca. She's a keeper!"

"Luca actually does really well with his bar," Cate says.

My dad actually bursts out laughing, slapping the table. "Did you hear that, darling? She stuck up for her man! I love that quality in a girlfriend, don't you Luca?"

My dad slides his glass of wine in front of my mom and my mom takes it, sipping it right away. He orders another bottle, though Cate and I don't really touch our wine. Cate spends the next hour praising Luna and defending me. I spend the whole time quietly watching; she seems to have things well enough in hand.

By the time my parents leave, drunkenly staggering to a cab, my father has decided that they love Cate. "She's a keeper," he intones. "You've got to put a ring on that one, son. Best decision you could make."

He hiccups as I roll my eyes.

"Okay, Dad." I tuck his head into the backseat of the cab, feeling an incredible sense of relief when it finally pulls away from the curb.

I look down at Cate, a sigh on my lips. "Thank you. You saved the night, somehow."

She blushes and looks away. "It's alright."

"No, it's not. I owe you an apology. I've misbehaved since we hooked up. But you..." I shake my head. "You saved me tonight anyway."

"Yeah, well." Her lips twitch and she glances up at me. "It wasn't that bad for me. As it turns out, they just want to hear about how great Luna is."

I groan. "Yeah. They've always been like that. My parents could not be more self—involved, except for cheering on Luna."

Her smile falls. "I am really sorry that you have to deal with that, Luca. I mean, I would argue that at least your parents are alive... but I don't think you have the same kind of relationship with them as I did with mine."

I frown. "No. Not even remotely."

There is a flash in my head, of Cate and her mom

arguing just before Cate got into my car years ago. I wish I had a parent that cared, even just for a little while.

Cate surprises me by pushing up on her tiptoes and kissing my cheek. Then she steps back, her face burning.

"What was that for?" I ask, perplexed.

She shrugs. "You just seemed like you needed it. That's all."

Before I can say anything, my phone starts vibrating in my pocket. I dig it out, trailing after her toward the Attic. It's one of the band managers that I have desperately been trying to get in touch with.

"Shit, I should take this," I say, although Cate is a few feet ahead of me by now. "Do you want a ride home in a bit, though?"

She flashes a grin over her shoulder. "Yeah, that'd be great."

Then she disappears into the front door of the Attic, leaving me to argue on the phone.

Chapter 20

Cate

C–

Had to leave early to make a partner's meeting at work.
See you there later.

$-L$

I stare down at the note Luca left for me, my mouth pulled into a frown. It's not a big deal that I didn't get a ride to work.

No, my issue is that I'm starting to feel like he knows me a little too well. Especially when I found the note pinned to the coffee maker.

Yeah, he would've had to have known my morning routine. He set this note out and ground some coffee just for me...

And I don't like it one bit.

I mean, I would've figured out that Luca had left

even without this note. And the coffee filter and pre-ground coffee just seem mocking to me.

That, or like Luca thinks that he has a grasp on me and what I like. The thought makes me vaguely nauseated.

This is only supposed to be for four more weeks. That's one month. Then things go back to normal, whatever that means. And one thing that is normal is that Luca and I hate each other...

Certainly the feeling I have in the pit of my stomach, which is not hate and is instead some mixture of lust and longing and a drizzle of starry eyed wonder... I am not supposed to feel this way.

Non-hate feelings were never part of the arrangement.

I still have hours before I have to be at work, so I ignore the coffee Luca laid out for me. Instead, I take the bus back to my grandmother's house. While I'm on my way there, I lapse into daydreaming a few times.

Well, by daydreaming, I mean remembering what sex with Luca was like.

Every time my mind wanders off and ends up in the gutter, I pinch myself on the back of my hand. It's the same technique that I used to stop biting my nails...

But it isn't working, thus far.

When I finally get to Grandma's house, I have to hunt her down. I finally find her in her outdoor greenhouse, kneeling between rows of mint and sage. It smells heavenly out here, especially when I pluck a tender shoot of mint, crushing it between my fingers.

Grandma turns around at the sound of my footsteps approaching.

"Cate!" she says, beckoning me closer. "Just the person I need. Here, grab a pair of gloves and help me weed." She yanks a weed from the row of sage. "These damned weeds."

I pick up a pair of gloves, kneeling beside her. "Hi Grandma."

"Hello, sweetheart. Grab that tool there, will you?" She points to a hand tool and I pick it up. "Mmm. Doesn't the earth smell good today?"

I can't argue with that. "Yep."

Pulling some weeds out by the roots, I toss them in the pile she's made. Grandma presses her lips together, glancing at me.

"How are things going with your man friend?"

All the while her hands are busy, using the tool to dig up a fresh clod of earth.

I blow out a breath. "Complicated."

Grandma's lips lift. "They usually are." She pauses, yanking on a particularly intractable weed until it comes free of the earth. Then she tosses it onto the pile. "I was under the impression that you didn't like him. What is his name again? Luke?"

"Luca," I say. I grunt as I tug at a weed. "And I don't. Or at least, I didn't."

My grandmother slides me a look. "You know, your parents hated each other before they became a couple."

I stop pulling a weed. "Mom and Dad?"

"Mmm-hmm." Grandma sits back, adjusting her hat.

"Your mom was conservative at the time. In the way she dressed, in the things she did, how she voted too, probably. I think having me for a mother, the biggest hippie that you could find in Seattle, was hard for your mother in some ways."

I don't say anything, not wanting to interrupt her remembrance. But I do put my hand on her back, rubbing small circles into her flesh. Grandma gives me a sad smile.

"Anyway, your father came along. He was very different, from a military family but rebelling against what he came from. He was laid back where your mother was strict, mellow where she couldn't be. She was a devout Catholic, he couldn't be bothered with any church. You get the idea."

I frown. "How did two people who believed such different things end up married?"

My cheeks stain, because I realize people could ask me the same question about Luca and I.

"Eventually I think they met in the middle in most things," Grandma says with a shrug. "But for a while there, all I heard about him were complaints. 'Charlie did this, can you believe it?' and 'Charlie said that! I wanted to smack him!'" Grandma dusts off her hands. "Then one day, the script flipped. 'Isn't Charlie handsome?'"

She chuckles, then gets up, her knees popping.

"Careful there," I say, steadying her.

She waves me off. "Come on. We need some hot cocoa. I've already set up the pitcher just inside the back door. We should sit on the back porch while we warm ourselves."

She marches toward the back porch, leaving me to follow her.

"Mom and Dad really seemed happy together," I muse.

"They were." She climbs the steps to the back porch. "Sit yourself down. I'll grab the cocoa."

I take one of the ancient wooded rocking chairs as Grandma returns with two steaming mugs full of cocoa. Thanking her, I sip mine experimentally.

Grandma is a lot of wonderful things, but a good cook is not one of them. To my surprise, it's well-balanced, the dark bittersweet chocolate offset by the buttery milk fat. Somehow, the notes are in harmony.

"I didn't make the cocoa," she says, smiling as she sips it. "I'm sure you can tell. Carmine made a few batches for the house."

"I didn't say anything," I protest, warming my hands on the mug.

Things are quiet for half a minute, then Grandma speaks again. "You said things are complicated with you and your man friend. Why do you feel that way?"

"Oh." I blow out a breath. "I met his parents last night. I mean, I've met them before as Luna's parents, but they barely noticed me. Last night though, they were paying attention and it was..." I pause, searching for the words. "A little bit terrifying, to say the least."

She arches a brow. "How so?"

"Mr. Leone was... I don't know, commandeering?

And imperious? And Luca's mom... she was nice but she drank a lot. A lot. Thank god they're gone a lot, but... I can't imagine growing up with them as parents."

My grandmother nods. "You were lucky, I think. Having the parents you had..."

That phrase makes me a little sad. Had, in the past tense. "Yeah," I say, my shoulders slumping. It's a little weird to even be having this conversation about my parents.

Then she smiles slyly at me. "So have you told Luca yet?"

My brow pulls down. "Told him what?"

"That whatever he's doing, it's working. You're smitten with him, I can tell."

A bloom of heat rises in my cheeks. "What? No. Ugh."

I roll my eyes but Grandma just grins at me. "Oh yes. You like him. Grandmothers have a sixth sense about these things."

I shake my head. "Nope. This conversation is over. Cancelled!"

"Mmm-hmm." Grandma looks down at her cocoa, pleased with herself. "We can change the subject but I don't think that will change the way you feel."

I stand up. "I should probably get going anyway."

"Oh, come give me a hug." She stands up and hugs me, brushing my hair back from my face.

Long after I leave though, I'm still turning over what she said.

Am I really smitten with Luca? I mean, we have been

in pretty close quarters for almost a month and a half now. And close quarters did bleed over into us having sex once…

I don't want to be one of those girls that goes all goo-goo eyed over a guy that she's had sex with, though. That's so not me.

Then again, neither was having sex with Luca in the first place.

I'm still turning the thought over and over in mind my mind when I reach the Attic. I head to the employee locker room, getting ready for work at a snail's pace. Bradford comes into the locker room, waving several envelopes in the air.

"Honey, please get these checks out of my mailbox," he says. "They've just been piling up out there. The other employees take theirs home the second they get them."

He hands me three envelopes. I frown at them, shaking my head a little. "I thought that you guys just dealt with this stuff somehow. I didn't realize that I had checks waiting for me, I guess."

"Well, you do. And they should be pretty substantial, especially since you have all your credit card tips on your paycheck."

I flush a bit. "Right. Thanks."

He waves, already on his way out of the locker room. "See you in a while!"

I stare at the checks in my hand, then sigh. Ripping open the first one, I scan for the amount listed.

Net pay… $1709.16.

My eyes bulge out. Surely that has to be a mistake!

No way in hell did I actually earn that much. Tearing open the other two checks, I find that they're for even more.

Nineteen hundred dollars and twenty four hundred dollars.

That can't be right! I mean... I don't remember talking to Luca about what I would earn hourly, but this is... some kind of charity, surely.

I mean, there is just no way that I've earned that much. Bursting out of the locker room, I practically run to the bar. Bradford looks up from a stack of receipts, arching an eyebrow.

"Something wrong with your paychecks, darling?" he drawls.

I shove them at him, my expression grave. "That can't be right," I say, pointing at the dollar amount. "There is no way that I have earned that much working less than twenty hours a week."

Bradford smothers a sigh and takes the checks, looking at my paystubs. "I mean, that looks right to me. I would estimate about that if someone asked me how much a waitress or a bar back makes here."

My heart thunders. "How much money does the bar make every night?"

He crosses his arms, pressing his lips together. "Way more than you thought, apparently. What is your issue here? Do you feel like you make too much? Because let me tell you something, dear. I guarantee you that other people, people who have to actually pay rent and bills, would kill for that issue. There are a lot of people in the world that are struggling to make ends meet."

My eyes widen. I didn't mean to complain at all. "I was just trying—"

Bradford holds up a hand to silence me. "Do you have an actual issue with your paychecks?"

Coloring, I hesitate then shake my head. "No."

"Good." He hands me back the checks. "If there isn't anything else, I am trying to finish up some paperwork before the shift starts."

I nod meekly. "Of course. I'll be right back, just let me put these checks in my locker."

Bradford smiles lightly but his eyes go down to the paperwork before him. I know a dismissal when I see one.

Slinking back to the employee locker room with my checks, I feel a little chastised. I really didn't mean to make a big deal out of nothing, especially not with one of Luca's business partners. And doubly so with someone that is essentially a stranger.

I shove the checks in the back of my locker and close the door. It just doesn't seem right that I should have so much when there are so many people that actually need to earn what I've accidentally stumbled into earning.

With that thought now weighing heavily on me, I head out to start my shift.

Chapter 21

Luca

I pull my SUV into a spot at the marina, turning the engine off. The morning is just getting bright. Even through the car windows, the briny smell of the ocean takes over my senses.

Cate looks at me, her suspicion evident. "What is this?"

I roll my eyes. "See all the boats and the docks? We are at a marina. Not a shabby one, either."

She gives her head a shake. "That's not what I mean and you know it. Why did you have me pack for two nights away?"

I wink at her. "You'll have to grab your bag and come with me to find out."

She looks out at the yachts bobbing in water, her brow pulling down. But when I get out of the car and grab my bag, she follows suit.

"Come on," I say, closing the trunk of the Porsche.

"It's a reward for being so helpful the other night. I know my parents can be a handful."

She looks uncertain, but I lead her down to the docks, weaving around some of the larger yachts until I stop in front of Tonight's Promise.

It's more of a schooner than a yacht, but it's plenty big enough for the two of us. Plus I got it at the last minute, because inspiration for this little trip only struck yesterday morning.

"Surprise!" I say, glancing at her to gauge her reaction. She looks warily up at the ship.

"Please tell me you didn't buy me a boat."

I smirk. "You wish. This boat costs more than a normal person makes in five years." The way she glares at me makes me laugh a little. "Relax, princess. I rented it for the next two days. Come on, let's head on board."

I walk up the wobbly plank that leads onto the boat, putting my bag down and helping her on board. She looks around, obviously fretting about something.

"What?" I ask. "Come on, it's fine. I covered our shifts at work, if that's what you're worried about."

She looks at me, gripping her tote bag and steadying herself on the boat's railing. "I've never been on a ship before," she confesses. "Or a boat or even a canoe."

"What??" I say. "We're in Seattle! The water is so close to us!"

Her cheeks color. "I know. We just grew up very differently, you and I."

That is undoubtedly true; Luna and I spent whole summers when we were kids navigating the seas and making sure our mom didn't fall over the railing when she'd had too many glasses of wine.

"Well, that's okay. It really just takes some getting used to," I tell her. "Here, let me show you around. Then we can head out to sea."

I point her toward the staircase that leads down into the sleeping quarters, tiny kitchen, and bathroom. She starts moving toward it like she's walking on the surface of some new planet and is not sure how gravity works here.

"You can drive this boat?" she asks.

"Yep. I have a license."

I follow the clatter of her footsteps down the stairs. She stops short when she sees the bedroom. With two round windows spilling bright light into the room, it's barely large enough to contain a double bed.

"This is it?"

I sling my bag onto the bed. Then I take hers and toss it onto the bed too. "Yeah. There are bigger boats with more room, but I figured if I rented something lavish you would really freak out."

She looks at me. "But there is only one bed!"

I roll my eyes. "There is a hammock hanging upstairs behind the steering wheel. I'll sleep there if necessary."

She exhales and looks at the bed again. "I don't know, Luca..."

I move a little closer to Cate, looking down at her with a stern look. I wish that I thought she would respond to being kissed or caressed, but something tells me she would be off of this boat so fast my head would spin.

So I just settle for almost touching, here in this confined physical space.

I touch her arm, moving my hand down to her elbow. Not a caress, just resting my hand on her body.

"Just trust me, okay? Give it one day. If you hate it after today, we'll sail back tomorrow."

She looks up at me, biting her lip. Her nostrils flare, her pupils dilate a fraction. She licks her lips, blushing.

"Okay," she says, her voice breathy.

I stare down into her eyes, liking the willingness I find there. "Okay." There is a moment of real connection there, hanging there between us. A moment that reminds me of just how it felt to have her in my arms, how it felt to hear her quiet moans and throaty pleas. A moment where her gaze dips down to my mouth and I lean closer, sober as a judge, ready to take her breath away.

But then that moment stretches a bit too long and grows awkward. Cate glances away and I take a step back, clearing my throat.

"I'll just go—" she starts.

"I should go—" I say.

We both give each other a bland smile. Turning, I hustle out of the room, climbing the compact staircase to get back to the upper deck.

Why are both of us so damn awkward together? I wonder as I head for the captain's chair. I guess that some leftover feelings are involved on both our parts, and none of them are good.

It's all bitterness that is pulling us down, threatening to make us sink. This mini-vacation will act as a test, telling me whether or not we can leave that bitterness in the past or whether we are just stuck in our ways.

I fire up the schooner, carefully guiding it out of the marina. For a while I am alone on the very top of the boat, up inside the steering cabin.

Setting the course for a nice, leisurely cruise on the Pacific Ocean, I hang out in the captain's chair for a bit. That turns into hours, the sun getting brighter and then starting to slip from its place in the middle of the sky. I hear nothing from belowdecks, not a single peep.

Eventually though I start to worry about Cate, so I head back downstairs.

I find Cate at the top of the stairs, sitting and looking out at the water. "I see you found a shady spot."

She surveys me, blocking out the sun with a hand. "I did."

"Do you want to come tour the captain's chair? Or are you hungry yet?" I ask.

"Why did you bring me out here?" she asks.

I shift my stance. "To thank you for handling my parents so well the other night. I already said that, I think."

She narrows her eyes. "Anybody would have done the same."

I smirk. "No, they wouldn't have. A lot of girls would've turned tail and fled." I glance out over the deck, to the gorgeous blue-green water. "It actually has me thinking that I should make sure to find someone that can handle my parents, when the time comes for me to settle down."

She frowns, considering my words. "Is that what you're looking for in a woman?"

I pause. Something tells me I should watch myself here.

"Well... yeah. In the broadest sense." I cross my arms. "It's a little like this. Three years ago, my friends and I went crazy and bought the building that would become the bar. So I try to bear that in mind when I'm meeting potential partners. I'm a successful bar owner. I'm rich. I'm handsome. I'm fit. I want someone who is all of that, but more."

Her eyes narrow. "Oh, is that all?"

I shrug. "When it comes to marriage? Yes. I need someone who challenges me to do more... but at the same time, they have their own things going on. I don't want somebody that is always waiting around to see what I'm up to. I don't want to be tied to someone that stagnates."

"I see." Her mouth flattens. "What else do you see for your future?"

I furrow my brow. "That's more uncertain. I know that I would like to own a few more bars. I want to travel a lot, preferably with my wife. I haven't ever visited Asia or Australia, so they're on my bucket list." I pause, thinking. "And if I have children of my own, I'll treat them a thousand times better than my parents ever treated me."

Cate nods. "Those are respectable goals."

I spread my hands wide. "What about you?"

She glances at me. Then her lips quirk. "Can I ask you for a favor?"

I lean against a ballast. "Sure. Shoot."

She blushes but doesn't look away. "Will you kiss me again? I just want to test something—"

That quick, I shush her. "Ssh. Come up here."

She clambers up from where she's sitting. Cate loses her balance for a second. I step forward and slide one hand around her waist.

"Don't worry," I murmur, looking down into her eyes. "I've got you." She stares up at me, her cheeks flushed, her mouth parted.

In her eyes, desire is written as plain as day. She pushes up onto her tiptoes as I growl and press my lips to hers.

She tastes as incredible as I remembered, like mint and honey and a savage sort of lust.

Cate moans into my mouth and I flick my tongue against hers, my whole body tightening.

I need this, I realize. I need her, at this very moment in time.

Breaking off the kiss, I peer down at her, brushing a wisp of her dark hair back from her face. "Does that answer a question for you?"

She doesn't answer. She just reaches for me again, her lips seeking mine, her curves feeling just right under my hands.

"Let's go to the bedroom," she whispers.

I pause, then lift her into my arms.

"Your wish is my command, princess."

Moving toward the stairs, I kiss her again, stroking her tongue with mine.

Chapter 22

Cate

Luca moves back to look at me, and I see the fire raging in his eyes. A fire that I feel too, a fire that could consume us both for all I care. His gaze drops to my lips, and I lean forward, lips parting. He moves to kiss me, his lips firm and demanding.

This is no peck on the lips. This is a searing kiss, one that makes my head spin and my heart beat faster. His lips are hot and urgent, his tongue invading my mouth, claiming every inch.

I'm breathless, overwhelmed, completely lost in his touch.

He pulls back, his eyes blazing with lust.

"I want you," he growls, his voice rough.

I can't stop myself from moving toward him. My hand cups the back of his neck, drawing him close. Our lips meet, and the kiss is wild and desperate, fueled by a primal need.

He grabs my hips, pulling me against him, his cock hard and straining.

"Fuck, sweetheart," he mutters. "You feel so fucking good."

My fingers tangle in his hair, tugging him closer. The kiss deepens, our tongues tangling together, a clash of heat and need.

He breaks the kiss, his eyes locked on mine. "I want to taste every inch of you."

His words send a shiver through me. He drops to his knees, his hands gripping my hips.

"Lie back on the bed," he commands.

I comply, my body buzzing with anticipation. His hands run along the sides of my legs, slowly pushing my slip up. When he reaches the apex of my thighs, he pulls my panties down, tossing them aside.

He spreads my legs wide, his breath hot against my skin. His tongue darts out, licking the length of my slit. I gasp, arching against him.

"God, yes," he groans, his fingers digging into my hips. "So fucking wet."

He continues his exploration, his tongue swirling around my clit. I squirm and writhe beneath him, the sensation overwhelming.

"Luca," I pant, unable to form any other words.

He chuckles, the sound vibrating through me. He sucks and teases and laps up my wetness, taking me to the brink of ecstasy and then backing off, leaving me desperate for more.

"Please," I whimper, my body shaking.

"We have all day, princess," he growls, his hands roaming up under my slip, cupping my breasts and tweaking both of my nipples at the same time with his calloused fingers and thumbs. "No need to rush this."

I cry out, the dual sensation of his mouth and hands driving me wild. He continues his exquisite torture, his tongue circling my clit and his fingers pinching and pulling. I'm on the edge, loving every second, every touch.

"Luca, please," I beg, my voice a hoarse whisper. "I can't..."

"You can," he says, his deep voice vibrating right through me. "You will. You'll be good for me, won't you?"

I moan, the feeling of his fingers plucking at my nipples making me shudder.

"Yes," I gasp, not even sure what I'm agreeing to.

"Good girl," he praises, and the words make my whole body flush with pleasure.

He moves his hands down, cupping my ass, holding me still as his tongue flicks against my clit. The sensation is almost too much to bear, and I can feel myself start to unravel.

"Oh God," I moan, my voice a low whine as I thrust my hips up to meet his amazing tongue. "Luca, yes... so good."

He grunts, the sound sending a jolt of electricity through me. His fingers dig into my ass, and his tongue slides inside me again.

The sensation is indescribable, and I can't help but buck and writhe beneath him, completely losing myself.

"Please," I beg.

He growls, his mouth never stopping, his tongue thrusting in and out. I'm trembling, my body tightening.

"So close," I gasp, then whimper in frustration when he rises up in front of me, taking that magical tongue away.

"Stay there," he orders me.

He begins to undress, taking off his shoes, pulling his tee shirt off over his head. His torso ripples as he does, and I admire his light dusting of dark chest hair. He's also got a trail of hair that leads down from his belly button and disappears into his waistband. His arms flex as he unzips his jeans, but he stops there.

I get a tantalizing peek into his unbuttoned pants as he comes closer, just for a second.

He moves onto the bed, kneeling at the end. He considers me for a moment, like he's trying to decide what to do with me. "Come here."

I shiver as I move closer, feeling like I'm under a microscope. He narrows his eyes and runs a single fingertip across my collarbone, down under the remaining strap of my slip. He draws the strap off of my shoulder, and then rolls the top of the slip down until my pink nipples are exposed to the air.

His touch is electric but surprisingly gentle, his movements slow and deliberate. My breathing is shallow, my pulse racing.

Luca leans in and places a kiss on the skin just below my collarbone. Then another, and another, his lips leaving a trail of fire in their wake.

I'm aching for him, desperate for more. He keeps moving, kissing his way down to my breasts.

He swirls his tongue around one nipple, and then the other, his eyes never leaving mine.

"So perfect," he murmurs, his words sending a shiver through me. "I've thought about doing this so many times."

He continues his exploration, his lips grazing every inch of exposed skin.

I'm trembling, the anticipation almost too much to bear. His hands grip my hips, and he presses his body against mine, his cock hard and straining against his jeans.

"Fuck, Cate. You have no idea how badly I want you."

The raw need in his voice makes me weak in the knees. His hands slide down, cupping my ass and lifting me up so that I'm straddling him.

I can feel the heat and pressure of his cock between my legs, the fabric of his jeans providing delicious friction.

My head is spinning, and I can barely think straight. All I know is that I want him, and I don't want to wait another second.

"Luca," I gasp, his name a plea on my lips.

He groans, and I can see the fire burning in his eyes. "You want this, princess? Tell me what you want."

He dips his head low and I open my mouth to answer but then his teeth graze my nipple and all coherent thought leaves my mind.

All I can do is feel and pant and moan. I roll my hips, the movement instinctual. He's so hard, and the friction sends another jolt of pleasure through me.

"Luca, please," I beg, not even sure what I'm begging for anymore, just that I need more of him. As much as he'll give me.

"What do you need, sweetheart?"

I can hear the smile in his voice. He's enjoying watching me squirm.

"I need you," I whisper that simple truth, my voice coming out in a husky purr.

He kisses me again, hard. His tongue invades my mouth, exploring and claiming as I open myself to him.

It's a kiss that leaves no doubt about who's in control here. He's got me exactly where he wants me, and he's not letting go. I whimper into his mouth, and he grins.

"Tell me you want this," he commands.

I nod, breathless. "I want it. I want you."

"Good."

And then his hands are everywhere, his fingers tracing patterns on my skin.

He kisses and sucks his way down my neck, across my collarbone, and down to my breasts again, but he doesn't stop this time. Instead, he trails kisses and little nips down my stomach, and then his fingers are gripping my thighs, spreading me wide.

Rocking back on his heels, he fixes his hungry eyes on my exposed pussy, making me shiver.

"So pink and perfect," he murmurs. I think for a moment he's going to go down on me again, to finally give me the release he's been teasing me with, but he doesn't.

He slips a finger inside, making my whole body buck when he crooks it just right.

"Fuck, Luca," I gasp, my head falling back against the mattress.

"You're ready for me to fuck you?" he teases, and I groan in frustration.

"Please," I whimper, desperate for it. For him.

"Tell me what you need," he demands, his voice thick with lust. "Let me hear you say the words.

"You," I moan. "I need you. Need you to fuck me."

"Good girl."

And then his finger is gone, and before I can even catch my breath, he's shoving his jeans and underwear down and pressing the head of his cock against my opening.

He groans, the sensation making him grit his teeth. He takes a moment, and his dark eyes find mine. "You sure about this, princess?"

I know he's teasing me again but I nod anyway, my voice a throaty whisper. "More than anything."

"Then let me give you what you need."

And with that, he's pushing inside me, stretching and filling me in the most perfect way.

"Oh, fuck, baby," he groans, his hips rocking against me, his cock buried to the hilt. "So fucking tight."

I moan, overwhelmed by the feel of him inside me. It's pure bliss.

He starts to move, slowly at first while my body

desperately tries to accommodate his thick length. But it doesn't take long for us to find our rhythm, our bodies moving in perfect sync.

"So good, Luca," I gasp, each thrust pushing me higher and higher, the pleasure building and building.

"Fuck yes," he groans, his voice husky. "That's it, sweetheart. Take all of me."

I wrap my legs around his waist, pulling him closer. I can't get enough of him. Our bodies are slick with sweat, our breaths mingling as we move together in this tight space. It's intense and intimate, and it feels like we're the only two people in the world.

I can feel him throbbing inside me, and I know he's close. The thought is almost enough to send me over the edge, but I'm trying to hold back, trying to wait for him.

"You close, baby?" he asks, as if reading my mind.

"So close," I whisper.

"Come for me," he growls, his hand sliding down between our bodies, his thumb finding my clit.

And that's all it takes. The pressure is too much, and I tumble over the edge, the orgasm ripping through me. I cry out, my nails digging into his back, as the waves of pleasure wash over me.

He keeps going, his hips snapping, his thrusts rough and urgent. And then he's groaning, his body tensing, his cock pulsing inside me as he finds his own release.

He slows at last, half-collapsing on the bed with me. He turns me over, kissing me tenderly. I cling to him, feeling...

Loved? Freshly fucked? Overwhelmed?

I lay on his chest, listening to his rapid heartbeat as it begins to slow. My eyelids begin to droop, and my breathing evens out. I'm not asleep per se, but I'm not far from it. When he speaks, it startles me.

"Ready to go again?" he asks, his voice barely more than a rumble in his chest.

I open my eyes and squint at him. "Again?"

He chuckles, brushing my hair back from my neck. He places a long, lazy kiss on my bare skin. "You want me, don't you?"

I bite my lip, but we both already know my answer.

It's yes. It will always be yes, for him.

Chapter 23

Luca

The next forty hours are a mind-blowing amount of sex, coupled with intimacy and a healthy dose of laughter. Cate is surprisingly witty when she's not fucking my brains out. As long as I feed her and make her coffee, she is surprisingly cool with anything else I want to do to her.

On the way back to the marina, she stirs from drowsing. I look over at her, smiling faintly.

"What?" I rasp.

She kisses me, twining her fingers with my own and pulling away the blankets from her body. There is an urgency in her kiss; I'm not sure if she just woke up and wanted me or if she knows that our time is drawing short.

I grab her by the waist and haul her up on the lofted bed, spreading her thighs and bringing us together. My mouth descends upon hers, hungry and demanding.

There is a fire burning inside me, and I can't seem to get enough of her.

She arches her back, moaning against my lips, and I lose control.

My fingers tangle in her hair, tugging her head back, and I bury my face in the curve of her neck, sucking and biting at her soft skin. She writhes beneath me, her hips bucking against mine, and the heat and friction send me into overdrive.

"Fuck," I mutter, my voice rough with need.

I trail kisses along her jaw, down her neck, and across her collarbone as I slide the thin strap of her dress off her shoulder. She gasps, and I grin, loving the way she reacts to my touch.

"I need you, Luca," she whispers, her voice hoarse.

"I'm right here, sweetheart," I murmur, my lips grazing the shell of her ear.

I kiss her deeply, my tongue exploring her mouth, savoring her taste. My hand slides up her thigh, under her dress, and my fingers brush against the lace of her panties.

She moans into my mouth, her hips bucking against mine, urging me on.

"Luca," she whimpers, her hands clutching at me, pulling me closer.

"Shh," I murmur. "Just relax."

I slip my hand inside her panties, my fingers finding her wet and ready for me. I stroke her gently, circling her clit, teasing her until she's trembling with need.

"Please," she begs, her voice a desperate whisper.

"Not yet," I growl, my voice thick with desire.

I pull back, and her eyes flutter open, her pupils blown wide with lust.

She looks at me, her cheeks flushed, her breathing ragged. She's so beautiful, so perfect. I want nothing more than to make her mine.

"Luca," she breathes, her voice a plea.

"Shh," I murmur. "Just enjoy it."

I press a finger inside her, and she gasps, her body arching against mine. I work her clit with my thumb, my finger pumping in and out of her.

She moans, her head falling back, her fingers tangling in my hair.

"Fuck," I mutter, the sound almost involuntary.

I add another finger, stretching her, and she cries out, her body shaking.

"Yes, Luca. Please, please. Don't stop. So good."

Her words are like music to my ears, and I keep going, pushing her closer and closer to the edge.

She's close, and I know it. I can feel her body tensing, her muscles clenching around my fingers.

"That's it, sweetheart. Come for me."

She whimpers, her hips thrusting against me, and I keep stroking her, my fingers working her clit.

She cries out, her body spasming, and I watch in awe as she comes apart beneath me.

It's the most incredible thing I've ever seen, and I know I'll never get enough.

When her orgasm fades, I pull my fingers out and lick them clean, savoring her taste. She shudders, her eyes locked on mine.

"God, Luca," she gasps.

"I know, princess," I say, grinning down at her. "You're fucking amazing."

I capture her mouth with mine, kissing her deeply, letting her taste herself on my tongue. Her eyes flutter open when I pull back. She looks dazed, but there's a small smile on her lips. "My turn now," she says, reaching for my waist. "I want to taste you this time."

Her fingers fumble with the button on my jeans until I move to help her, repositioning myself on the bed next to her as I finish stripping.

As soon as my jeans are off, she's on top of me, straddling me, her lips seeking mine.

Her kiss is hungry, demanding, and I can't help but moan as she grinds against me.

My cock is already hard and aching, and I can feel her wetness against my skin. I'm more than ready to slide inside her, but she seems to have other ideas. She's the one doing the teasing this time.

She trails kisses down my neck, her fingers tracing patterns on my chest, making my skin tingle.

I grab her hips, pulling her closer, the heat and friction almost unbearable.

"Cate," I growl, my voice strained.

She glances up, a wicked smile on her lips. "Yes?"

"Fuck. Just don't stop."

She laughs, and I know I'm a goner. This girl is going to be the death of me. But damn if it won't be worth it.

"Don't worry," she murmurs, her hands sliding down

my torso, her fingers wrapping around my cock. "I'm just getting started."

She pumps her hand up and down, her grip firm, her pace slow and steady.

I groan, my hips thrusting, my body desperate for more.

She moves lower, her breath hot on my skin. She flicks her tongue against the tip of my cock, and I swear I see stars.

"Fuck, Cate," I mutter, my hands tangling in her hair.

She keeps going, her tongue swirling around the head of my cock, teasing and torturing me.

I'm barely hanging on, the sensation almost too much to bear. She's relentless, and she knows exactly what she's doing to me.

"Shit," I growl, my fingers tightening in her hair. "I'm close."

"Mmm," she murmurs, her mouth still on my cock. "Don't come yet..."

Her words trail off as she takes me deep into her mouth, her lips wrapped tightly around my shaft. She bobs her head up and down, her pace increasing.

"Cate, fuck," I bite my lip, trying to hold on as the pressure builds inside me.

She hums in response, her hand and mouth working in tandem, pushing me closer and closer to the brink. It's fucking torture, but the best possible kind.

I fist my hands in the bedsheets, squeezing my eyes shut as she takes me deeper and deeper, squeezing the base of my cock and massaging my head with her tongue and throat. "Fuck, oh fuck."

Just when I think I can't possibly last another second, she eases back, panting to catch her breath as my balls churn and I thrust up into the empty space where her sexy mouth was.

"Jesus," I exhale as she flashes a too-sweet smile. "You're driving me fucking crazy, sweetheart."

She laughs. "Payback is a bitch, huh?"

Now it's my turn to laugh. "Is that what this is?"

"Payback for all the times you've made me beg and plead."

I shake my head. "We both know you enjoyed each and every one of those times."

"Maybe," she says, her eyes twinkling.

I pull her up, kissing her deeply. "Your turn now," I growl.

"Hmm, what are you going to do to me?"

"Whatever I want."

"Mmm, yes. I like the sound of that."

"Good," I murmur, flipping her onto her back.

"What are you—"

But before she can finish her question, I've already got her wrists pinned above her head, my lips crashing against hers.

She moans into the kiss, her body arching against me, and I can't help but smirk.

I know she's ready for me, but now I'm tempted to draw this out a little longer.

I kiss my way down her neck, my tongue and teeth

leaving marks in their wake. She's writhing beneath me, her breath coming in short gasps.

"Luca, please," she pants, her hips grinding against me.

"Please what?" I ask, trailing kisses along her collarbone.

"Please, I need you. Inside me. Now."

Yeah, fuck holding back. I need this, too.

I kiss her one more time because I'm fucking addicted, then line myself up with her eager, wet pussy. "Since you asked so nicely."

I press forward, filling her completely with one long, smooth thrust. "Holy fuck, gorgeous," I mutter.

She cries out, her eyes rolling back. "Oh, God," she gasps, her legs wrapping around my waist, pulling me deeper.

I thrust again, and again, the friction and heat between us building to an inferno.

I let go of her wrists and move my hands down to her hips, gripping her tight.

"So good," she moans, her nails raking across my back.

"Damn straight it is," I growl, slamming into her, our bodies moving in perfect sync.

We're lost in the moment, the world disappearing around us, everything fading away except for this intense connection between us.

"Luca," she whimpers, her body trembling. "I'm close."

"Me too, sweetheart," I grit out, feeling her tighten around me.

She cries out, her muscles contracting, and I lose control, my hips bucking wildly as the orgasm hits.

"Shit, Cate," I groan, spilling inside her, my body shaking.

The pleasure is blinding, overwhelming, and I ride the wave, lost in the sensation.

We come down slowly, our breaths mingling, our bodies still joined.

"Holy shit," she murmurs, her eyes hazy with lust.

"Yeah," I pant, resting my forehead against hers. "That was…"

"Amazing," she finishes for me.

I chuckle. "Yeah. That."

We stay like that for a few minutes, our bodies entwined, basking in the afterglow before I collapse onto the bed next to her.

She smiles at me a little sadly. "We have to go back to real life soon."

I tuck a strand of her dark hair back. "I mean, unless we don't. We could be like my parents, living on the coast of Greece and yachting full-time."

Cate laughs softly. "I don't think that is an option, even if you have the resources. I'd miss Luna and my grandma too much. You would miss your bar and your friends."

I pull a face. "After a while, sure. But for those first few months…"

She gives me a skeptical look. "Months? You think we would last a week without ripping each other to pieces?"

I shrug. "We made it for two days. Why not two months?"

Cate props herself up on her elbow. "All we did was have sex the entire time."

I act hurt. "You clearly forgot that I made you fruit salad, salmon, and potatoes."

Her lips lift at the corners. "I haven't forgotten. But other than that, we haven't done anything else but nap and have sex. People can't live like that."

"They can and they do."

"Fine, I couldn't do it. I would get bored being your little... kept pet."

"You were doing just fine being a kept woman back on land," I tease. "It's not like you don't live in my big house and eat what I put in the refrigerator."

I mean it jokingly, but I can see that it lands wrong. Her jaw tenses and she sits up, tucking the blanket around her torso.

"It's only temporary. And I only do those things because you asked me to."

I roll my eyes. "I was only kidding. I like having you live at my house."

Reaching for her, I grab her face and kiss her lips. But just like that, the spell is broken. She doesn't smile or kiss me back. She pushes me away.

"Yeah, well." She scoots to the edge of the bed. "You were worried about your ex coming to visit, but I don't think she's going to. I think you might have misled me."

I pull a face at her. "It's not my fault that Madisyn is a flake."

"Well, my time with you is almost up anyway. I should probably start planning for when I'll move back into Grandma's house." She finds her rumpled dress and pulls it on over her head.

I glare at her. "You have big plans for that day, huh?"

Cate just shrugs. She doesn't look at me at all. "Maybe."

"Great," I say, getting up. My pants are nearby in a wrinkled pile and I pull them on, my mood gone sour. "Can't wait. I guess I'll go back upstairs. We should be at the marina soon anyway."

"Fine," Cate snaps. "We'll be out of each other's hair soon. Madisyn's wedding can't come fast enough, personally."

I grab my shirt from the bed. "Fine."

I stomp upstairs, not entirely sure what we are fighting about. All I know is that Cate is right about one thing.

Soon enough we'll be out of each other's hair — and lives — for good.

Chapter 24

Cate

I'm spoiled. Living with Luca has ruined me.

I realize this when I stomp downstairs the next morning, bemoaning the fact that I'm still in Luca's house, only to find that we are out of coffee.

"No. Way!" I hiss, rattling the empty bag. I'm sure I look like a monster, thrashing around the kitchen in my kitty cat pajamas. But I don't care.

I want coffee. This house is so fancy, but it has zero coffee. How is that even possible?

The fact that it isn't here and already made peeves me. I throw the bag in the trash and miss the can, meaning that my little tirade ends with excess coffee grounds all over the floor.

And the kicker is that for a second, I think about leaving the kitchen like that. Coffee grounds on the floor, trash can in the middle of it all.

After all, some invisible person will just come along

and clean it up. I don't have to be the one that does it, right?

That is the moment, holding the trash can in one hand and staring fiercely at it, that I realize.

What am I thinking?

I don't really believe that just because I happen to live somewhere with a maid, she should be responsible for the mess I just made... right?

Disgusted with myself, I take two minutes to clean up the coffee grounds. The whole time, I'm just thinking about Luca and how I've let his lifestyle bleed into mine.

This is not my best self. This is some stranger that is impolite verging on boorish.

Honestly, my Grandma would be ashamed of me.

I storm back upstairs, looking at my calendar on my phone. It's a Wednesday, not a day I work. I'm supposed to be shopping with Luna today.

But I can't do that. I can't go and spend money on myself, not when I've been acting like this.

My phone rings, making me jump. I pick up my phone, not recognizing the number.

"Hello?"

I hear crinkling on the other end. "Cate?"

My brow hunches. "Rachel?"

Rachel Black sometimes volunteers at the women's shelter with me.

"When are you getting here?" she asks. "We have almost everything set up already, so I assume you are going to be working one of the booths."

My mouth opens. The carnival. The one I helped to

organize, to raise money for the shelter. I can feel my face start to heat. "That's today?"

More crinkling. "Sorry, I'm sewing these fracking taffeta table decorations and they are so loud. What did you say?"

"Nothing!" I say. "I'm sorry, I overslept. I'll be right there."

"Yeah, okay..." Rachel says. "Before you go though, do you know anybody willing to have pies flung at them? William went missing and we already have like a hundred whipped cream pies already made up. I'd hate for them to go to waste..."

"Uhh..." I scrunch my face up, hunting for some fresh clothes in my dresser drawers. "I'll put some feelers out, okay?"

She sighs. "Sure. I'll talk to you when you get here."

After we get off the phone, I scrounge around for clean clothes. But of course, there are no modest clothes that are clean. Just my work clothes.

Fuming, I put them on. If I wasn't about to be late, I would actually do some laundry. But I am, so I just put my black knee socks on with my short black dress and my long grey coat over it.

Hoping I look cute rather than like a stripper, I slip on my shoes and grab my purse. Dashing downstairs, I run into Luca. He's perfectly dressed as usual, wearing black jeans and a Sigur Rox t-shirt. He arches a dark brow at me as I rush past him.

"Where are you running to?"

"I'm late. The women's shelter is having a carnival," I call over my shoulder. "I totally blanked on it."

He sets down the glass of water he's sipping. "You want a ride?"

"No!" I yell. That is literally the last thing I want, but I don't have time to get into a fight with him over it. "Later!"

The entire time I am waiting for the bus and riding into the city, I'm just sort of glum. The thought of moving out of Luca's house as soon as we attend his ex's wedding... in what, a week and a half? Yeah, that stresses me out.

Why exactly I can't say. But the future really doesn't hold anything worth looking forward to. Especially not moving back into my grandmother's house.

Don't get me wrong, she is lovely. But after being at Luca's, it will be a tough transition. Being in a place with so many other bodies... and so much competition for the bathroom at all hours of the day... that isn't the greatest draw. Maybe I should use a little bit of the money I've made to find myself my own place.

Or at least some place with less than six people living there. And a private bedroom.

That's fair, right?

When I get to the women's shelter, it's a zoo. The big gymnasium is divided into twenty little booths, each set up for a game or an experience. I walk by people putting the finishing touches on a ring toss game, pass two older ladies dressed as fortune tellers. It's actually all come together pretty well, no thanks to me.

I spot Rachel, holding a plastic baggie full of water and frowning. She's petite but elegant, always impeccably dressed. Even now in the middle of the fair, she wears a black pantsuit with a pearly necklace that just screams *I have expensive tastes.*

"Are you sure that it's alive?"

I start toward her just as she gives the bag a jiggle. There is a little blue flutter in the corner of the baggie. The man Rachel is talking to points to the blue flutter. "I swear, the betta fish are all alive. Most of them are just asleep. Dead fish float."

"Okay," Rachel says, a skeptical expression on her face. "If you say so..."

She sees me and the relief on her face is nearly comical. "Oh, Cate! There you are!"

Rachel comes over to me, giving me a tiny hug. "I'm so glad to see you."

"I'm so sorry I didn't help put all this together," I say, looking around. "It looks amazing."

"Hah!" she says. Brushing a lock of blonde hair out of her face, she smiles. "Don't worry about it. Most of the work was done by my fiancé Grayson anyway. He's..." She looks around, then points out a tall, lumberjack-looking guy with a well-groomed beard. "There he is, moving that stack of boxes."

My eyebrows rise. "Wow. He is very handsome." I grin at Rachel. "Well done, you!"

Rachel blushes. "Thanks. I put up with him." She puts her arm around me, turning me toward an empty booth. "We are still missing William. Like I told you before, the pies are all made up and the booth is covered in plastic so that the pies won't get everywhere... but we don't have anybody to throw the pies at."

"Oh, no problem! I can do it. I feel like I deserve it anyway." I slip my shoulder bag off with a grimace.

Rachel purses her lips, looking me over. "Yeah... don't take it personally, but I really want a guy. Women should take out their feminist rage on him. I would volunteer Grayson, but he's helping to run Pin The Tail On The President." She pulls a face.

"Ah. Totally." I look around, trying to think of who I should call. Gosh, who do I even know well enough to ask them to do this?

In the back of my head, I'm still kicking myself for not being here yesterday. Maybe if I had, I could've planned something out...

"Hey."

I whirl. Luca is right behind me, all leather jacket and dark, tousled hair. Seeing him makes my heart beat double time.

"What are you doing here?" I ask, frowning.

"My sister said you were going to be here for a fair. I figured I should come down and see what the fuss is all about while the shelter is open to the public." He looks around the gym, assessing. "Somehow, it's exactly how I thought it would be."

I shoot him a little glare. "We aren't even in the building that I usually go to."

Rachel speaks up from right behind me. "Do you know this guy? Because when I think about someone I would throw a pie at, that guy is definitely close to what I imagine."

I sigh. "Yes, I know him. But there's no way he'll let us fling desserts at his head."

Luca approaches, looking around. "Are you running one of these booths, Cate?"

Rachel smiles, interrupting. "Why yes, she is! Say, what are you doing for the next few hours?"

Luca glances at me, then shrugs. "I don't know. What do you need?"

Rachel looks at me with a grin. "See? Problem solved! Now you can work the booth and your boyfriend can let people lob pies at him." She pats me on the shoulder. "I should go check on Grayson."

"Wait..." I try to call after her, but she's already on her way across the gym. Glancing at Luca, I shake my head.

"What are you doing here?" I ask.

He shrugs. "Luna said you would be here. I figured I would come down and see what the fuss is about."

I scowl. "Normally you shouldn't hang out at a women's shelter. In case you haven't noticed, you are a guy."

He looks around, shrugging. "I see guys here today."

Rolling my eyes, I head over toward the empty booth. "That's not really the point, is it?"

Luca stops me by touching my elbow. I look up at him, feeling conflicted. On the one hand, I'm glad that someone is here to help...

On the other hand, why does it have to be him?

"Do you want me to leave?" he asks earnestly. "I came here to try to apologize."

He looks down at me, all traces of his usual smugness have vanished.

It's not fair, the way he's looking at me. My heart falters. My mouth goes dry. I don't trust myself to speak.

So I just shake my head. He gives me a tiny smile, his lips lifting up at the corners of his mouth.

"Okay then. What is it that you've got me doing again, exactly?"

I can't help but grin at that. "Oh, you're going to hate it."

Grabbing his hand, I lead him over to the pie booth.

He eyes the booth with a skeptical look. He looks at the sign hanging on the front of the booth that just says, "PIES 2 TICKETS EACH".

"What is this? Why is most of this area all lined in blue plastic?"

"Oh, you'll see." Behind the counter set up there are several metal trays covered with a blue plastic sheet. I lift one corner of the cover, pulling it back to show him the contents.

Luca's bros furrows. "Is that a pie?"

"Yep." I grin.

He gives me a suspicious look. "What, are we selling pies?"

"In a manner of speaking. I'm selling these whipped cream pies. And you... you're getting them thrown at your face."

His look of surprise is practically perfect. "What?"

I laugh. "You should see your face. Does it really surprise you that women would want to throw pies at your face?"

His mouth turns down. "No, I guess not."

I give him a measuring look. "I think you'll want to take that leather jacket off, at least. I don't know how leather responds to whipped cream, but I imagine that you'll want to put it somewhere safe."

He gives me a look as he unzips it and takes it off, but he doesn't say anything. He just stows his jacket under the front counter and finds a comfortable position on a stool placed in the middle of the plastic sheet.

As people begin filing in the gymnasium, I keep an eye on him. The first customers I see rush to the tarot reading booth or the miniature cat paintings both. I bite my lip, looking at Luca.

"What are the chances of getting a coffee brought to me?" He looks vaguely grumpy.

I smile a little at that. "At the women's shelter when you, a white man, are supposed to be raising money for battered women? Yeah, roughly the same odds as a whale falling out of the sky right now." I cock a brow. "You can hire someone on an app though, I'm sure."

He pulls out his phone, ignoring me in favor of scrolling through it. I turn back to the crowd, trying to induce some customers.

"Throw a pie at this guy! Just two tickets..." I call out. I glance back at him. "You know you want to... I mean, pies are the only thing that stops him from mansplaining and man spreading! Two tickets!"

Several women stroll by, looking interested. But no one seems to want to throw the first pie.

"Your plan doesn't seem to be working," he observes dryly.

I shoot him a look. "You know what? I will personally pay four tickets to shove a pie in your face."

Luca smirks at that. "Oh yeah? Bring it, princess."

I pull a crumpled wad of bills out of my pocket, slapping them down on the table. Then I grab one of the whipped cream pies, grinning at him as I approach.

"You ready for this?" I taunt him. I sidle up to him, stopping right in front of his face and adjusting the pie in my hand.

His eyes shine. "I can take anything you throw at—"

He gets a big old face full of whipped cream. I make sure to rub it in, too. When I pull the pie tin away, he wipes whipped cream out of his eyes and away from his lips.

I beam at him. "That was amazing."

He grabs my waist and bends me back, kissing me. His lips feel hot and hard under the frothy cream. He gets whipped cream all over my face and in my hair before he lets me go.

A couple of ladies burst into spontaneous applause, making my cheeks burn.

"Give him another pie!" an older lady hoots.

I demur, wiping the cream from my face. "I just wanted to open the gates!" I exclaim, red-faced. "Now please, throw some pies at this man."

"It is for a good cause..." Luca says to the crowd, laughing.

After that, we have a good steady business. Lots of ladies come up to our booth and have me snap photos of them as they chuck whipped cream at Luca. So many, in fact, that we run out of pies in just over two and a half hours.

Which is good, because Luca has to leave shortly after that for work. Before he does though, I help him clean the whipped cream off of himself. I wipe a smudge from his eyebrow, thinking to myself that I'm glad that he came today.

Luca looks at me, taking my hand and bringing it down to cup his jaw. "Have you forgiven me officially yet?"

My lips curl upward. I brush my thumb along his jaw, looking him in the eyes. "I suppose so."

He bites his bottom lip, his eyes shining. "Good."

He kisses me one more time, then stands to leave. "There is a late-night party at the bar tonight. We're all dressing up in costume. You should come, if you want." He gives me a once over, his eyes lingering on my body. It seems like his gaze heats up my bare skin. "I'd like it if you were there."

Then with that, he turns and heads out, carrying his leather jacket so that it doesn't touch his whipped-cream covered body. I sit on the corner of my booth table, watching him and sighing.

I shouldn't go to the bar later and yet... I know I will.

Chapter 25

Luca

The bar is busy as fuck around eleven p.m. People are dressed in whatever costumes they feel like: Owen came as the vice president, Bradford is dressed in short-shorts and a tied up gingham shirt as Daisy Duke, and I've donned a set of fake pointy teeth as a member of the Lost Boys. Everyone else is in costume too, standing in the bar right now as a mix of clowns, sexy nurses, and a weird number of adult bumblebees.

The party is a success, maybe almost too much of one. It gets so hectic that I step behind the bar and start filling drink orders, my head down, bobbing along to the dance music we have on in the background.

But really, in the back of my mind, I'm just wondering where Cate is. I'm pretty sure she'll come, but I've been wrong before.

Especially about girls who pique my interest in the

exact way that Cate does. My thoughts sour for a moment as Madisyn pops into my head.

I was really into Madisyn and she played me like a well-strung violin. Cate seems different than Syn, but... maybe I just pick women that want something from me. After all, I've kept Cate close by offering her money...

Bile hits the back of my throat. Could I have set myself up for failure here?

Cate slides behind the bar, hip checking me. "Hey!"

I glance up at her. My eyes widen when I see what she's wearing.

A tiny red plaid skirt, an oversized white men's button up that's tied up at her waist, gray knee socks. I can see a flash of her belly button... and I can almost see her ass in the short tartan skirt. And the kicker is that her dark hair is in two neat plaits.

"You're a Catholic schoolgirl?" I blurt out, unable to take my eyes off of her.

She blushes. "Yeah. I mean, Luna helped me pick it out." She toys with her shirt. "I hope you don't mind, I borrowed your dress shirt."

I give her a steely look. "Hold on."

For three quarters of a minute, I have to focus on finishing the drink order in front of me. I look at the ticket again, cracking two beers and pouring out a measure of tequila.

Then I push the drinks across the bar to the waiting patron. He tries to give me his card but I wave him off. "It's on the house. No charge."

"Oh, sweet. Cheers!" he says, but I've already turned

away. I find Cate pulling a rack glasses out of the dishwasher.

Coming up behind her, I grab her hips and pull her ass back against my hips.

She shoots me a look. "Are we not working, then?"

She straightens up so I lean down, whispering in her ear. "God, I hope not. Because I'm going to have trouble paying attention to anything that doesn't involve your legs, your tits, and your ass."

Her cheeks go pink. "Is that right?"

"Unquestionably," I murmur. My lips graze her ear and she shivers as she looks up at me.

"What will we do, then?"

Her words are a suggestion, or maybe a challenge. But I'm not ready to give up and go hide in my office with her. Not yet.

For the next little bit, she's my wife. I want to show her off some.

Plus, I have a good feeling that dancing and drinking may have a certain kind of effect on her. Pressing her against my body as we move on the dance floor might be a new kind of foreplay, if I do it right.

And I intend to do it perfectly. I kiss Cate's ear and then spin her in my arms. "Let's get a drink first. Then I think the dance floor is calling."

Cate looks surprised. "We are going to dance?"

"As surely as we are going to fuck later." I smirk. "Here, let me get us drinks."

I pour her a glass of champagne and grab a whiskey

for myself. Then I take her hand and lead her out from behind the bar.

As soon as we move toward the dance floor, the beat of the bass vibrating in my ears, we run into Luna.

Literally run into... her blonde head turns and her eyes widen a bit as she takes us both in, her gaze lingering on our clasped hands. She's dressed as a witch, wearing a little black dress and clutching a drink in one hand and a broomstick in the other.

"Look at you two!" she says, smirking.

"You look..." I narrow my eyes on her dress. "Like you're wearing as little as you can get away with."

Luna rolls her eyes. "And you are what, some sort of guy wearing dark clothes so that you didn't have to try anything out of your comfort zone?" She chuckles. "Please."

Drawing myself up to my full height, I pull Cate a little closer. "I'm one of the Lost Boys." I gesture to my mouth. "See the teeth?"

Luna pulls a face and looks to Cate. "Honestly, how do you even live with my brother? He thinks he's too cool for school."

Cate goes red, glancing at me. "I mean... we're not, like..."

She tries to tug her hand from mine, but I hold onto it. "Luna is just being silly. I'm sure she didn't mean anything by it."

Luna smiles. "It's true, I was just talking trash." Someone catches her eye from across the room, a tall dark haired guy in medical scrubs. "Oh, that's my boss. I need to ask him about the schedules for next week. Catch you guys later...”

Cate raises her eyebrows at Luna’s receding figure. “That was very odd.”

I start to pull her toward the dance floor. “I’m not really worried about it, to be perfectly honest.”

Cate favors me with a look. “No?”

I shake my head, pulling her into my arms and moving slowly with the rhythm. “Nope.”

She smiles up at me. “Well, if you’re not worried...”

She sways with me, sipping her champagne. I drop my free hand to her back and press her up against my body, smiling as I take a drink from my glass. She snakes a hand around my neck, her fingers warm against my bare skin.

It feels good to be this close, to feel her tits rubbing against my chest, her abdomen and thighs brushing against my cock. But what feels better than that is the way that she looks at me just now. Her head thrown back, a smile tugging at her lips, her eyes sparkling.

Damn. If she looked at me like this more often, I would probably do anything she asked. I would go into battle for her if she asked me right now. I’m like a lovelorn teenager or something.

She finishes her glass of champagne and breaks away from my body to put the empty glass down on a table. I shoot the rest of my whiskey and do the same. Then my hands are free to pull her close, her little body soft against mine.

She stares up at me with those dark eyes, her brow smooth and unworried. "You're a good dancer."

I grin down at her, gripping her waist. "You sound surprised. I'm good at nearly anything I put my mind to."

Her lips quirk. "Yes, you do seem to be good at a lot of things."

Bending down close to her ear, I whisper. "I'm not the only one who is good at things. I think we're both very skilled in certain areas."

Her breath stops for a second. She turns her head, looking at me, her expression practically dripping sex. "Oh yeah?"

"Oh, yeah." I chuckle. "And you know what they say... practice makes perfect..."

Cate surprises me by pushing up onto her tiptoes and kissing me. It's no coy kiss either; long and deep, it invites me to do much more.

My hands find her waist. I sigh against her lips, growing frustrated that I can't just bend her back and strip her right here.

Cate leans against my torso, reaching up to be kissed. My office isn't that far away. We can have a modicum of privacy there, enough that even Cate probably won't have anything to say.

I turn her around, ready to start walking her back towards the office. I look up, glancing directly into Madisyn's crying face.

"Oh, Luca!" she sobs. Completely ignoring the fact that I'm holding Cate, she latches onto my arm, seeming to have trouble standing up.

And fool that I am, I let go of Cate to steady Madisyn. Cate steps back, her expression guarded. I look down at Madisyn, who flattens herself against my body with a howl.

"He's such a bastard!" Madisyn cries.

"Err..." I try to create some distance between the two of us, but Madisyn acts like she's suctioned to my body. "Get off of me, Syn."

Madisyn just starts bawling harder and clinging to me more insistently. "He did me wrong, Luca! Reggie cheated on me! You should go beat him up..."

Making a face, I force Madisyn to step back. "I don't even know what you're talking about, Syn."

I glance toward Cate. She's biting her lip with a frown, just beginning to turn away. "Cate, don't go anywhere."

Cate shoots me a glare and then heads back toward the bar. I need to get rid of Syn, as soon as possible. Otherwise, I'm afraid that Cate will leave the party altogether.

Or worse, she'll pack her shit and leave my house.

"Madisyn, what the fuck?" I complain. "You just alienated my..." I stop, fumbling for what Cate is. "Stop cock blocking me."

Madisyn wipes at her mascara which is running down her cheeks. "But Reggie cheated on me! And I know that you are still hung up on me—"

A sharp bark of laughter escapes me. "No, I'm not. Now if you'll excuse me—"

Madisyn digs her nails into my arm. "You aren't over

me. No one is ever over losing the best thing that's ever happened to them. And I am definitely that for you."

She tries to kiss me then, ignoring my body language. "Madisyn, stop!" I push her away, anger boiling up from somewhere deep inside. "I don't want to kiss you. And by the way, you weren't the best thing I've ever had. If anything, you leaving was better."

She screws up her face, rage showing in her eyes. "Luca, you better be careful how you talk to me. I swear, one more word and I won't take you back..."

Her chest heaves. She looks like some kind of demented clown, trying to clutch at my arm.

I shake my head and start to back away. "You're not listening. I don't want you, Syn. I'm happier without you. Now I've got to go and find my... my wife."

Madisyn grimaces as I turn and walk away. "Don't you dare leave, Luca! Luca!! I won't come back..."

I put my head down and keep moving through the crowd of partiers, looking for Cate. I spot her dark head disappearing into the back hallway and I speed up.

I have to catch her before she tries to leave.

Chapter 26

Luca

"Cate!" I call out. I walk down the darkened back hallway, spying her as she pushes the door to the parking lot open.

She turns around in the doorway, her dark eyes fiery. "What? What could you possibly say to me right now?"

"I didn't want that," I say, gesturing to the front of the bar. "I had no way of knowing Madisyn would be here."

Her lips pull into a frown. "So what, she just showed up?"

I sidle closer to her until I close the gap between us. She shivers and licks her lips, gazing up at me. I widen the opening of the door by placing my hand over our heads. "I swear. I didn't want her to. I told her to fuck off."

I scan her face, trying to guess what she's thinking. Her brow is knitted. She's sucked her lip between her teeth and stares at me.

I can hear my heart beating in the silence between us.

"Luca," she exhales at last. "I need more than this."

I reach out, gently grabbing her hip and pulling her body towards mine. "More than this?"

Cate puts her hands up and pushes at my chest. "Yes, Luca." Her eyes bore holes into my face. "I thought that something purely physical would be enough, but it isn't."

I see just the beginning of tears forming in her eyes. Gripping her waist more firmly, I try to placate her fears.

"This isn't just physical," I say.

Her breath leaves her in a huff. "It isn't?"

Shaking my head slowly, I back her up, pushing the door wide with our bodies. "Nope. It's a lot more than that and I think you know it."

I expect her to ask more questions. Or maybe I'm dreading the moment when she asks me to define just what our relationship is, I don't know.

But she doesn't say anything.

Her dark eyes are large and mesmerizing, her face sweetly heart shaped. I cup the side of her face in one hand, pushing back some of her wild hair. Her lips are luscious and inviting, and they part ever so slightly when my gaze drops to look at them.

I don't honestly know whether I move first or she does, but we both surge forward. My lips find hers, hesitating at first. But once I get the taste of her in my mouth, the scent of her in my nose, I go wild.

The door slams closed behind us, and my hands slide

down her body. I pick her up, and her legs wrap around my hips.

We break the kiss and she gasps, the cool air hitting her mouth and making her lips even pinker. I turn her, slamming her back against the wall.

She grunts. I kiss her again, more aggressively this time, my tongue tangling with hers. Her fingers tangle in my hair, pulling my face closer.

She bites my bottom lip, tugging on it.

"Oh, fuck," I growl, my hands cupping her ass. "You're driving me fucking crazy, beautiful."

Her legs tighten around my waist, her body rubbing against me. I groan, the friction almost too much to bear.

"God, Luca," she pants, her breath hot against my ear. "I need you. Now."

I can't argue with that. My hands move down, sliding under her skirt. Her panties are wet, the fabric soaked through.

"Jesus, you're so fucking wet," I mutter, sliding a finger under the lace and dipping it inside her.

"Not here," she moans, still grinding against me in spite of the words coming out of her mouth. "Where... where else can we go?"

I set her back down on her feet and kiss her again, already tugging her toward the parking lot. "My car," I murmur between frenzied kisses.

We stumble through the parking lot, our hands all over each other. We finally reach my car, and I open the door, pushing the driver's seat up to give her some room to climb in.

Her brow furrows as she looks down at the small backseat of my Porche. "In here? How are we both going to fit?"

"Easy." I lean in to nip at the soft, fluttering spot at the base of her neck. "You're going to be on top of me."

That's all it takes to get her moving.

She scrambles into the car, her skirt riding up to give me an enticing view of her ass.

I reach for her because I just can't get enough, but she's already moving to the far end of the seat. "Come on," she gestures. "I don't know how this is going to work, but I know I need you in here with me. Now."

My cock throbs at her insistence, and I struggle to get in with her, molding my six-and-a-half foot frame to a backseat that definitely isn't made for two. "Straddle me," I say, but she's already on top of me before I can get the words out. "Fuck, I need to be inside you."

She leans in to kiss me. "Yes, Luca. Please," she whimpers, her lips grazing mine.

I kiss her, hard and deep, my hands sliding down her back, tugging at the fabric until my fingers find the hem of her skirt. I push it up, exposing her bare ass.

She moans into the kiss as my hands caress her skin. I grip her hips, pulling her closer, and she grinds against me, the friction driving us both wild.

We break the kiss, our breaths mingling in the space between us.

"Jesus, Cate," I growl, my voice low and thick with lust. "You feel so good."

"So do you," she breathes, her hands tugging at the

hem of my shirt. "But we need less clothes between us. Take your shirt off."

I sit up as best I can, helping her pull the thin white dress shirt over my head. It's a tight squeeze, and I grunt as we manage to remove it.

"Much better," she murmurs, her nails grazing the bare skin of my torso.

"You too," I say, my hands reaching for the buttons of her shirt.

I make quick work of the buttons, revealing her smooth, perfect skin inch by inch. When I get to the bottom, I push the fabric off her shoulders, leaving her in just her bra and the skirt that's hiked up around her hips.

"God, you're so fucking beautiful," I whisper, my eyes roaming over her.

She blushes, the color spreading across her cheeks and down her neck. She looks almost shy, but there's no mistaking the desire in her eyes.

"You're not so bad yourself," she says, her fingers trailing along my chest, leaving goosebumps in their wake.

I reach around to unhook her bra, letting it fall away and freeing her breasts. They're perfect, and I can't resist leaning forward and taking one nipple in my mouth.

She arches against me, her breath coming in short gasps as I suck and tease her nipple.

"Luca," she groans, her hips grinding against mine. "That feels so good."

I can feel her heat through the thin material of her panties and my pants. The sensation is driving me crazy, but I'm not ready to take my mouth away from her deliciously perfect breasts yet.

She writhes on top of me, her fingers tangling in my hair, tugging me closer. I bite her nipple lightly, and she cries out, her back arching.

"Yes," she gasps. "God, yes." She reaches back to palm my cock through my pants, squeezing the hard length. "I need you, Luca. All of you."

"Soon," I promise, switching my attention to her other nipple.

"Now," she insists, her voice low and husky. "I can't wait another second."

I finally pull away from her breast and look up at her, her dark eyes full of desire. She looks wild, her breasts heaving, her hair mussed. She's never looked sexier.

"Okay, sweetheart," I murmur. "Let's do this."

I help her wriggle out of her panties, and she immediately goes for my pants. She fumbles with the zipper, finally managing to free my cock.

She strokes me, her hand firm and sure. "Oh god," she moans, her thumb swirling around the head. "You're so big."

I growl, gripping her hips. "And you're gonna take every inch in that tight little pussy."

"Yes," she whispers, positioning herself over me. "Oh God, Luca. Please hurry. Need you to fuck me."

She knows how it drives me wild to hear her beg and whimper like this. I usually draw it out, selfishly wanting more of her sweet, pleading voice. Not this time, though.

I need her just as much as she needs me, and I can't wait another fucking second.

I watch as she slowly sinks down, my cock stretching her tight pussy. It's the hottest thing I've ever seen, and I have to fight the urge to thrust up into her all at once.

"So good," I groan, my fingers digging into her hips.

She starts to move, riding me, her pace slow and steady. She throws her head back, her dark hair spilling down her back, her breasts bouncing with each movement.

She's the most beautiful woman I've ever seen, and the sight alone is enough to push me over the edge. But I don't want it to be over yet.

I slide a hand between our bodies, finding her clit with my thumb. She gasps, her movements faltering as I rub tight circles around the sensitive bud.

"Oh God, Luca," she moans, her nails digging into my chest. "Feels so good when you do that."

"Good," I murmur, leaning in to kiss her neck. "Because I want to make you feel good, sweetheart. I want to make you come."

She gasps, her pussy clenching around me, and I know she's close.

"That's it, sweetheart. We're almost there," I growl, sucking and nipping at her collarbone.

"I'm so close," she whimpers, her hips rocking against me. "Don't stop, Luca. Please, I'm gonna come."

"Come for me, princess," I urge her. "Let me feel you come apart."

Her movements grow frantic, and I can feel her pussy tightening around my cock. She lets out a scream, her whole body shuddering as she comes.

"That's it, sweetheart," I groan, holding her tight as she rides out her orgasm. "So fucking beautiful."

As she comes down from her high, her movements become slower, more deliberate. She stares down at me, her eyes dark and hungry.

"Your turn," she says, her voice low and husky. "I want to feel you come inside me."

Her words are enough to push me over the edge, and I can't hold back any longer. My hips buck, and I come with a roar, my cock pulsing deep inside her.

It's a release like nothing I've ever felt before, and for a moment, all I can do is cling to her, my body shuddering. I slow, then stop, trying to catch my breath. She lays sprawled across my chest, her breathing rapid, covered in a layer of sweat. Not just hers, but mine, too. They've mixed, become something more than just sweat.

Cate pulls down her skirt and reaches for her top, trying to make herself presentable as she drags in her breaths. "We should cover ourselves up. I don't want Owen or Bradford to walk out here, looking for you."

Instead of listening to her, I cup the back of her head and kiss her thoroughly. "The windows are fogged up, princess. We're safe from prying eyes for a few minutes."

A chill runs through her body. She looks at me, passion still thick in her eyes. "I like when you call me that."

My mouth curves upward. "What, princess?"

She bites her lip and nods. "Yes. It's a little... dirty. You only say it when you have sex on your mind."

Her cheeks color. She twines her fingers with mine. I rub little circles into the palm of her hand with my thumb. "I'll have to keep that in mind."

She looks down at our clasped hands. "This is nice."

"The fucking?" I ask.

"No," she says, frowning at me and shaking her head. "I just meant... when we don't fight, it's nice to just... be together."

My lips quirk. "See, I think that the fighting feeds the flame. Like if we didn't bicker, our sex wouldn't be as hot."

Her brow furrows. "What would happen if we didn't fight, then? Do you think that we would just... lose interest in each other?"

I pull her hand, moving her incrementally closer. "I don't think I will ever lose interest in you, princess. Maybe you'll drive me crazy. Maybe I'll say the wrong thing and you'll run. But lose interest in you?" I kiss her, long and slow, flicking her tongue with mine. "I don't think we'll ever have to worry about that."

Then I roll her over, so that I'm on top of her body. I start kissing her again, my fingers sneaking up to her breasts, pushing the fabric away once more.

"Luca!" she says. I can tell despite her breathy tone that she's complaining, so I bury my face in the crook of her neck.

"What?" I murmur.

"Can we please go home first?" she asks. I catch her nipple with my fingers, rolling it, making her moan.

"Not a chance in hell, princess."

I kiss her, silencing any further protests.

Chapter 27

Cate

The next morning, I slip out of Luca's bed. Without even looking at the calendar, I already know why my heart is so heavy.

It's the last day of January.

Five years ago today, I lost my entire family. One distracted driver who was looking at his phone. One foggy afternoon in the hills surrounding Seattle. And one curvy road...

Together, those things made me an orphan. I can't bear to think of it, much less talk to another person about why I'm forever broken and desolate. I almost weep just thinking about it.

That's why I am better alone, today especially. So I steal out of Luca's bedroom and to my own, getting dressed. I stuff a huge wad of tissues into my coat pocket and shoulder my purse, then leave Luca's house quietly.

I order myself an Uber, just as I have the four years before on this date. As I watch out the window silently, the Uber navigates through fog and a little rain, toward the highest point in the city. It's early on a Sunday and the weather is bad, so there is hardly anyone out. It's so foggy as we climb the final stretch that I can barely make out the road ahead.

I can see the street beside me, though. That's all that counts. When I see Dorie's Market coming up, I say so to the driver.

"Do you mind stopping right here?" I ask. "Please, on the right. I can walk from here."

"Of course," she says cheerfully. She pulls over, letting me out. "Have a great day."

I say nothing, my chin wobbling. It's still hard to accept that other people don't know that this monumental, world-changing thing happened.

My mom and dad died and no one is the wiser. Everyone just carries on with their humdrum little lives as if nothing had ever happened.

I take a deep breath, my feet carrying me toward the little market. I push open the door, cringing at the sound of the bell overhead. Dorie's Market is just the same as it was five years ago. It's still stocked high with canned goods and a small produce section. It still smells most strongly of lemon, like wood polish maybe.

And most importantly to me, it still has fresh flowers. Right between the heads of lettuce and the berries are a few bouquets of flowers.

I choose the one with the most color, selecting the bouquet that has pink ranunculus, yellow daisies, dark red roses, and baby's breath. My mom would have loved this arrangement; she always preferred bright bursts of color over more muted flowers.

My eyes well up at that. I rush to the counter and pay for them, then get out of the store as quickly as I can manage.

I step out into the morning chill, my eyes settling on the cemetery. From here, I can just barely make out the big wrought-iron gates.

Cavalry Catholic Cemetery lies just beyond, though the fog makes it impossible to see just now. Taking a deep breath, I step out into the road, crossing the cobblestone street toward the cemetery.

It's a little uphill walk. I reach the gates with minimal huffing, but then I stop. Looking up at the broad arch made of wrought iron, I swallow.

"Just go in," I tell myself. "You can do it..."

I always have this trouble at this particular point. Knowing what lies beyond prevents me from entering the gates with any kind of ease. But sooner or later, guilt will win out. It just a matter of time.

I hear a car door slam. As I am trying to psych myself up, or maybe just let my guilt overwhelm me, I hear a familiar voice.

"Are you stuck?"

I turn halfway. There is Luca, walking up the last few steps of the hill.

"What on earth are you doing here?"

Luca shoves his hands into his jacket pockets, looking at me with a careful expression on his face. "I followed you here."

My mouth twists. "Why?"

He shrugs a shoulder. "Because. I want to know things about you." He looks up at the cemetery gates. "I didn't realize that you were coming here, obviously."

I look down at the flowers I'm holding. My fingers tremble. "You should leave. This is private."

I can't bear the thought of Luca watching me grieve.

Instead of listening to me, he moves closer and touches my arm. "Hey. Will you look at me?"

Glancing up into his face, I feel so exposed. Tears gather in my eyes again. This whole day is always emotional for me and being vulnerable in front of him is only making me more sensitive.

Somewhere nearby, church bells begin to ring out. I suck in a breath.

I am so ashamed to be crying in front of him. It's not the first time by any means, but that doesn't make it less excruciating.

Luca doesn't waver though. He moves closer and runs his hand over my back. His dark eyes bore into me.

"I'll wait for you out here if that's what you really want. But I'm also ready to go inside the cemetery." He nods at the high gates. "If you were hoping to get through today alone though, you're out of luck."

I sniffle, looking down at my flowers again. I'm just so sad right now about so many things. Too many things to even list. But Luca doesn't make me sad.

Angry at times, yes. And lord knows that he frustrates me. But he makes me giddy sometimes, and I laugh at his jokes when we're not fighting. Then there's the incredible, not to be missed sex we've been having...

And he's also showing remarkable kindness to me right this second. So I make a decision, right here and now.

"You can come," I say. My voice sounds miserable, but at least I said something. At least I made a decision.

Luca nods, his expression somber. He takes my arm and guides me through the gate that I was stuck outside of. Graves rise up on either side of the cement path, some mausoleums and some more austere and small grave markers. I point to the left.

"We'll have to go that way."

We walk through the morning chill, passing through the oldest section of the cemetery. I can only make out the path a few hundred feet in front of us. Everything else just sinks back into the gray and foggy morass.

We come to a fork in the path and I turn right, pulling Luca along with me.

Soon I see a towering tree, its branches bare this time of year; my parents are buried just beneath it and I always look for it to navigate here.

I cut down one of the aisles, being extremely respectful of the graves as I go. Soon we reach the tree, a colossal oak whose branches twist into the sky.

I look down to find the graves of my parents right next to each other. The stones are a boring gray granite. His name and her name, with the dates of their births and deaths. The inscriptions just say beloved father and beloved mother because I couldn't even come up with anything to say at the time.

I couldn't stop crying then and I can't hold back my tears now.

Luca stops a few paces behind me. I feel self-conscious as I lay the flowers between my parents' graves and sniffle.

"Hi Mom. Hi Dad." I fight to keep my composure. Looking back behind me, I see Luca waiting, his expression patient.

He's too close for me to talk to them like I usually do. I scrunch up my face but before I can say anything to him about it, he raises his hand.

"I'll be over there," he says, pointing to the path we left a few minutes ago. "Take your time."

I bite my lip and watch him walk away, nearly disappearing into the foggy morning light. He stops and stares off into the distance, hovering just on the edge of my vision.

I turn back to the graves, my brow furrowing. A dead leaf blows onto my father's grave and stays there. Stepping closer, I remove it, stuffing the leaf in my pocket.

"So that was Luca," I say, glancing back at him briefly. "You met him, actually. I think you did anyway. The Christmas before..." I stop, correcting myself. "The Christmas before I graduated high school, I mean. I was at the Leone's party. You both went to a movie and swung by the Leone's house to pick me up. Luca introduced himself, even though I think it was brief." I sniff. "Anyway, he's a good guy. I know, I sort of hated him for all the years that you were... you were here."

I bow my head, sadness overwhelming me for a moment. My tears roll down my face, dripping off freely. It takes a minute to master myself again.

"Sorry," I rasp. I produce the wad of tissues, wiping my face and blowing my nose. "I just... I miss you guys both so much. It's hard..." My voice cracks. Tears blur my vision. I bow again, going through the entire process. Let the tears overwhelm me, tamp down on my emotions again, blow my nose.

"It's hard living without you guys. Dad, you'll be glad to know that I kept volunteering at the women's shelter. Just like we used to do when you were alive. Mom, you'll..." I pause. "Well, you'll be glad to hear that I am still going to mass every week. You would be less excited to know that I've been living with Luca... but not everything is about church."

I look back at Luca, blowing out a breath. "Actually, I'm married. Well, not like... married married. But I married Luca after I had too much to drink. Don't worry, I think we're going to annul it. That should make you feel incrementally better about me living with someone. He is my husband."

For now, at least...

Sighing, I purse my lips. "Grandma is good. She's doing well. Luna is good. She's working at the University of Washington Medical Center, doing her medical school rotations and stuff. Oh! And Harper got a job with a big publishing house. She has a fancy office downtown."

I think about what else they would like to know. "I realize that you guys probably are already aware of all of this... being up in heaven and all. I just... I wanted you to hear it all from me, I guess. Isn't that silly? Feels kind of stupid, to be talking to your graves like you are actually here."

The church bells ring out again briefly, drawing my attention for a split second. It's cold out here; I hunch down into my coat. And spend a few minutes staring at the ground in silence.

"I guess I should go," I say at length. "Just know..." Tears well again. "That you are very missed here. And you are still very loved. And although I have plenty of time left on earth, a lifetime will be over when you blink. We'll all be together again in the afterlife. Okay?"

I blow my nose again. "I'll try to come see you guys in a few months, when it's warmer outside. Okay? I won't wait a year this time." I wipe at my eyes. "Bye, Mom and Dad."

Turning away from their graves, I steel myself as I walk back down the row toward the path.

I find Luca sitting on a bench, staring out across the graveyard. The morning is starting to warm up and with the warmth goes the fog. When he sees me walking toward him, his lips thin.

"Hey."

I sit down beside him on the cement bench, looking out across the graveyard. "Hey."

A moment of tension blooms between us as I try to

find the right thing to say. Something nice, something to erase the frown on his lips.

"I'm sorry about your parents," he says.

I'm surprised by that. "Oh. Well... it was a while ago."

He sighs. "Yeah, I know. But the time passed obviously doesn't make it better."

I narrow my eyes. "No. The pain fades but it doesn't disappear."

I look down at my hands, rubbing them together for warmth. I'm still at a loss for words, it seems.

Luca looks up at the sky. "I imagine that planning things is harder. Like big life things." He slides me a glance. "Getting married, for instance. How do you throw a wedding when you know that your parents won't be there?"

I suck in a long breath. "For me, it isn't that, exactly. It's more like..." I stop to think for a few seconds. "Why date someone? Why get married? Why have kids? When my parents died, their love just... vanished. One day, just poof." I gesture with my hands. "I'm so afraid to... to love anything or anyone like that ever again. It just seems like a surefire way to open yourself up to heartbreak."

Luca looks at me for a long moment. I expect him to disagree, to roll his eyes. To dismiss my feelings.

But he doesn't. Instead he reaches his arm around me, drawing me close. And I burrow into his warmth, appreciating his silent presence more than I think he knows. Putting my head on his shoulder, I try to control the way my eyes well up again.

He puts his arm around my shoulders, holding me close. "It's okay to cry, Cate."

For some reason, his words make a sob rise in my chest. But he doesn't shush me or pull away. He just brushes some hair back from my face and rubs my shoulder a little bit.

I bury my face in his leather jacket, breathing in his warm scent and crying like a little kid. His touch never changes, although I do notice that he does start rocking me a little bit.

Consoling me, as it were. And to my surprise, it works a little. That, or I just expend all my energy here on this bench, clutching his jacket and sobbing.

When I'm done, I am beyond spent. And Luca seems to know it somehow.

He helps me up off the bench and guides me out of the cemetery, putting me in the passenger seat of his car. Then he drives me back to his house and takes me to my bed.

I curl into a ball on my bed, exhausted. And Luca stays with me, rubbing my back lightly until I fall asleep.

Chapter 28

Luca

I am wondering, at this precise moment in time, what it would be like to keep Cate. I've been thinking about it for a couple of days. But right now I'm looking at her while she makes coffee in my kitchen, wearing a set of snowflake-patterned pajamas and a forlorn expression on her face. She puts her arms on the counter and leans down, watching the coffee drip.

She is sexy, yes. And pretty easy to be around when she finally runs out of smart remarks. But seeing how she handled my parents the other night... how they basically loved her and paid almost zero attention to me... that was such a relief that I am now wondering how I could keep her around.

And seeing her break down at the cemetery... there was a sad sort of magic there in the air. She was vulnerable and raw, I was silent and supportive...

It was kind of odd but also kind of impressive that we were both so fucking adult about everything. It gave me a glimpse into what we could be if *we* were actually a thing.

So yeah, I want to explore that feeling. And I think it will take longer than the five days we have left before Madisyn's wedding.

I mean, what I assume is Madisyn's wedding... I haven't exactly checked up on her or anything. Frankly, I would pull out of going altogether, but I don't want to upset the delicate balance Cate and I seem to have just now.

I look at her, pouring steaming coffee into two mugs and adding a splash of cream to each.

I don't want to pay Cate for additional time.... I don't want that sort of arrangement. Just... I don't know. It would be nice if she were just to *want* to stick around. I would just have to convince her that we — me and her — are worth sticking around for.

What would happen if I told my lawyer not to file the annulment paperwork? Or not yet, at least.

She turns and slides one of the mugs of coffee to me. "Here."

I take the coffee, watching her as I take a sip. It's burning hot but creamy and delicious. Smiling, I take another sip.

"Thanks."

Cate looks at me, her gaze calculating. "I'd like to take you to a place."

Setting my mug down, I wrinkle my forehead. I tease her. "You're going to have to be more specific before I'll agree to it. You could be planning to take me to the industrial part of downtown where you'll drug me and steal my kidneys."

She rolls her eyes. "Luca, seriously."

My lips lift. "I seriously like having both my kidneys, Cate."

She snorts. "You are impossible."

When she picks her coffee mug up like she's going to leave the kitchen, I snake my hand around her waist. "Wait, wait. Tell me more about where you want us to go."

A mischievous look settles on her elfin face. "Nope. I'm not going to tell you anything. I want to give you the address and have you drive there first."

I pretend to think about it. "Hmm. What will you give me in exchange for this huge amount of trust you're asking of me?"

Her lips quirk. She sets down her mug and pushes up onto her tiptoes, brushing her lips across mine. "I don't know. What did you have in mind?"

I kiss her neck and she giggles. Cupping her breasts through their brightly-colored flannel covering, I whisper in her ear. "I bet I can make you beg me to fuck you."

She rolls her eyes and grins. "I don't know about that."

Kissing her again, I release her. "We'll just see about that. One mystery trip will cost you one hour with me, doing whatever I want."

She bites her lip, a salacious grin on her face. "That sounds fair. It's a deal. Get dressed and meet me at the car in ten minutes."

I drink my coffee as I put on a clean white t-shirt, dark blue jeans, and my leather jacket. What sort of place is Cate taking me to? I honestly can't imagine.

On the ride there, I try to guess.

"Is it a motorcycle sales place?" I ask.

Cate slides me a look. "It's definitely not that."

"Hmm." I purse my lips. "The other day, you showed me a video of a celebrity whose husband brought a sloth into her bedroom just because she loves sloths."

She wrinkles her nose. "So?"

"So are you taking me to a secret sloth sanctuary or something?"

She rolls her eyes. "No, definitely not. And by the way, her husband only got her the sloth experience because he knew how much she loved them. And because her crying at seeing the sloth was so adorable. Somehow, I don't think you feel the same way about sloths."

I shake my head. "No, I don't."

She sighs heavily. "I think you're getting the wrong idea about this place anyway. It's more of a... mmm... a thing that revolves around me. I'm just taking you with me because I want you to see what I'm going to spend your annulment money on."

I raise my eyebrows. "Wait, really?"

She looks out the window, her expression unreadable. "Yep."

I turn that over in my head for a bit. We start to go through a neighborhood that I know for some reason. Large brick houses that have mostly seen better days. I squint and I try to remember why I know the address Cate gave me.

Then we pull up outside the house she lived in with her parents. I turn off the engine, trying to understand why we're here.

She turns to me, excitement on her face. "It's stayed the same, don't you think?"

I lean down and look at the house. It's actually in worse repair than I remember it being in. The gutters are overflowing with leaves, the concrete path leading to the dingy front door has several breaks in it.

"Do you not own this anymore?" I ask, slowly piecing things together.

Cate shakes her head. "No. My grandmother had to sell it when my parents passed away." She looks at the house longingly. "But look." She takes a worn piece of paper out of her purse, unfolding it and smoothing it out. I look at it carefully and see that it's a real estate listing for the house. "It's for sale!"

I give her a puzzled look. "Why are you showing me this place?"

"Because I want you to know what I am planning on spending the ten thousand dollars on. That money, plus my own money that I've saved... they'll go into buying this place." She scrunches up her face. "Well, once I earn a little more money. I think I'm about ten thousand short but I'll earn that pretty quickly working at the bar."

Of all the things I thought she might show me, her escape route from this marriage wasn't one of them. I'm silent for a few beats. My eyes scan her face and she frowns.

"I thought you were going to be more supportive about this."

I lift a brow. "About you buying a crumbling property that I have nothing to do with?"

She glances out her window, biting her lip. "I wouldn't call it crumbling."

I sigh sharply. "The house is in obvious disrepair, Cate. I hope you didn't tell me about it as a way to tell me that I should buy it. Because aside from you having an emotional attachment to it, the house might as well be razed."

"First off, I was not trying to get you to buy it. I don't know where you came up with that idea. And why are you being so mean right now?"

I shrug, feeling out of my depth here. "You say I'm being mean, I say I'm being a realist. This place is barely standing up, Cate."

"It is not!" She hits my arm.

I look at her, my expression stony. "Are you saying that you're ready to move out?"

She looks taken aback by that. Cate shakes her head. "No. I mean, I'll move out when you want me out. Or when our annulment comes through, whichever comes first."

I take a deep breath, looking at the house again. "Is that it? We push forward and get the annulment so that you can move out?"

She stares at me, a little stunned. "I didn't realize that there were any other options, Luca."

My forehead wrinkles. "There are, though. I mean... there should be, at least." I glance straight ahead, my hands coming up to the wheel. "I care about you, Cate."

I just thrust the statement out into existence, my stomach twisting. It's how I feel, yes. But I don't know about how Cate feels so there is every probability that she's going to be appalled.

"What does that mean, exactly?" she asks softly. She touches my arm, drawing my gaze.

I look at her, my stare intensifying. "I don't know," I admit, my voice a low rumble. "But I think you feel it too. That this could be something, if we just let it grow a little."

She blushes but she doesn't look away. "I care for you too, Luca. It's just..." She pauses, a muscle twitching in her cheek. She swallows. "I know I'm not very good at talking about how I feel. But that doesn't mean I don't feel anything."

She lowers her gaze, her hand falling away from my arm. I shift toward her, cupping her face and turning her gaze back to me. She looks at me, brows furrowed, her teeth biting into her lower lip.

Ever so slowly, I brush my kiss across her lips. Her eyes sink closed as she opens her mouth against mine. She tastes amazing, her vanilla cinnamon flavor bursting across my tongue. I need more of it. My hand slips around her waist as I pull her close.

I always need more when it comes to Cate. More of

her drugging kisses, more of her quiet moans. More of her soft body burrowed against mine as we rest, my arms shielding her or caging her, I don't know which.

She's the first to pull back, her pupils dilated, her breathing ragged. "Take me to your bed, Luca."

I nod, frowning. "We're not done with this conversation though, are we?"

She bites her lip, hard white against soft, plush pink. "Not unless you want to be done."

Smiling stiffly, I start the car and throw it into drive. All the way home, I turn over the words she said to me.

I care for you too, Luca.

Is that enough for us to take a chance on?

I don't know, but I'll be darned if I don't want to find out.

Chapter 29

Cate

I want him, I think. *I want him bad.*

I miss a step somehow, tripping and dropping half the towels, sprawling towards him. He reaches out to keep me from falling, grabbing me by the shoulders.

"Ooh!" I say, my breath coming out in a whoosh.

"Easy," he says, steadying me. I shiver again as I stand up straight, and he looks at me with a very serious expression. "We should get you out of these wet clothes."

I let my head fall back, looking up at him. He stares down at me, bringing his hand up to push back a couple of pieces of hair that are plastered to my forehead.

I don't dare to breathe. I don't dare to speak. I'm frozen under his beautiful green gaze, waiting for him to make a move.

Luca cups my cheek, running his thumb roughly along the outline of my lips. He bites his bottom lip; for the first time since I've met him, I know without a doubt what he is thinking.

He wants me.

Suddenly I push up onto my tiptoes, bringing my lips a fraction of an inch from his. I gaze into his eyes, asking him a wordless question. Is it worth it?

Almost begging. His gaze flickers down to my lips. I can feel his breath against my mouth, his warm breath fanning across my skin.

Then he closes the distance, his expressive eyes closing. His mouth presses against mine, warm and soft. He kisses me with no trace of the hesitation he must feel. No, his kiss is hard and dominant and full of passion reawakened.

He slides up a hand around me, pulling me the last step toward him, my soft body hitting his hardened frame. My hands come up to his chest, clutching his shirt.

His free hand begins unzipping the hoodie, peeling it off along with my cardigan. I shiver, from nerves and from being cold, and he senses it.

Without a word, he sweeps me off of my feet, carrying me up the stairs to my bedroom. I wrap my arms around his neck, feeling so small and delicate in his grasp.

He automatically goes to the master bedroom, which is the same one I use. Inside, the room is very girly. The bed is made of cedar wood, four posters with white lace curtains and an ivory coverlet.

But he ignores the bed, heading to the en suite bathroom. With only its clawfoot tub, I don't see what he wants with the bathroom, but he carries me over to the tub anyway.

Luca sets me down, turning on the taps. Then he proceeds to undress me, pulling at the strings of my wrap dress. I step out of my shoes and help him with my dress; soon it falls to the floor, and I am left shivering in my matching white lace bra and panties.

The steam starts to fill the room, its heat very welcome. Luca kneels to take off his Converse, then looks up at me.

"I've imagined this a hundred times," he admits, his voice thick with emotion. "I've thought of a thousand different scenarios, different positions. Imagined which ones would give you the most pleasure."

I shiver again, but this time it's not from the cold. I bite my lip, afraid that if I speak, I will break the spell.

"You know what I want, more than anything right now?" he says, reaching out and caressing my hip.

"What?" I say, my voice barely more than a whisper.

"Take off your bra and panties, and sit on the side of the tub for me."

My heart thunders in my chest, but I obey him. I unclasp my bra, letting it drop to the floor. Then I shimmy out of my panties and step forward, perching on the side of the bathtub.

Luca stands up, towering over me. He runs a hand through my hair, and I look up at him, my lips parting.

His eyes flash with desire, his pupils dilating. He cups my breast, massaging the soft flesh. His fingers find my nipple, teasing and tugging the sensitive bud.

I can't help myself. A soft moan escapes my lips, and his lips curve into a smile.

"You're so responsive, sweetheart," he says, leaning down to press a kiss to my neck. "I love the way you react to my touch."

"And I love the way you touch me," I say, my body aching for more. "Please, Luca."

He stands up straight again while his free hand finds my other breast, mirroring the movements of his other hand.

"Fuck, Cate," he groans. "You're so sexy."

I'm drowning in the little jolts of pleasure he's sending from my nipples right down to my core. My body is on fire, and it's almost too much to bear. But at the same time, it's not enough.

I want more. I want all of him.

I reach out and grope him through his pants, his thick length straining against my palm. He's towering over me, looking down at me with heat in his eyes, and I can't wait another second.

I need him. Now.

"Let me taste you, Luca," I gasp, tugging at his pants. "Please. I need you."

He chuckles softly, stepping back to let his pants drop. His cock springs free, and he wraps his fist around it, stroking slowly.

"You want this, sweetheart?" he asks, his voice thick with lust.

"Yes," I whimper. "Need to suck you. Need you so bad."

I can't take my eyes off his cock, his fist sliding up and down the shaft. It's so big and thick, and I'm practically drooling at the sight of it.

Luca leans in, his hand leaving his cock and moving to grip my hair. "Well, I'm not going to deny you, princess."

His voice is pure sex, and I can't believe this is happening. He's everything I've ever wanted and more.

"Thank you," I whisper, licking my lips.

"Don't thank me yet," he says, giving my hair a gentle tug. "You have to earn it."

His words send a shiver down my spine, and I'm ready to do whatever he asks of me.

"Anything," I promise, staring up at him.

"Good," he murmurs. He releases his grip on my hair, stroking the soft strands. "Now reach down and touch yourself. Spread yourself wide for me. Let me see all of you."

My cheeks flush with heat—both from embarrassment at being so exposed and from the thrill of knowing he's getting off on seeing me like this. I obey, parting my legs and exposing my most intimate parts to his hungry gaze.

Luca groans, his cock throbbing in his hand. "Fuck, sweetheart. You're so beautiful. Make yourself feel good. Moan for me."

As he watches, I run a hand down my belly, slipping it between my legs. I find my clit, rubbing tight circles around the sensitive bundle of nerves. My hips buck involuntarily, my body begging for more.

"Oh god, Luca," I moan, my eyes fluttering shut.

"That's it," he says, his voice rough. "Keep going."

I'm so close already, and I'm desperate for release. I'm teetering on the edge, but I want him inside me when I come.

"Luca, please," I beg. "Need you."

He chuckles softly. "Beg some more, princess. I like it."

"Please, Luca," I whimper. "Please let me suck your cock. I'm so close, I-I don't think I can wait much longer."

"You beg so sweetly, sweetheart," he murmurs, stroking himself. "You want this, princess?"

"Yes," I moan, my finger picking up speed. "Yes, please."

He steps forward, his cock inches away from my lips. "Then take it," he says.

I lean forward, my tongue darting out to taste his tip. He's salty and musky, and I want more. I open my mouth wide, sucking his head between my lips.

He groans, his hips bucking, pushing his cock deeper into my mouth. "That's it," he grunts, his hands fisting in my hair. "Jesus, your mouth feels good."

His words are music to my ears, and I double my efforts. I swirl my tongue around his head, sucking hard. This is what I've been waiting for, been begging for, and I'm determined to make it good for him.

He moans, his cock throbbing in my mouth as I bob up and down on his shaft, taking him as deep as I can.

"Fuck, sweetheart," he groans. "Just like that. So fucking good."

His words are like gasoline on a fire, and I'm burning up with need. My pussy is aching, begging for his touch, and I slide a hand down again, desperate for some relief.

My clit is so sensitive that I almost come immediately. I'm so close, but I have to hold off. I don't want to come without him deep inside me.

I slip a finger inside, pumping it in and out. It's not enough, but it helps take the edge off.

Luca pulls my head back, his cock popping out of my mouth. I gasp, panting, looking up at him with confusion.

"Why'd you stop me?" I ask, my voice raspy.

"Because I don't want to come in your mouth, sweetheart," he growls.

"Yes," I breathe, nodding desperately. "Please, Luca. Fuck me."

He doesn't need any more encouragement. He picks me up, carrying me back into the bedroom and easing me down onto the bed.

My whole body is humming, and I'm so ready for him. He looms over me, his hands stroking my body, sending little sparks of pleasure all over.

"Yes, more," I beg. "I need you. Need you so bad."

"I know, princess," he murmurs, kissing my neck. "I know. Just let me take care of you."

His hand slips between my legs, finding my clit. He rubs the sensitive nub, making me writhe beneath him.

"Fuck, you're so wet," he groans.

"All for you," I gasp. "Only you."

His fingers dip lower, teasing my entrance. I buck my hips, desperate for more.

"Yes, God," I moan. "Right there. Keep... keep going."

He slides two fingers inside, stretching me, filling me. It's exactly what I need, and I'm right on the edge again.

"Luca," I cry, my voice high and thin. "Yes, Luca. Don't stop. Please don't stop."

He leans in, capturing my mouth in a kiss. He's fucking me with his fingers, and it's almost too much. I'm spiraling out of control, and I never want it to end.

"Come for me, sweetheart," he murmurs against my lips. "I want to feel you come apart."

And I do. I explode, fireworks bursting behind my eyelids, my body shuddering. I've never come so hard, and I'm screaming his name, begging him to fuck me.

He doesn't disappoint. He climbs onto the bed next to me, then positions himself between my legs, spreading them as wide as they'll go.

"I need you, Cate," he says, his voice rough.

"I need you, too," I breathe, my body still trembling. "Please, Luca. Now."

He lines his cock up with my entrance, his tip just barely touching my sensitive skin.

"Look at me," he commands.

I open my eyes, looking up at him. He's staring down at me, his eyes full of desire.

"I want you to remember this," he says. "Every time you look at this bed, you'll remember this moment. Remember how good we are together."

Then he thrusts inside, and it's like nothing I've ever felt before. He fills me, stretching me, and it's pure ecstasy.

"Luca," I gasp, wrapping my legs around his waist, urging him deeper.

He starts to move, and it's heaven. He sets a steady rhythm, his cock sliding in and out of my wet pussy, his thumb circling my clit.

It's too much, but I still can't get enough. "Yes, yes, yes," I moan, my head thrashing from side to side.

"Fuck, sweetheart," he groans, his movements becoming faster, more urgent. "You're so fucking tight. Feels so good."

I can feel myself losing control, and I'm powerless to stop it. I'm falling over the edge, and he's right there with me.

"Yes, yes," I chant, my body quivering. "God, Luca. Yes. More. Harder."

"You want more?" he asks, his voice ragged. "You want me to fuck you harder?"

"Yes," I cry. "Please, Luca. Give me everything."

He grunts, picking up the pace, pounding into me. "Gonna fuck you so hard," he says, his voice strained. "Gonna make you come all over my cock, beautiful."

"Yes," I sob, tears leaking from the corners of my eyes. "Yes, Luca. Make me come. Please, please, please."

He leans down, his face inches from mine, his cock driving into me.

"That's it," he says. "Come for me, princess. Let go."

"Yes," I scream, my nails digging into his back. "Oh, god, yes."

And then I'm falling, falling, falling. Waves of pleasure wash over me, and I'm lost. I'm floating, weightless, adrift in a sea of bliss.

And Luca is right there with me. He's groaning, his cock pulsing deep inside me, his hips bucking as he comes.

"Fuck, Cate," he growls, his body shuddering. He rests his forehead against the pillow to my left, breathing openmouthed for a long second. My racing heart begins to slow.

Luca kisses me then, long and languorous. He tastes like his sweat, but I don't mind it one bit. I sigh into the kiss, bringing my hands up to cup his face.

We rest like that for a long time, until I slip off to sleep.

Chapter 30

Luca

I lie on my side watching Cate sleeping beside me. Her lower body is burrowed against mine but her spine is twisted so that her face is angled away. It looks uncomfortable to me but she seems to be sleeping peacefully.

The early morning light streams across her still figure, throwing shadows across half of her body. I look at her delicate dark eyebrows, the sweep of her black lashes against her cheeks, her sweetly bow-shaped mouth. Her face is in profile, the light making it seem more angular than it actually is.

She stirs for a moment, pulling the blankets up and murmuring something softly. She turns away from me and I sigh.

Tomorrow is Madisyn's wedding. Not that I give two fucks about Syn getting married, but that's the entire structure of my marriage to Cate at this point.

What happens after the wedding? The future slips

through my fingers like sand through an hourglass. Everything is tentative. Our entire relationship seems to be held together by half-spoken promises.

I woke up in a mood about it and it isn't going away. I know myself. I need a distraction or I'm going to brood about this for the next twelve hours. So I get up and get dressed, texting Owen as I go.

Drinks?

He responds in a couple of minutes. *I mean, it's the daytime... but sure.*

I think for a moment, trying to choose a place that's equal distances from his house and mine.

Whiskey Soda Lounge, twenty minutes.

I grab my leather coat, leaving Cate a scrawled message. *Back soon.*

Leaving the piece of paper on my pillow, I head out to the bar. When I pull my bike into the parking lot, Owen is already waiting for me.

"Hey," he says, scanning my face.

"Hey."

I push past him, heading in the front door of the bar. There are a couple of people drinking at the far end of the counter. The bartender gives us a nod, motioning for us to seat ourselves.

As we slide into a booth, I pluck a menu from the bracket on the wall. Owen does the same, watching me carefully. The bartender comes over and takes our order.

After I don't say anything for a minute, Owen sighs. "What's up, man?"

I favor him with a frown. "What, I can't just want a drink?"

Owen narrows his eyes at me. "You seem to forget that I've known you for too long. I can tell something is going on with you."

He's right, of course. But it still irritates me. "Mmm," I grunt.

The bartender brings our drinks. I don't taste mine, I just roll the amber liquid around in the glass.

"Things with Cate aren't going well, then?"

I exhale a long breath. "I don't know. She took me to see the house she wants to buy and live in once the annulment goes through." I take a sip of whiskey, making a face when it burns a little going down.

Owen shifts in his seat. "And that's bad?"

I glance at him, shaking my head. "I don't know. I mean... I offered her ten thousand dollars, contingent on her faking this marriage until Madisyn's wedding. But now the wedding is here, and I just..."

"Wait, you offered her ten grand?" he asks.

I nod. "Yep. I said we would sign the paperwork on the annulment after this wedding, and then I would pay her."

Owen purses his lips. "But you don't want things to change, I am guessing?"

"Yeah." I scrunch up my face. "Actually, I don't know. I just feel like Cate moving out isn't going to help clear things up."

He takes a sip of his drink and swishes it around his mouth. "Have you talked to Cate about any of this?"

I look at the ceiling, sighing. "Sort of."

"What does that mean?"

"We talked about it a little when she showed me the house. And then she kissed me." I bite my lip with a frown. "Actually, it's been like that for the last two days. I try to bring up the annulment and she kisses me."

A note of humor ripples across his face. "You're telling me that you can't resist her advances, or what?"

I shrug. "I guess I haven't wanted to. Not yet. What if I ask her to stay and she says no?"

Owen looks down at his drink. "Is it better to just keep doing what you're doing? Neither of you ever says anything real to the other because you are both emotionally stunted people?"

I shoot him a glare. "I didn't say that."

"Hm." He takes another sip of his whiskey. "Just tell her that you don't want her to move out. It's really simple."

I wrinkle my brow. "Just like that?"

Owen shrugs. "I think so. I mean, I don't know her, but that's what I would like."

I look at my watch. "It seems like a good idea, but..."

Owen makes a face. "It's between that and letting her leave, which you don't want. Just go. Go right now and tell her to stay. That way you can go to Madisyn's wedding and just... you know, be real."

I smile, imagining Cate and I hugging while we talk to Madisyn. "There is a first time for everything, isn't there?"

Owen rolls his eyes as he pulls a twenty dollar bill out

of his wallet. "I will buy your drink if you'll just go talk to Cate, man. Seriously."

I squint at him. "Yeah, alright." I start sliding out of the booth then pause. "Thanks, man."

Owen just shrugs again. "Anytime."

With a determined frown on my face, I ride my motorcycle home. As soon as I get home, I call out to Cate.

"I'm back!" I announce. I head over to the fridge for a bottle of water.

Cate comes downstairs from her room, drying her hair with a towel. She's wrapped in maybe the ugliest old-lady bathrobe I've ever seen. Her lips are turned down at the corners.

"Hey. Where did you go?"

"Just went for an early drink with Owen." I open the bottle of water and chug it halfway down. "You looked like you needed rest."

Her eyes narrow. "Huh."

I set the water bottle on the counter, steeling myself for what I want to say. I don't know why I'm nervous, but I am. Heading into the living room, I snag one of her hands and lead her toward the sofa.

"Come here for a minute."

"Luca," she protests. "I have to get ready for work. I don't have time to hang out on the couch for a minute, no matter what you say."

I sit down on the couch, towing her in my wake. She sits down beside me with a huff. "We have to be really, really fast this time."

My lips quirk at that. "I like your thinking. But actually, I just want to talk."

Her eyebrows rise. "Oh, I don't think this is really the time—"

"I don't want you to buy that house," I say, cutting her off. "I don't want us to get an annulment right away and I don't want you to buy that house."

The only thing I read on her face is puzzlement. "Why not?"

I think for a second before I answer. "I think there is something between us and I want to find out. Which I don't feel like we can with our current arrangement. I need more time than that."

"It sounds like you just don't approve of me buying my childhood home," she says, tugging her hand from my grip. She crosses her arms.

"I don't, but that's not the point."

She gives me a disapproving look. "I think it very much is. How I spend my money is not ready for you to say, Luca."

A sigh bursts from my lips. I can feel myself getting hot under the collar. "Cate, it's literally falling apart. I bet you if you paid for an inspection, the inspector would laugh instead of giving you an estimate for repair."

She stands up. "I don't really need a lecture. I have work."

"Wait a second," I demand, my expression turning stormy. "I just asked you to stay with me here."

"But you demanded that I don't spend my money on

something I want at the same time." She grits her teeth. "That isn't fair at all, Luca."

Sucking in a breath, I stand up. "Fine, use your money how you want. Buy that house. Buy into a pyramid scheme. Do whatever."

"I will." She scowls.

"You know what? That sounds great. Why don't I just go get my checkbook right now? God, you and Madisyn really aren't that different, are you?"

Cate stills. "I'm sorry, what did you just say?"

I fold my arms across my chest. "Madisyn liked to invest too, did you know that? She bought fifteen thousand dollars worth of natural beauty supplies on my credit card. Apparently someone told her that she could sell it without a problem. Five months later, when she dumped me, I had to clean fifteen thousand dollars worth of Beyoutiful shit out of my garage."

"And?" Cate snaps. "How is that the same as me buying a house I've wanted for years?"

"You won't take money advice!" I shout, throwing my hands up in the air.

"But it's my money!" she cries. "Why do you even care about how I spend it?"

My eyes become slits. "It's not about the money. It wasn't about the money with Madisyn either. It was a symptom of larger problems within the relationship."

"What relationship?" She shakes her head. "You've told me you care about me, whatever that means. But you've never asked me to be your girlfriend."

"That isn't fair and you know it. We're already married for god's sake!"

Cate looks so mad, as if she would burn down everything I've ever loved if given the chance.

"I don't know anything, apparently. Maybe the reason that Madisyn dumped you was that you were a tight-fisted jerk."

Startled, I take a step back. "I can't believe you just said that."

Cate glares at me. "I could say the same thing of you, Luca. Maybe you would be better off with someone like Madisyn. She seems shallow, but maybe that's what you need. That way you don't have to guess at her objectives."

"At least her objectives aren't secretive and weird."

"Is that what you call dating men exclusively for their money?"

I glare at her. "You know, you may be better off becoming a nun. The only marriage you should be in is to God. Leave the rest of us mortals alone."

Cate sucks in a breath. "Are you saying that you don't want to be married anymore? Because that can be arranged very easily."

I lash out. "Maybe I am, Cate!"

The wounded look in her eyes is unmistakable. "Fine. I'll start moving out tonight."

"Oh no," I say, shaking my head. "You're going to that fucking wedding with me tomorrow. You're going to dress up and look hot and smile. Then and only then are you released from this marriage."

She leans in close to me, lowering her voice. "Fine. I

hope you enjoy having a wife for the next twenty-four hours, because after that I'm done."

My fists bunch. I squint down at her. If I don't get out of here and blow off some steam, I am going to lose it. "You should go to work."

Brushing by her, I head for the front door.

"Where are you going?" she calls.

"Out!" I shout back. "Before I put my fist through the wall."

I don't hear a response so I go outside, slamming the door as I go.

Chapter 31

Luca

I shoot a sideways glance at Cate as we exit the limo outside the Foundry, the fancy as fuck place that Madisyn has chosen for her wedding. She looks unbelievably gorgeous in her wedding finery; I know for a fact underneath that heavy black coat she's wearing a barely-there pink velvet dress. When I first saw her in it, I swear to god my mouth started to water.

Yeah, I'm definitely going to have to rip that off her later when we fuck. But at the moment, she looks frosty and remote.

I offer her my arm as we climb the steps to the rustic wood building. She gives me a deadpan look and then huffs a little as she accepts.

"Still mad, then?" I ask.

Cate narrows her eyes on my face. "Yeah, I'm still mad."

I shrug. "All right. Later, then."

We both said some pretty bad things to each other

yesterday. Words spoken out of anger and frustration more than anything. I know I need to apologize, but I also want her to act like she's even a little bit sorry.

Is that too much to ask?

She just rolls her eyes at me. Normally I would try to talk to her, but now is neither the time nor the place for apologies or explanations.

It'll just have to wait.

As we step into the converted barn, I look around. Plants and string lights hang from the ceiling beams. There is a bar set up with people in tuxes and elegant dresses milling around to my left. Straight ahead are two aisles of neatly arranged chairs and an elaborate cupola set up at the very opposite end from where we are standing.

"Hello," a well-dressed man greets us. "Welcome to the Hartwell-Rivers wedding. Here's a program. May I take your coats?"

Cate glances at me as she slides her coat off her shoulders, revealing creamy skin everywhere. Her neck, her upper back, her amazing fucking legs. Pretty much everywhere that the little pink dress she's wearing doesn't touch is bare and dewy. I arch a brow and look her up and down.

She shoots me a look but doesn't respond to me. Instead she hands her coat over to the man, accepting a program in its place.

"Thank you," she says prettily.

Undaunted by her frosty attitude, I trade my coat for

a program too. Cate looks at me in my tux, hesitating for the barest second.

I smirk. "You can't even stay mad at me for one day, can you?"

She jerks her gaze away, lifting her head and straightening her spine. Rather than answer me, she just pretends like she didn't hear me. "I think I need a drink."

"Best idea you've had all day," I say. Motioning to the bar, I usher her along. "After you, wife."

She sniffs and stalks ahead of me, giving me plenty of time to stare at her ass in that little dress. I grin, thinking about how hot the sex is going to be tonight.

Actually, maybe I should let her keep the dress on. And those little silver heels, too.

When we reach the bar, I order her a glass of champagne and myself a whiskey. Handing her the champagne flute, I grab my tumbler and look around.

"I guess we're supposed to be talking to people," I say, sipping my whiskey.

Cate tilts her head to the side. "I don't know anyone here. Do you?"

I look around at the crowd. "Yeah, but there's no one I really want to talk to."

She shakes her head a little bit and sips her drink. "Why are we even here, Luca?"

Giving her question a casual shrug, I glance around again. "To bug the shit out of Madisyn, mostly."

At the sound of my ex's name, Cate flinches. She immediately guzzles her champagne, finishing it in mere seconds.

"Going big, huh?" I tease her.

She just scowls at me. "I'm going to get another drink. I'll leave you to figure out what to do with yourself when I'm not around."

With that, she whirls and disappears behind a crowd of people near the bar. Pulling a face at her antics, I sip my whiskey and wander away from the crowd.

Glancing around again, I take in the rustic decor. With a sigh, I admit to myself that this is going to be a long afternoon.

"Luca?"

I turn around and find a harried-looking young woman. She's dressed up but she carries a clipboard and wears a headset. If I had to guess, I would say that she works for the venue.

"Yeah, that's me..." I admit.

She smiles, but her distress is clear. "Would you mind coming with me? The bride wants to see you for a second."

I frown, glancing back to see if Cate is in view. "I don't want to leave my wife here alone. She doesn't know anybody."

The young woman presses her lips into a firm line. "It'll just be for a second. She won't even notice you were gone."

She holds out her hand, ushering me forcefully toward a back hallway. I scrunch up my face, shaking head.

"This had better be good," I mutter. "I don't like being segregated from the other wedding guests like this."

My words have no effect on the young woman, who just clears her throat and clutches her clipboard tighter. "If you'll just head into the second door on the left..."

She hurries me down the darkened hallway. I roll my eyes as she shepherds me to a bright red door, gesturing that I should go ahead.

I open the door to find Madisyn standing at the window in a white silk robe.

"Oh, I don't think—" I say.

The door closes behind me, the young woman that ushered me here nowhere to be seen. Madisyn turns away from the window, tears and mascara running down her cheeks.

"Luca, you came!" she cries.

I back toward the door. "Madisyn, I don't know what you are planning, but I want nothing to do with it."

"Luca," she sobs. "I'm so scared of getting married..."

I bump against the door, but find the doorknob locked. "Madisyn, let me out of here."

She ignores me almost entirely, collapsing on a white couch. "You're married. How do you do it, Luca? I'm really freaking out over here."

I turn and bang on the door. "Hey! Let me out!"

Madisyn starts sobbing. "What if we don't get along forever? What if... what if some girl comes along someday and Reggie can't resist her?"

I try the door knob a final time, then sigh. Turning to face Madisyn, I frown. "Syn, you can't just trap me in here."

She looks up at me, grabbing a box of tissues from the

table beside her and wiping at her tear-stained face. "I need your help. You are the only one who can talk me down. Please, Luca. Allay my fears!"

Stepping toward her with a doubtful expression, I sigh again. "If you have doubts, you should be talking to Reggie about them. Not your ex. And especially not against his will."

Madisyn blows her nose. "I'm supposed to just go on blind faith that Reggie loves me and will be faithful to me? Hah!" She turns to me, beseeching. "You were faithful, weren't you?"

I sit on the couch, crossing my arms. "Yep."

Madisyn moves closer to me, sniffling. "How did I ever dump you, Luca?"

I shoot her a glare. "Publicly and loudly, as I remember." I shift on the couch. "Now I really think you should get your little flying monkey outside to let me out of this room."

I see her bite her lip, but when she launches herself into my lap, I'm not really for her. She climbs on top of me, trying to force her mouth on me.

"Fucking hell," I say, pushing her back.

But Madisyn isn't worried about my resistance. She locks her arms around my neck, anchoring herself to me.

"Madisyn—" I bellow.

In the next moment, Cate bursts through the door, looking wide eyed. "Luca—"

She freezes, her eyes locked on Madisyn and me. I panic, pushing Madisyn off.

"Cate, this is not what it looks like," I warn, rising to my feet.

Cate looks at me, her eyes filling with tears. When she speaks, it sounds as cold as ice. "We're through."

She whirls and runs out of the room. I'm not far behind her, but Madisyn is right on my heels, clutching at my arm. "Stay with me!" she screeches.

"Let go of me!" I roar. "Jesus Christ, woman! How can you not get it through your head that I've moved the fuck on?"

Madisyn claws at me, holding on desperately. "You came to my wedding. You were going to interrupt the ceremony!"

I grit my teeth. "You are fucking insane, you know that?"

"We could run away together," Syn says, her eyes wide. "Just think how romantic it would be!"

I break free, backing away from her. "Coming here was a mistake. I don't want you. I could never want you." I shake my head. "The only girl who deserves my heart just ran out that door. So thanks for that, you fucking crazy woman."

I storm out, ignoring Madisyn's pleas for me to come back. I'm so mad that I am actually trembling. Looking around the hallway, I spot the assistant hovering at the end, looking scared.

"Where did my wife go?" I snarl, stalking down the hall toward her.

She just points to the front door. I look at all the wedding guests, who have stopped talking and now are just staring at me. I rush to the front door, calling over my shoulder.

"Madisyn just tried to seduce me!"

And then I burst outside into the cold afternoon air. I look both ways, searching the street for Cate. I come up empty, though... there is no one out on the street at all.

God, she must think the worst of me right now.

But what I shouted at Madisyn was one hundred percent true. Cate is the only girl who's won my heart.

I have to tell her that. It will go a long way toward undoing the damage that coming here has done.

The only problem will be finding her first...

Chapter 32

Cate

"Cate?"

I glance up from my seat in the hospital's emergency room, wiping at my tear stained face. Luna is coming toward me, wearing her dark blue scrubs and looking puzzled.

"They paged me to come here but they didn't tell me why," she says, frowning. "What's wrong? And where is your coat?"

She stops in front of me. I stand up and throw myself into her arms, sobbing and hiccupping.

"Luca..." I cry, inculpable. "He... he... we... the w-wedding..."

She embraces me, her hand cupping the back of my head. "Okay. It's okay. Maybe we'll just get you somewhere more private and let you calm down a little first."

She starts steering me back the way she came from, scanning her identification badge and letting us behind the door marked "Staff Only".

"I'm so sorry!" I blubber. "I know that you're at work—"

Luna tugs me into a lounge room off of the hall, sitting me down on a couch. "Don't worry about it. You're actually catching me right after my shift, not that it matters at all." She sits beside me and grabs a warm throw from the back of the sofa. "Here. You must be freezing!"

Honestly, I don't even notice how cold I am. I hunch down into the fleece throw blanket, but I'm too busy being miserable to worry about it.

"Thanks," I say, trying to contain myself.

Luna looks at me, tucking a strand of her blonde hair back. "What's going on Cate?"

I blow out a breath, wiping at my face. "Luca took me to his ex's wedding..." I take a deep breath, my chin wobbling. "And then I walked in on him practically getting a lap dance from his ex!"

Luna's eyes widen. "He didn't!"

I nod, tears threatening to overwhelm me again. "He did."

A sob escapes me. Luna tries to comfort me.

"I'm sure that can't be right. Luca is a lot of things, but he's not a cheater."

I hiccup. "We broke up yesterday. I... I said he would be better off with someone like Madisyn. And then not twelve hours later, I find her sucking his face."

A little bell chimes. Luna pulls her phone out of her pocket, bites her lip, and then puts the phone back. "That's him, looking for you."

"Oh no. No, I'm not interested in confronting him." I

dash away tears from both my eyes. "He didn't even let me move out first! He just... he just did exactly what I was afraid of."

Luna takes a big breath. "I'm so sorry. I feel bad that I sort of... encouraged you guys to get together." She pauses to think. "I'm going to need more details from you. Like... way more details. But first, I think we should get out of the hospital. There are way too many prying eyes here."

Sagging back on the couch, I frown. "If we go to your house, he'll follow us there. If he hasn't already been there, it's surely on your brother's list of places to look."

She sighs. "Well, we're not hiding from Luca or anything. But I get your point. Lucky for you, I'm house sitting for my boss. And he has a huge empty house with all the wine, Netflix, and ice cream anyone could want."

"Really?" I ask, sniffling.

"Really. Let me grab my stuff and we can go straight there." She flashes me a perfunctory smile and pats my arm.

An hour later, I am standing inside Luna's boss's lavish living room, folding the little pink velvet dress up. Luna gave me a set of scrubs to wear and she eyes me while she hunts around the couch for the remote.

"You should've gone into medicine," she says. "You look hot in those scrubs."

I give her a wobbly smile and collapse onto the white leather couch, pulling a big throw blanket on top of myself. "Oh yeah?"

"Aha!" she says, finding the remote. She flicks the

huge flat screen on and sits down beside me. "Yeah, we would've taken the hospital by storm."

She looks at her phone, which is buzzing again. I stare at it, frowning.

"Is that Luca?"

She glances up at me. "Yes."

I pout. "Let me guess, he's saying I don't know what I saw."

After a moment, she flips her phone over and sets it aside. "Pretty much, yeah."

"I know what I saw." Wrapping myself more snugly in the blanket, I sit back.

Luna flips the channel on the television and mutes it. "Okay. You have to explain it to me again. You two fought yesterday night?"

Nodding, I scrunch up my face. "Yeah. I took him to see my old house and we got into it."

Her eyes narrow. "Your old house?"

"Yeah. I'm planning on buying it. Or I was, until all this happened." My mouth turns down at the corners. "I wanted to show him what my next step was. Little did I know, he got all up in arms about it."

She looks thoughtful. "So... you're telling me that you basically showed my brother the future... but you haven't outlined his part in that future to me. Where does Luca fit in to the vision you have for your future?"

My cheeks color. "Well... I don't know. I figured we would just... umm..." I pause, thinking about it. "I actually haven't given it that much thought. That would mean that I had planned part of his future, which I don't feel like I have any right to do."

Luna leans back, stretching. "Yeah, that's not how normal wives behave. And you are his wife, Cate. Until those annulment papers are signed, at least. Everything you do affects Luca."

Her words give me pause. "I... I guess I'd never thought of it that way."

"So you took him to rub his nose in a future he won't play a part in." She gives me a frank look. "Not your best move. What happened next?"

"He told me not to buy my old house and that it wasn't a good investment. And then we started to fight about how I planned to spend my money.... Which somehow morphed into us arguing about whether or not he belonged with someone more like Madisyn."

"Yeesh." She makes a face. "That sounds tough."

"It was. We ended up breaking up during the argument. Except your brother is a bullheaded jerk so he insisted I still go to Madisyn's wedding with him." I sigh. "And then lo and behold, we're not at the wedding for twenty minutes when I catch him cheating on me. Or... maybe not cheating, but—"

Luna holds out her hand. "Hold on, hold on. According to his texts, he was sitting on the couch and Madisyn jumped on top of him."

I huff. "Which is what a cheater would say!"

"Has Luca ever given you any reasons to distrust him, though? And before you say that I'm on his side, just know that I am pointing this out not because he's my brother, but because you clearly love him." She crosses her arms.

I wrinkle my nose. "Being in love is horrible. It's like…" I start to get tears in my eyes, just saying the words aloud. "I opened my heart to him, Luna. I tried to let my defenses down. And just when I do, Luca pushes me away." I sniffle. "That's why I know that love sucks."

"No, love is a gift." She gives me a look, rubbing my hand. "And since you didn't answer me, I'm going to assume that you have no reason to distrust Luca in particular. It sounds like you're just taking out issues you've had in the past on him. Which is funny, because I would accuse him of the same thing."

I tilt my head. "Huh?"

"He's all worked up over you not including him in your big purchasing decisions because Madisyn screwed him over so badly, financially and otherwise. You left Luca out and there was no space in your life plan for him. And you were hurt in the past so you are lashing at my brother." She purses her lips. "You two are actually perfect for each other, if you would quit being so silly about everything."

I scowl at her, wiping at my eyes. "I thought we were supposed to hide out and eat ice cream today."

"We can." She cocks her head. "But if you think I'm not going to try to help you see what is right in front of your face, you're crazy."

I don't know how to argue with that, so I just change the subject. "You are a total pain in the behind. I hope that the tables are turned sometime soon."

Luna looks at me for a few seconds, then slides over and hugs me hard. "I love you. You know that, right?"

Surprised, I just hug her back. "I love you too."

"I just want what is best for you. Always. I hope you realize that."

"I do, Luna."

When she finally pulls back, she tucks a strand of hair behind my ear. Her lips quirk. "Tell me that you'll think about what I said. Then I'll hand you the remote and go get us some ice cream."

"I will." My quick response makes her narrow her eyes. "No, really. I will. I just need some time to cool off before I can even consider Luca's point of view."

"Hmm." She stands up, grabbing her phone. "All right. I'm going to go raid Dr. Smith's freezer. You're in charge of the remote. Pick something good."

While she pads off to the kitchen, I stare at the remote.

Is what she said right?

Am I being unfair to Luca by painting everything with the same broad brush?

And if I am, what am I supposed to do about it?

A sigh on my lips, I shake my head and start browsing through the channels.

Chapter 33

Luca

I glance at my phone for maybe the thousandth time. Adjusting my bow tie again, I try not to pace around the ancient stone floors of the cathedral. I'm not normally anxious, but the stakes here are high.

"Stop fidgeting," Owen says, looking up at me from his place in the first pew. He closes the hymnal in his lap and sets it aside, rising. "I'm wearing a tuxedo because you asked me to and I'm not fussing with it. I'm sure you can do the same."

Yeah, fuck it. I start to pace.

"This was a terrible idea," I lament. "Cate is going to hate it when I ask her to marry me again. Why did I let Luna talk me into this?"

"Because Luna promised she has softened Cate up for you for the last two days." Owen looks thoughtful. "I don't know why you and Cate are so spiky with each other. She's perfectly nice to me."

I shoot him a glare. "It's not always like that with us. Besides, I'm trying to leave that spikiness behind."

He trots up the steps to the altar, looking around a little. "Do you think that is part of your thing? I mean, that's one of the reasons your sex is hot, right?"

Raising my eyes up to the cathedral's vaulted ceiling, I sigh. "Can we talk about something else?"

He shrugs. "Sure. This whole day is just about you two."

I pace some more, though it's not helping my stress level at all. "Let's go over the plan again. Luna is going to get her here. Then..." I trail off, frowning.

Owen comes over to me, standing in my way. He puts a steadying hand on my shoulder. "Then everyone else will fade into the background. I'll be right outside. It'll just be you two in here until you call to me."

I take a deep breath. "That just leaves the key piece to me, then. I have to figure out what the fuck I'm going to say to her."

He raises his brows. "Yeah, now would be a good time to practice whatever you're going to say."

My mouth turns down at the corners. "I love her. Even when she's being mouthy. Even when she's crying. I still love her. That's the main point I want to focus on."

"That's a good one." He smiles ruefully. "I wish I had what you have, man."

I eye him. "What about you and Chloe?"

I only have to mention her name and his cheeks color. Instantly, Owen turns from a confident man into a bumbling fool.

"Oh, Chloe and I are just friends," he says firmly. He clears his throat, clarifying. "We could never be anything more than that without damaging our friendship."

My phone buzzes in my pocket. I pull it out, glancing at the screen. As expected, it's Luna.

We are in the parking lot, heading to you.

I glance up at Owen. "Luna says that they're here. This conversation is paused, but it's not over."

He rolls his eyes at me. "Whatever you say, man."

Owen heads to the back of the cathedral, disappearing through one of the dark wood doors. I head to the end of the first pew, sitting down.

My heart beats loudly in my ears.

Will Cate listen to what I have to say?

Or will she just give me the cold shoulder?

When I hear Luna's voice at the back in the cathedral, I tense.

"Just come on," Luna says. "I know it's not one of your church days, but I think you'll find it worthwhile..."

It takes an inhuman amount of inner willpower not to turn around. Especially not when I hear Cate's voice.

"I don't think—" She stops mid-sentence. "Luna, what is your brother doing here?"

"Don't be mad," Luna says. She raises her voice to call out to me. "Luca, I got her here!"

I rise, turning to face them. Cate looks breathtaking in a simple black gown; Luna is dressed fancy too in a lemon-colored dress. Dressing up is part of what I asked Luna to do.

Cate is pale, a distrustful frown on her face. Luna

bites her lip, walking backwards toward the rear of the cathedral.

"Luna!" Cate snaps. She turns to see my sister retreating. I watch her swallow heavily as her gaze returns to me. "What do you want?"

I approach her slowly, seeing her sizing me up as I get closer. She licks her lips nervously and tucks a strand of her hair behind her ear.

"I want to tell you that I'm sorry. Sorry for the fight, sorry that I ever made you walk into Madisyn's wedding with me." I pause, frowning. "I didn't actually want to go. But I was worried that if I didn't keep that date as a tentpole, our relationship wouldn't be able to bloom."

Her eyebrows rise slightly. "Is that what it is? A relationship?"

I prowl closer. "That's what I want it to be. We were obviously drunk when we wed, but... I think my subconscious knew something I didn't."

Her eyes narrow as I take the last few steps to stand before her. "What would that be?"

I reach out and take her hand. Looking her in the eye, I kneel.

When I pull out the ring box, her look of shock almost makes me smile. I just hold the ring box, not quite ready to open it yet. I have to explain myself first.

"I think I knew that there was a spark, Cate. You knew it too. But we both had reservations. Things that had to do with our pasts. I was still worried about Madisyn. You were guarding your heart because you'd been hurt." I smile ruefully. "We were both dim. But especially me."

Cate, for her part, is staring at me like I've gone mad. "Luca—"

"Cate," I interrupt her. "I love you."

Her eyes go wide. "You do?"

I nod. "I realized it a while ago, I think. But I've never felt it more strongly than when you ran out of Madisyn's wedding. I was furious with her for plotting to break us up, yes. But I was even more mad at myself for letting us both be put in that position." I take a deep breath. "I realized then that I am pretty obsessed with you."

Her cheeks stain with color. "You are?"

Expelling a breath, I nod again. I snap open the ring box, then take her hand again.

"Cate De Rose, you mean so much to me. We may fight, we may disagree on so many things... but at the end of the day, there is no one else who I would ever want to call mine."

Her eyes fill with tears. "Oh, Luca... I feel the same way."

I pull the ring free of its box, holding it up to her, an offering. "Will you be my wife? In truth this time."

She presses one hand to her heart. "Yes, Luca. Yes."

My heart soars. I am too tongue tied to say anything, so I just slide the ring on her finger. I'm about to stand up when Cate launches herself at me, kneeling to kiss me.

Her lips are hot and sweet under mine. I twine my hands around her body, sinking my fingers into her hair as I kiss her breathlessly.

Her grin mirrors my own as she pulls back, tears on her face. "I love you, Luca Leone."

I brush some of her hair back from her face, relishing this closeness.

"I love you too, Cate."

She looks at the huge diamond on her finger. "You didn't need to get me this, you know. I would've said yes without it."

I kiss her again. "I know. That's something that I love about you. I just wanted it to be official. I figure we can do it properly this time. A big white dress, this cathedral, me in a tux... the whole nine yards."

She sucks in a breath. "You mean it?"

I chuckle. "If it makes you happy, we'll do it. I would marry you on a beach. I would marry you in a ditch. It doesn't matter to me. We have all the time in the world to decide."

Standing, I help her to her feet. She beams up at me, her tears drying. "I love that, Luca."

I stick my elbow out, offering it to her. She takes my arm and I usher her toward the back of the cathedral. "Owen is here somewhere. I think we should tell him and my sister first... then we should go somewhere."

Cate's brow knits. "Like to your house?"

I smile, shaking my head. "No. Somewhere more exotic than that. And while we're on our mini-vacation, I'll contact my real estate broker about buying your old house."

Her steps falter. "You said it was a bad investment!"

I stop, staring down into her face. "It's meaningful to you. That's all that matters."

She frowns. "I don't need to you to buy things for me, Luca. That's not why I married you in the first place."

I cover her hand where she touches my arm. "I know. But I can. And I will. Then we will never argue about that again." I smirk. "Although I'm a hundred percent certain that we will find new things to fight about."

Her lips lift. "I'm still paying the down payment on the house. You can put up a fuss if you really want to, but I feel pretty strongly about it."

Pulling her close, I seal my lips over hers briefly. "I would expect nothing less, princess."

A little chill slips down her spine even as the nickname makes her smile. "It's a deal."

And with that, we head to the back of the cathedral, both bathed in the glow of our own love.

Chapter 34

Cate

As I walk down the aisle of the cathedral, the audience is standing up, looking at me in my wedding finery. I wobble a little, but Carmine is right beside me. He pats my hand and wheezes a little, smiling at me.

I only have eyes for one person, though. I can't stop staring at Luca. His dark blue, tailored tuxedo and crisp white shirt perfectly accentuate his tan and the bold lines of his face and body.

Even from this distance I can see the stubble on his face. My heart squeezes. Luca is normally fastidious; he must have been so busy this morning that he'd forgotten to shave.

I force myself to smile and nod at the people on either side of the aisle. I don't really see anyone's face, but I know they are there. I can hear people whispering and see a few waving at me.

We had wanted a smaller wedding, but that had been

impossible, considering Luca's social prestige and my grandmother's friends. Mostly the cathedral is packed with people who know the Leones, but I don't mind. As long as my grandmother is here, and Harper and Luna are acting as my bridesmaids, I'm not too stressed.

Luca's mother and father had put up an unholy stink about it when we broached the mere idea of a small, intimate wedding. They also turned up their noses at my wanting it to be in a church though.

Luca put down his foot and told them we would bend on the guestlist but I got to pick the place. So here I am, walking down the aisle.

I smile at my grandmother and her friends as I reach my spot by the groom. They smile back at me, which is the little bit of encouragement that I need right now.

Luca's mother, liberated by my husband's departure and excited by the prospect of a grandchild, had even quit drinking. She had been sober for three months now, and a far better person for it. Luca's father is, well, he is still an asshole, but he is making an effort to at least be respectful to Luca and Luna.

I reach my groom's side. Luca beams at me.

All other worries and thoughts cease. All I can see is this man before me. Luca takes my breath away.

The wedding ceremony goes by in a blur. All I remember is when the priest asks Luca and I to join hands and recite our vows. When Luca gently slides the wedding band onto my finger, and his eyes gleam with unshed tears as he speaks.

"Cate, you have been a revolution in my life. No

matter where we've gone, or what we've done, we've always been able to come back to each other. You are kind, beautiful, smart, strong, good, and loyal. I vow to love you, honor you, respect you, support you, and protect you. I vow to be faithful and kind. I vow to never forget how lucky I am to be marrying my best friend."

He stops for a second, gathering his breath. My heart swells; my eyes blur with tears.

"I only have one regret, which is that it took me so long to figure out that I was in love with you. I think, in my mind, I kept seeing you as that scruffy little girl that Luna first brought home... and then one day, I looked and I suddenly saw this incredible, beautiful woman before me."

I beam. "I'm glad you changed your mind," I quip.

He laughs. "Cate, I know you've had to struggle before, but no matter what comes our way, I vow that you won't struggle alone ever again. Your troubles will be mine, your joys my own. Everything I have is yours."

I feel the tears running down my cheeks like rain. Suddenly, all my anxiety seems to melt away, leaving only an overwhelming sense of love and gratitude. I take the large gold wedding ring and place it on Luca's finger.

"Luca... first, those vows were amazing. I don't know how I could ever top them. But then, I don't have to, do I? We're together now, and everything that strengthens you also strengthens me."

"You know it," he affirms, squeezing my hands.

"You've been my best friend too. I can't even remember a time when you weren't in my life. I feel like you encourage me, protect me, reassure me, and grow with me. But I was blind to you, just like you were to me."

Luca brings one of my palms to his lips for a kiss, but otherwise doesn't interrupt. I swallow heavily and then continue.

"Once I realized I was in love with you, it felt like someone had turned on a light within my soul. I vow to cherish you, and that light. I vow to love you and honor you. I vow to always be grateful for the blessing of your love. And I'll protect you, too, whenever I can. I vow to be by your side for the rest of our lives together. I love you and I'm honored to call you my husband."

The priest smiles and says, "By the power vested in me, I now proclaim you man and wife. You may now kiss the bride!"

As people stand and applaud, Luca's strong hands wrap around my waist. I turn my face up to his and he seals his lips over mine. I feel more happy and protected than I've ever been, here in his arms.

Forever and ever.

Chapter 35

Luna

Coming up next...

I swallow nervously as I climb the steps of the drab little office building. I pause in front of the dark wood front door. Hoisting my medical bag, I smooth my dark gray skirt.

"You're going to do well," I tell myself. Moisture pools in my armpits. I normally wouldn't wear such a formal black top, especially not on this warm Seattle day.

But today is a job interview.

No, not an interview. *The* job interview. I really need this internship to put on my resume during this summer while I transition from medical school into my residency. It's vital for the doctors in charge of assignments to find me impressive, from what I hear.

Of course, my medical school only accepts a few positions as resume-worthy... and I found out about all of this two days ago. And this is it, the only position remaining.

I look at the building one more time, biting my lip.

Aurora Borealis Charters, the sign above the door reads.

Blowing out a steadying breath, I open the door. A gust of cool air buffets my face as I step into the dreary office. Everything is just shades of brown in here. The faded carpet, the worn drapes, the chipped office furniture.

I swallow again. How is this place still open and making money?

There is a young woman seated at the reception desk. She looks up at me from an ancient PC, her expression puzzled.

"May I help you?" she asks.

I step fully inside the office, closing the door behind me. "Yes. I have an appointment with Daniel Byrne?"

The receptionist's brow furrows. "In what regard?"

I set down my heavy medical bag with a soft thunk. "It's a job interview. You're still looking for someone with medical expertise, right?"

"Ohhhh," she says, pushing herself to her feet. "Sorry. You just look too young to be a nurse."

I scowl at her words. "I actually just graduated medical school," I say, keeping my tone as even I as can.

"Oh!" She flushes. "Sorry. Let me just go tell him you're here."

I bow my head. "Of course. Thank you."

She goes through the only doorway, only bothering to partially close the door. "Daniel! The medical attendant is here!"

I fidget with my bracelets. Each one is a silver bangle from Tiffany's, chosen with great care. One for each year of college.

I graduated with my two best friends, Cate and Harper, and wanted something to commemorate the time.

So I got us all matching bangles. It may be silly, but it really bucks me up to think about the meaning of the bracelets on days like this one.

The receptionist sticks her head out of the doorway. "Mr. Byrne will see you now."

Smiling graciously, I pick up my medical case and head back toward her.

She ushers me down a hallway to a cramped office, where a shockingly handsome man sits behind his file-covered desk. He wears slacks and a tropical shirt, his salt-and-pepper hair cut close to his scalp. He stands up to shake my hand and I notice that he is quite tall and muscular to boot.

I flush as our palms touch.

"Daniel Byrne," he announces.

"It's a pleasure. I'm Luna Leone," I say. The color in my cheeks flames higher under his measuring gaze.

I wonder what he sees when he looks at me.

A little rich girl?

Someone too young to be a doctor?

I hope not.

"Sit, sit," he says, resettling himself in his seat. "Let's see..." He digs through the piles of papers on his desk, unearthing a file. He flips it open and leafs through the pages. "You're from Mercy Southwest, right?"

I sit down in the only chair, setting my case down beside me. "Yes. I just graduated medical school in the top half of my class."

Okay, I was number fourteen out of thirty. So what I told him was not a lie... it just wasn't exactly the whole truth.

My lie draws his gaze up from the page. "Really?"

I shift in my seat, trying not to give in to my urge to fidget. "Yes."

"Mm." He looks down at my file again. "We usually don't get the first draft of med students in here. Or second, or the third." He smiles ruefully. "Actually, we usually only get the people that just barely graduated by the skin of their teeth. Cruising to Alaska and living on a boat for an entire summer doesn't really appeal to a lot of people, I guess." His brow hunches. "Especially not women."

I blush again. "I see. Well, you were on the approved list of placements that my school gave me..."

He rocks back in his seat, studying me. "Why are you really here? Is this your backup or something?"

My cheeks are stained bright pink. "No, sir. This is the only place that I've applied." I gulp. "I just found out about the program this week, though."

He cocks a brow. "Ahh. So you ran out of other options, then."

God, kill me now. "I prefer not to think of it that way, Mr. Byrne."

Daniel's gaze is heavy on me for a moment, then he rocks back in his chair again. "I think that kind of attitude will get you a long way, Miss Leone." He looks down at my file again, sucking at his teeth. "Mercy West has never steered us wrong yet. I'll just need you to fill out a million papers saying that you won't sue us if anything goes wrong."

"That's it?" I ask, surprised. I start to stand up because he does, but he waves me back down.

"Yep. As long as you are qualified, we'll take you. I just need to bring my son in to meet you. He captains most of the charters that we take out so he'll be your direct boss."

Relief floods me. "Oh, thank you Mr. Byrne!"

Daniel gives me a hooded smile. "We'll see if you're still thanking me when you're actually out at sea, with waves rolling below deck and no land in sight."

My eyes widen, but he heads out of the office. I used to spend every summer on my parent's yacht when I was a kid... but it's been fifteen years since then.

Do most of the medical staff that this place hires deal with seasickness, then?

"Dad, I really don't have time for this," a gruff voice says.

For some reason, every hair on my body stands on end at that voice. I don't know why it sounds familiar though.

I hear Daniel answer. "Just poke your head in, Gabe."

I turn my head just in time to see a decades-younger version of Daniel appear. He's probably only thirty, more muscular and fit than his father. His hair is jet black, like the t-shirt he's wearing. But his eyes...

He looks at me with eyes the exact color of seagrass, that faint blue-green shade.

How could I ever forget those eyes?

It's been six months since I got drunk and hooked up with a stranger in Vegas for my birthday. We didn't use names and he left before I could ask for his number...

But I will never, ever forget those eyes. Or the things that his calloused hands made me feel that night... He made me scream his name four different times... then he vanished while I was drowsing.

Gabriel. Saying his name inside of my head excites me. I can feel my pupils begin to dilate.

"I—" he begins.

"You—" I start.

We both stop. My heart is suddenly beating hard enough to hear it in my ears.

"Gabe, don't stop in the middle of the damned doorway," his father chides. "Come on now."

Gabe looks at me, a silent plea on his face. He clears his throat.

"I don't think we should hire a girl," he says loudly. "Remember the last one we brought on? She didn't even make it for two hours before we had to turn around and drop her off. Women aren't cut out for the life."

I raise my eyebrows. "Excuse me?"

Daniel doesn't seem to notice the tension between his son and me. "That was eight years ago, Gabe. Get with it. Women can do anything they want to do now."

I narrow my eyes. "You look familiar, Gabe."

He actually blushes. "No, I don't think so. I don't see any reason I would. You must be confused."

My brow hunches. From his guilty tone, I can guess that he's flat-out lying. I don't know why, though.

"Gabe, I just wanted to introduce Miss Leone to you." Daniel looks at his watch. "Would you two excuse me for a moment? I need to take my pill and I think I left the bottle in my car." He turns and heads out. "I'll be right back!"

Gabe and I are left there, staring each other down.

"What the heck is going on?" I ask.

Gabe slides his gaze out the door, then whispers his answer to me. "You should not work here, little girl."

I make an offended noise. "Uhh! I should work anywhere I want to, Gabriel."

He narrows his eyes. "Seriously. You should get out of here. I don't have time or attention for someone... someone like you."

I huff. "That's funny. I think that you don't want Mr. Byrne to know that you slept with me. Why would that be?"

Gabe reddens. "Get. OUT!"

Normally I would leave. My mother always taught me that a woman should only be in places where it was clear that she was wanted. Desired, even.

This is definitely not one of those situations.

But if I don't take this internship, I'm out of options. And I'm damned sure that Gabriel isn't going to stand in the way of me getting a good rotation when school starts again.

I fix him with my gaze. "No. You probably don't know this, but the school looks at these next few months when they are determining who gets what position next year. This internship is my last chance not to end up at the bottom of the pile."

Gabe leans back against the wall, peering outside again. "I don't care."

"Well, you should." Grasping at straws, I pull out my only ammunition. "Otherwise I... I will tell your father about the drunken night we spent together."

The corner of his mouth turns down. "So?"

Oh, fudge. I start to sweat, even in the air-conditioned office.

"I think you care what he thinks," I accuse. "If not, I'll just... I'll march out of here and tell him!"

Gabriel studies me, not too different from the measuring gaze his father gave me earlier. Then he shifts his stance.

"Fine," he says, gritting his teeth. "Just keep your mouth shut, all right?"

That actually worked? He's just... letting me work here?

"Okay," I agree hastily. "You have my word."

He snorts. "You've already blackmailed me. Do you really think your word is worth anything to me?"

Gabriel pushes himself off of the wall, heading out of the tiny office. I look at him as he goes, feeling a weird ripple of guilt.

"Wait!" I call.

He pauses, already out the door. "What?"

Swallowing, I try to think of what to say. Surely I can reassure him somehow. Explain that I'm really a good person, I just need this job.

He starts to move away, shaking his head. So I blurt out the first thing I think of.

"You... you won't be sorry," I manage.

Gabe turns his head, disgust written plain on his features. "I already am."

What does that even mean?

Then he's gone, lumbering down the hall. I jump when I hear him slam a nearby door. Standing and clutching my medical bag, I swallow.

I got the internship, yes.

But at what cost?

I fidget with the silver bangles on my wrist, thinking of how angry Gabriel was.

How did he get like that?

And what do I have to do with anything?

Daniel soon returns, ushering me to sit. But I'm left churning those same questions over and over again in my head.

And remembering those steely sea glass eyes...

Chapter Thirty-Six

Thank you for reading Sinful Fling. If you loved this book, please consider leaving a review. It's the best way to let me know that you want me to write more books like this one!

I'm so excited for what's next. I know that if you liked this, you'll love Sɪɴꜰᴜʟ Bᴏss... It's Gabe and Luna's story. Forbidden love is very close to my heart... and I am very excited to be able to present this combination of some my favorite tropes: Billionaire romance, accidental marriage, fake relationship, enemies to lovers, forced proximity, grumpy/sunshine, spicy. I'm over the moon to write the stories that I've been longing to write for years.

He was her boss on the high seas. She was the intern he couldn't stop thinking about. A shared secret led to a summer of forbidden temptation.

When she signed on as medical staff for a summer internship on a yacht bound for Alaska, she never expected the captain to be him. Tall, dark, and impossibly handsome, he was also the mystery man she'd hooked up with in Vegas a few months ago.

He insisted their fling stay buried, but their undeniable chemistry refused to stay under wraps. Long days on the water and stolen moments of tension made keeping their distance impossible.

As a breathless longing built between them, the pressure of their forbidden passion threatened to explode. Could they keep their relationship a secret? Or would they crash and burn?

Tropes: Workplace romance, forbidden love, second chance, forced proximity, grumpy/sunshine, summer fling, slow burn, spicy tension.

Grab Sinful Boss **right now!**

* * *

Loved Luca & Cate? Fall for the rest of the couples in this series!

Sinful Fling - Aiden & Olivia - Brother's best friend
Sinful Enemy - Luca & Cate - Enemies to lovers

Sinful Boss - Gabe & Luna - Workplace
Sinful Chance - Grayson & Rachel - Second chance
Sinful Teacher - Carter & Eve - Student-teacher

About Vivian Wood

Vivian likes to write about troubled, deeply flawed alpha males and the fiery, kick-ass women who bring them to their knees.

Vivian's lasting motto in romance is a quote from a favorite song: "Soulmates never die."

Be sure to join her email list to keep up with all the awesome giveaways, author videos, ARC opportunities, and more!

Vivian's Works

Wildflower Lane
Small Town Rom Com
The Accidental Honeymoon

Say Yes to the Nemesis

Cape Simon
Small Town Romance
The Grumpy Boss Agreement
The Fake Fiancée Proposition
The Playboy Rival Arrangement

Sinfully Rich
Steamy Billionaire Romance
Sinful Fling
Sinful Enemy
Sinful Boss
Sinful Chance
Sinful Teacher

Billionaires Ever After
Steamy Bad Boy Romance
His Best Friend's Little Sister
Claiming Her Innocence
His Fiancé To Keep
His Lovely Virgin

Hush Hush Club
Forbidden Billionaire Romantic Suspense
Such A Good Girl
Such A Spoiled Brat

Married At Midnight
Forbidden Billionaire Romance

Deal With The Devil
Wed to the Devil
Vow to the Devil

Ruined Castle Trilogy
Forbidden Billionaire Romance
The Single Dad
The Nanny
The Caress

Broken Slipper Trilogy
Forbidden Billionaire Romance
The Patron
The Dancer
The Embrace
Possessive

Fifth Avenue Villains
Fifth Avenue Devil

Dirty Royals
Forbidden Royal Romance
Cruel Heir
Sinful Princess
Pretend Princess

King's Capture Duet
Dark Billionaire Romance
King's Capture
Queen's Sacrifice

Addiction Duet

Angsty Dark Romance
Addiction
Obsession

Other books

Wild Hearts

For more information....
vivian-wood.com
info@vivian-wood.com